Pauline

Praise for *An Enemy Within*

'In this compelling book, Ciarán Roche offers an insight into a dangerous reality. As a society, we have only begun to understand the extent of the cause and effect of child abuse, and yet this book is about so much more. It is a story, too, about a cast of characters who try to make life better for others in their community. Such courageous people bring this book to life as they face, unflinchingly, the enemy within.'

Liz McManus

'Readers of crime novels will really enjoy this book. A devastating murder causes the hidden layers of life in a small country town to be peeled back. Joan, reconnecting with her childhood friends, supports Detective Sergeant Kevin Brady's drive to solve the crimes, until an unexpected twist further complicates things. A gripping read that shines a spotlight on a crime none of us want to believe happens in a civilised society. Ciarán Roche deserves our gratitude for such a powerful read.'

Pól Ó Mhurchú

An Enemy Within

First published in Ireland 2025 by
Dingle Publishing Services,
Ard na Caithne, Ballyferriter, Dingle, Co. Kerry
www.dinglepublishing.com

Dingle Publishing

British Library Cataloguing in Publication Data.
A CIP catalogue record for this book is available from the British library.

ISBN 978-1-7397813-6-1

Project Management: Dingle Publishing Services
Design: Anú Design, Tara
Set in 11 on 16 point Garamond

Printed and bound in Ireland by Walsh Colour Print, Castleisland, Co. Kerry, using paper from sustainable forest resources only.

An Enemy Within

CIARÁN ROCHE

Dingle Publishing

Ciarán Roche is the author of a number of plays for which he has received widespread recognition. He was shortlisted for the RTÉ P.J. O'Connor Radio Play Award for *A Tangled Web*.

Born in Drimnagh, Dublin, he is the second child of nine. Having left school at 15, he moved to England, where he qualified in disability and psychiatric nursing before working as a mental welfare officer. He subsequently worked in Ireland as a social work manager, branching out to develop alternative support services for children and their families. He is currently the chairperson of three not-for-profit companies providing support for individuals and families.

Ciarán divides his time between his home in Co. Wicklow and the Dingle Peninsula in Co. Kerry. *An Enemy Within* is his debut novel.

PREFACE

It was only in the late 1980s and early 1990s that we began to fully realise the impact of sexual abuse on victims and that they needed help to come to terms with it. This book, set around that time, attempts to explore just a few of the ways in which abuse negatively impacts on our sense of ourselves.

Victims can be, and need to be, given the opportunity to open up about it in a healthy, therapeutic way.

That is the basis of this book.

CHAPTER 1

Kevin Brady was seething with rage. He was standing in a clearing deep within a dense public forest, the early morning mist rising unnoticed about his ankles as he looked around this small, bramble-enclosed area. He seemed totally unaware of the fact that his clothes offered only meagre protection against the elements. His brain, however, was racing, his mind contemplating a number of quite horrific facts. The quiet of the early spring dawn in this normally so lovely woodland was totally at variance with the rage inside Detective Sergeant Kevin Brady.

The wild animals and birds were unusually silent, unused to such early morning activity. Two policemen were moving briskly around the car park. They were stringing 'do not enter' signs across the pedestrian entrance, an act that of itself would bring the attention of passers-by to this wood, just off the N7. The tall trees muffled the sound of the traffic that at this early hour was just beginning to build up on the main Dublin–Cork road. The sombre mood of the police in the car park bore witness to the fact that a tragedy was afoot.

Some four hundred metres up a steep track above them stood three men. Their presence confirmed the actuality of a tragedy, as only a major incident would have brought those three to such a place at six o'clock on a midweek morning. The men, each used to dealing with the horror of sudden, unnecessary death, stood in mute tableau as the rising sun gave a little more light but no hope to this wooded clearance.

Dr Pat Fitzsimons was well known to those used to looking at the national news. As the State Pathologist, he was regularly featured at the scenes of crime. A middle-height, slim man, he was easily identifiable in his customary well-worn weatherproof wax jacket. The familiar tweed hat sat above his small face and the bag of his trade lay open beside his feet.

Con Doyle was no taller than the doctor. He stood, wrapped in his duffel coat, gloves protecting his hands, as he awaited the initial findings of his colleague. Kevin Brady, the last of the trio, looked every inch the policeman he was. A tall, dark, broad-shouldered man, he stood slightly apart from the other two, dressed in a casual jacket, an open-necked shirt and light trousers. His soft shoes were no match for the damp rising from the cold grass beneath them. But Kevin was immune to the damp and the cold. He wasn't just angry; he was seething with rage and his inner turmoil left him impervious to the weather. His anger was not external; rather, it was directed in on himself. His eyes were focused, fixed intently on what lay beneath him.

The naked body of a young boy lay rigid and vulnerable on the black plastic bag in which it had been dumped a few hours earlier.

Twenty silent minutes had passed during which Dr Fitzsimons had carefully cut open the black bag and examined the contents. He finally stood upright, straightening his stiffened spine, before quietly speaking.

'Well, obviously he is a boy, twelve or thirteen, I would guess. He died – was killed – some five hours ago, give half an hour or so either way.

'He suffered a hell of a lot before he died. The poor boy has marks of multiple bruising on large parts of his body. A number of bruises are a day or so old, but most were more recent, probably inflicted shortly before his death. He was also, I am sorry to say, sexually abused in the process. The bruising and tearing around the anus is very severe. I can show you this if you want.'

'No thanks,' said Kevin sharply. 'Hearing about it is bad enough.'

The doctor shrugged. 'It amazes me, Kevin, that after all these years you are still so squeamish. Anyway, I can say with some certainty that the cause of death was strangulation. There are clear marks of a narrow rope or twine around his neck and this probably cut off the boy's air supply, causing him to die. Whether it was done deliberately or it was a nasty perverted sex act that went horribly wrong, I can't tell. Maybe I'll know more when I have completed a formal autopsy back in the mortuary. By the look of it the poor kid was probably lucky to die when he did. He must have been terrified and in terrible pain from the abuse he was suffering. Whoever did this is a really sick, perverted excuse for a human being.'

Silence fell as the three men stood uncomfortably with their own thoughts. Kevin Brady shuffled more than the other two, his agitation showing in his jerky movements. It was Dr Fitzsimons again who finally broke the silence. 'I would say that he was a healthy, well-nourished young boy. He has good skin and all the indications are that he had been well cared for; clean hair, good nails ... just a nice young boy who was abused and then callously murdered. Any more will have to wait for the post-mortem.' After a pause, as the doctor bent down and with practised ease closed and picked up his bag, he added 'Look, lads, I have done all I can here. I'll organise for the body to be taken to the morgue, if it's okay with you.'

Kevin and Con both nodded silently. The doctor looked back down at the slight, lifeless body below them and continued: 'I am sure he wasn't living rough. He was healthy and well cared for, so I would think he is bound to be reported missing. It should be easy enough to identify him.'

'Ugh!' he added as he shivered. 'Thank God I don't have to do that part of the job. I wouldn't be up to it. I don't envy you guys the job of telling the parents.'

Con and the doctor turned and took a few steps out of the clearing, the doctor balancing his bag with accustomed ease in his left hand. Then they became aware that Kevin hadn't moved, so they stopped and looked back at him. Kevin tossed his head angrily, then, looking intently down in the direction of the car park, in a bitter, defeated tone he said, 'The boy's name is Barry … Barry Breen. He is thirteen years old. Actually he just turned thirteen two weeks ago. He is from Brownstown in North County Dublin. His parents are ordinary, decent people, leading happy, contented lives. That is until two days ago when their only son never arrived home from school. His dad is a machine operator and his mam stays at home caring for her family. I can guarantee that at this very moment she is lying awake in her bed finding a hundred reasons to blame herself for her only son going missing. Their lives are now irrevocably ruined. They will never recover from this … Who could?'

The bitterness in Kevin's tone stunned his colleagues as much as their surprise that he knew who the boy was. Kevin, like Con, worked in a special task force and missing persons were not normally within their brief. Con, who had shared many an investigation with Kevin, finally moved and, placing an arm on his tall friend's elbow, quietly asked, 'How the fuck do you know him?'

Silence stretched. The other two waited, their eyes fixed on Kevin's rigid face. Finally, with an angry shake of his powerful shoulders, he started to talk … to explain.

'Well, it's a longish story and I shouldn't even have got involved, but …'

Con, who knew Kevin only too well, did not need to be told that the 'but' summed up the soft side of his friend.

'About four years ago I was sitting in the office when a woman just barged in. She looked drawn and strained and desperate and … well, I didn't have the heart to put her out. Anyway, she told me her story, and a sorry one it was. Her son Frank had gone missing from practically outside his own front door. He was only eleven years old and hadn't been seen in over a year. I suggested that she should try Missing Persons and I had even reached out my hand for the phone to ring them when she cut across me and said that of course she had been in contact with Missing Persons. What sort of an idiot did I take her for? Actually she said that Missing Persons had been dealing with her from the beginning but … nothing. No sign or trace of her little boy had been found. Now, a year and a bit later, she accepted that her son was dead, had almost certainly been murdered. She asked me to take on the case and treat it as a murder investigation. More than anything, she wanted – needed – his body to be found so she could give him a Christian burial. She needed a grave and, as she said, a gravestone where she could go to talk with him. She was insistent that the least her baby deserved was a Christian burial.

'Well, anyway, she was a lovely, sad lady and I felt so sorry for her and her family that I sort of agreed to look into it. I shouldn't have, but anyway! I got nowhere, of course. Jean in Missing Persons gave me the file to read, but nothing: no trace, no clues and not even a glimmer of a suspect. Mrs Creamer regularly rang me and then a year ago she brought in a man with her. His son had also gone missing in very similar circumstances.'

Kevin walked over and looked down at Barry Breen's little body before continuing. His tone still held within it an air of defeat, but the anger that so dominated him was beginning to ease, as if the unburdening of his guilt was therapeutic in itself.

'Four years and I have got nowhere at all, not a single inkling. Mrs Creamer keeps hounding me. Two lovely families caught, grieving for their sons with no body, no process of resolution for their grief. Anyway, a month or so ago as a last resort I drafted a circular and sent it to every Garda station in the country. In it I asked to be contacted immediately if any young teenage boy went missing in suspicious circumstances. I emphasised that I needed to know promptly. Well, yesterday morning I got a call from a Garda in Brownstown and he told me about a local boy who had been reported missing. He told me that the missing lad's parents were in a terrible state. As I wasn't too busy yesterday, I rang the parents and went to see them. They gave me his history and some photographs. I also visited his school and the last place he was seen. This is definitely the body of poor Barry. I bloody knew as soon as I heard the phone ring this morning that it would be. Now I will have to go back again … and tell them … this.'

The doctor and Con were stunned into silence as the depth of their colleague and friend's involvement in the case was revealed. They paused, unsure how to respond. The birds, as if in tribute to young Barry's presence in their territory, continued with their silence. Con was the first to move. He gently took Kevin's arm and led him out and on to the path. The doctor followed on their heels.

'Kev, mate,' said Con softly as they walked, 'you take too much on yourself. You shouldn't have even seen them, not to mind getting involved. Look at you, blaming yourself for their boy's death. It wasn't your fault, Kev.'

'A great detective I am,' said Kevin as bitterness welled back up in him. 'Mrs Breen, I couldn't find your son, but I can tell you where his abused dead body is. Do you think she should be grateful to me … eh?'

'Stop it,' Con and Dr Pat said in unison as they gathered around their colleague. Con, as if to distract his friend, said, 'Listen, Kev. I have arranged to see the young man and his girlfriend who discovered the body. We are to meet them at half seven this morning before he goes to work. I know how you like to talk to people before they get caught up with retelling their story to friends. So we can go straight to the local station, get our thoughts together and then interview them … okay?'

Kevin nodded. Turning to look back up the track in the direction from which they had just come, he said, as his professionalism began to impose itself, 'Good – let's interview them first, though God knows that may well be a waste of time. Anyway, after we have seen them I better go over to Brownstown and break the news to the Breen family. I'll get one of the local Gardaí to come with me while I do it. And Con … let's make sure to get a news blackout from the TV and radio people if they arrive, at least until the parents have been told. God help them. The least they deserve is to hear the news in person. Then after that, I am personally going to find the bastard who did this and make sure he is locked up for life.'

Kevin made as if to move on, then stopped again and, looking all around him, said bitterly, 'I am also going to have every square inch of this wood dug up spadeful by spadeful, even if I have to do it myself.'

The three men walked on, Con all the while keeping a comforting, calming arm on his friend's elbow as they went. Then, just before they reached the opening to the car park, Con stopped. Quietly, his sharp Dublin wit coming to the fore as it so often did, he asked, 'Kev, I know you are a culchie, born and reared deep in the boglands, and you grew up working the land. But why would you be getting out your pick and shovel to dig up this place? It's huge, there's bloody miles of it.'

'Acres,' Kevin corrected with a small smile, as the first real sign of a break in the rage within him showed, before he added, 'Don't ask me why, but I really think that all three cases of the missing boys are somehow linked. My instinct tells me that the bodies of the other two boys could well be buried somewhere in this wood. I am going to find Frank Creamer's body if it is the last thing I do.

'Above all, though, I am going to find the perverted animal that could do such things to any poor defenceless young boy and make sure he is locked up for life. You know, it's a sick world we live in and sometimes, like on mornings like this one, I just hate this bloody job.'

CHAPTER 2

Kevin

Joe and Ellen were tired, excited and a little bit apprehensive when they arrived at the Garda station at 7.30 a.m. Kevin and Con were consummate professionals, though, and quickly settled them down. Joe was a talker and Ellen an interrupter, so once they had got going they needed only minor prompting to tell their story in a coherent manner.

Joe started. 'I finished work late last night. I had a rush job on and then I called around to Ellen's at about half nine.'

'It was nearer ten,' Ellen interjected. 'See, Joe is the maintenance fitter at our local factory. He is great with his hands. He just seems to know about mechanics and he needed to fix the machines after everyone else had gone home.'

'When I got to Ellen's,' Joe went on, 'the house was packed. All her brothers and their mates were there, so Ellen and I went to the local for a drink and some peace and quiet.'

'Joe and I have been going out now for a year. We only had a soft drink. I don't drink and Joe doesn't either except one or at the most two pints, and that's only at weekends,' clarified Ellen.

Joe smiled at her as, putting his hand over hers, he touched her into silence before he went on. 'We talked there with friends until closing time. Then, as we knew that her house would still be full and, well … my landlady doesn't encourage visitors late at night, so we went for a drive and then a walk in the wood.' This was met with revealing eye contact between the young people. 'We often go for a walk in the wood, so we're very familiar with it, even at night,' Ellen added.

'We were just walking back, quiet like, not talking, when we came around a bend in the track and suddenly in front of us we could see a shape. It was about thirty yards away.'

'I got an awful fright,' put in Ellen, 'and I cried out and held on tight to Joe.'

'We stopped,' Joe continued. 'I was trying to figure out what it was. I thought it might be a stag or some such, when suddenly it moved to the right. I heard a crash as something fell and then, just as I began to think it was an animal that had gone into the underbrush, out came a figure that was obviously a man, and he started to run away from us down the track.'

'I got so scared,' interjected Ellen. 'I begged Joe to stay where we were, but no, he insisted we should follow the person down the track. I was scared and Joe nearly had to pull me along with him.'

'When we got down to the car park,' Joe continued, 'we heard an engine start and rev up. We got there just in time to see it drive to the exit, where it had to stop for a few seconds as a car came by along the main road. Then it accelerated quickly and drove off in the direction of Dublin. In the lights of the passing car I noticed that it was a van, not a car: a whitish one. A …' Joe stopped, as if unsure whether he should go on or not.

'Say what you think, Joe. It doesn't matter if it turns out to be right or not. Tell me anyway,' Kevin said encouragingly.

'I think it was a Corsa … an '87 Corsa van.'

'How could you know that?' Kevin asked, surprised by Joe's answer.

'My Joe, he knows his cars, so he does,' Ellen answered for him. 'See, he fixes his own and most of our friends' cars, so he does.'

'Does he now?' said Kevin, smiling at her as the first glimmer of amusement crossed his face since the interview had started.

'And did you notice anything else about it?' he asked, turning to look at Joe.

As Joe started to say something, Ellen again cut across him and said 'Lightning!'

'Lightning?' Con and Kevin echoed in tandem, as all three men looked at Ellen. Slightly flustered, she tried to explain.

'The van was at an angle, and as the passing car's headlights lit it up, something on it reminded me of a flash of lightning … Well, it did!'

Joe shook his head as the detectives looked at him. 'I didn't see that. I was trying to see the licence plate. No go, I'm afraid. All I could make out was that it seemed to be M something. MM. M something, but I couldn't be sure. I was trying to see the registration number, so I didn't notice anything else. I'm sorry, and I know that can't be right as there is no such reg, but that is what I saw, or thought I saw!'

'That's okay, you can only tell me … us … what you thought you saw. The rest is up to us to make sense of it,' said Kevin, 'and you did great, both of you: just great.'

They beamed, then Ellen said, 'I wanted to go straight home, but no, my Joe insisted that something was funny about the whole thing. He wanted to get his torch out and go back up to the spot on the track, but I wouldn't let him. Let's go home,' I said.

'I'm often on call from the job, so I used the call radio in the car and told the fitter who was on the night shift where I was. I asked him to ring Jim Craven in the Garda station urgently, tell him that he needed to get here as quickly as he could. We know Jim well, you see. He was with us in no time, and we went up and found the black plastic bag that had been dropped. We found it no problem.'

'He wouldn't let us examine it,' interjected Ellen. 'Jim rang and called out the sergeant. He came and we waited in the police car until they discovered it was a dead body … the poor boy.'

'The Garda did exactly the right thing,' said Con.

Kevin added, 'And you two were brilliant, the way you handled the whole thing. I must say you showed great courage in following him down the track. I don't know if I would have been so brave.'

There was a lull while Joe and Ellen basked in the praise, then Kevin quietly asked, 'Tell me, how come whoever it was didn't see your car?'

'Oh,' said Joe hesitantly. 'Well, you see, there is a smaller car park up a narrow side track … more private, you see.'

'Yes, I see,' said Kevin as his mind ticked on and he hoped that this young couple had enjoyed their extra privacy before they took that fateful walk in the wood. Kevin was alive and energised now. His rage had been replaced by the determination of the hunter that he naturally was. Joe and Ellen had been of more help than he could reasonably have expected them to be.

The chase was on.

This was what he was trained for.

CHAPTER 3

Kevin

'Where the hell is Kevin?' Con asked of no one in particular as he looked down at the chaotic desk. Paper littered the floor as well as the desk, a sure sign that the normally tidy environs of Kevin's workspace had been well used already that morning.

It was 12.30 and Con, after his late-night call-out, had just arrived. A few hours at home, a cooked breakfast and a reinvigorating shower had somewhat set him up for the new day. Kevin had clearly got in well before him.

'That eejit is in the canteen playing with cards he's made – tried to get me to read them for him … as if I've nothing better to do! Told him to eff off, I did,' came from a disembodied voice at the other end of the large partitioned office that housed up to twelve detectives in the Garda headquarters. Con didn't bother to run the voice down. He just strolled off to locate Kevin.

As Con entered, Kevin was standing just inside the door of the still quiet canteen, squinting at a card propped up on the windowsill at the other end of the room.

'Great! You're here.' said Kevin, grabbing Con's arm. 'What do you think that number is, the one on the card over there?' he asked excitedly.

'Eighty-something,' Con answered, now understanding the 'eejit in the canteen' comment.

'No, no, not the numbers – the letters. What do you think they are?'

'M M … N N … or …'

'Or what?' asked Kevin urgently.

'Or WW, maybe.'

'Exactly, that's what I reckon as well.'

'Slow down, Kevin. What the hell are you up to?'

'Joe, the fitter we interviewed this morning – one thing Ellen said is that he really knows cars. She said she couldn't differentiate between a Ford or a Nissan if it hit her, but that if Joe said it was a white Opel Corsa van, he was bound to be right. She said Joe wouldn't make a mistake about that.

'But he also said that the car registration was MM, and there is no such registration. So I wrote out a number with MM on it the same size as a car plate and at this distance, fifty feet or so, it couldn't be MN, MH or WX, so it has to be WW. Nothing else fits.'

'That's a huge leap, Kevin, and anyway, where does that get us, even if you are right?' Con asked.

'I thought about this when I finally got in and showered this morning. See, Joe doesn't only know the makes of cars, he knows the years. He said it was a 1987 model van, so that's why I had to try my theory out. The registration WW looks like MM from the distance. It has to be a Wicklow car, and an '87 registered one at that. We've got the bastard. I mean, how many white Opel Corsa '87 vans registered in Wicklow can there be?'

'Slow down, Kevin. You're letting your imagination run away with yourself. It could be MN, Monaghan or WX, Wexford. You could be wrong. You're getting carried away and not, may I remind you, for the first time.'

'It's that bastard who is going to be carried away, Con. I know I'm right. I'm going down to the Wicklow County Council offices to go through their van registers. Are you coming?'

CHAPTER 3 - KEVIN

'For God's sake, Kev, this isn't even our case yet and if I don't finish the Jacobson report, which I was supposed to do first thing this morning only you had me out half the night, the boss will have my guts for garters. Why don't you just ring the council office?'

'No, it's too important. We have to go through them ourselves, and quickly. Come on, Con … please.'

'What about the Breens? I thought you were going to go there and break the bad news!'

'I … I rang Brownstown station and they are getting a female liaison officer to go with them. This is too important: we can't lose this opportunity. Come on, Con.'

'No, I can't. Look, you go if you think it's so important and I'll cover for you. I'll say you were out all night, which we both bloody well were. Now piss off before anyone starts asking for you. Oh, and say hello to your country cousins for me. Go.'

'Okay – I'll ring you later.'

Julie Downes was anxious. An Administrative Officer in Wicklow County Council, she had just been summoned to the County Manager's office, something that had never happened before in her fifteen years' service.

A tentative knock was answered by her boss, very much in command. 'Ah, Julie,' he said, waving her in. 'This is Detective Sergeant Kevin Brady, looking for our help.'

Kevin smiled as he shook Julie's hand. 'I am looking really urgently to identify a car, and all I know is that it is an Opel Corsa van registered in Wicklow four years ago, in 1987. I think it may belong to a small business in the county. It really is a very serious case, and I'd be so grateful for your help.'

Julie looked at the County Manager, who nodded encouragingly.

'A 1.3 petrol or 1.5 diesel?' asked Julie quietly, surprising Kevin.

'Now that I don't know,' answered Kevin, 'but if I had to I could find out.'

'If it's a business van it's more likely the 1.5. diesel,' Julie said as if thinking aloud. She then looked at the County Manager before continuing. 'When I took over the tax and registering section fifteen years ago it was a mess. Just one registration system and so much of our time was spent dealing with disputes over tax bands. Cars are taxed on their engine sizes and we had to keep going back to the main register. So I opened a new ledger that recorded them under car makes and engine capacities. Mind you, if we had the computers I keep asking for it would be a simple task,' she added, looking directly at her County Manager.

Kevin, not wishing that theme to be developed, quickly cut in. 'Would you mind if Julie showed me her system – it sounds very hopeful to me?'

The manager smiled at Kevin then, looking at Julie, said 'Fine, that sounds like a very good initiative of Julie's, and I hope it can help.'

Half an hour later Julie had a sheet of paper which she shared with Kevin.

'Only five diesels were registered in 1987. They were a new model then, so only a few were bought that year. They are much more popular now.'

'And these are the names and addresses of the owners?' Kevin asked.

'Yes.'

'I don't suppose you could tell me the professions of the owners as well?' he asked wistfully.

Julie smiled, then asked, 'Is it really that important?'

'And urgent,' Kevin added.

'Well, a lot of these vans are used by one-man companies, so we could try the local small business directory: they bring it out every few years and I keep a copy. Just a thought!'

'I'm deeply in your debt,' Kevin said as Julie hastily disappeared. Ten minutes later she came back smiling.

'The first one is a plumber in Arklow. Two and three are probably small farmers, judging by their addresses. Four is a tyre fitter in Greystones. Five is an electrician based in Colestown, just outside the town here.'

Kevin took the list from her and looked at it intently, trying hard to keep his excitement under control.

CHAPTER 3 - KEVIN

'I can't tell you how helpful you have been, Julie. You do know you are totally wasted here in your job,' Kevin said sincerely. 'I'll just call in to the County Manager and thank him.'

At seven o'clock Con was still at his desk when he answered his phone.

'Con, we've got him. It has to be him. Joe and Ellen were very observant. The van is parked outside a John Franklin's house in Colestown, just a few miles out of Wicklow town, and it's got a streak of lightning on each side of it. He's an electrician and it has to be him. Can you get the paperwork done so that we can get an arrest and search warrant tonight?'

'Tonight!'

'Con, we have to do it immediately. We can't give him any more chances to hide evidence, so we have to do it now, tonight. We'll sleep tomorrow.'

'Why do I not believe you!'

'Thanks, Con. Look, I'll go round to the Garda station here, inform the brass and get some reinforcements for when you get here. We've got the bastard. Thanks, Con. See you soon. I … I just know it. We're bloody geniuses, so we are!'

CHAPTER 4

Joan

I'm sure that I am not the first person to wonder how it is that we have no premonition of disaster as it falls into our lives. It had already happened that morning before I woke up, yet I went about my normal routine, getting my teenage son up, feeding us both, nagging him to eat a more substantial breakfast before a brief kiss on the cheek heralded the sound of the back gate banging and the bike being dragged into action as he left for school. Had I not put on my usual pop music station but instead listened to the early news bulletin, I would have left for work better prepared to deal with that morning's disastrous revelations.

The bank was open, but such were the shock waves that reverberated around the place that no business was being done. I have been a cashier, now a sort of assistant manager, for over fourteen years, but I was doing less work than anyone else, if that was possible. I too was shocked, but with much more reason than the other employees in the bank. To them John Franklin was a regular, familiar customer. He was someone whose van, with its sign showing a bold flash of lightning and bright red lettering, was a part of their everyday provincial town's life pattern. To me he was a friend, an integral part of my childhood. He was someone who, along with his wife and two children, I counted among my closest friends. I reread the national paper. Sensibly, an increased number of the morning editions had been delivered to all our newsagents. Idly I wondered what would happen to the early editions, now redundant, fodder no doubt for the dying art of chip-wrapping. Who in our town was going to accept a paper that morning that hadn't John Franklin's name emblazoned upon it? For the sixth or seventh time I reread the article in the vain hope that somehow, between the last reading and this one, the name and identity attached might have changed.

But nothing had changed. My life and the lives of old friends were changed by it. They were changed irrevocably.

COLESTOWN MAN ARRESTED AND CHARGED WITH MURDER OF TEENAGER

At one o'clock this morning, before a special sitting of the Wicklow District Court, Judge Joseph Smith remanded into custody John Franklin (37) of Colestown, Co. Wicklow, on foot of the charge that he did murder Barry Breen, 13 years old, of Brownstown, Co. Dublin on or about the 11th day of March of this year. Mr Franklin, flanked by two Gardaí, made no reply to the charge. He stood silent and impassive while he was remanded into custody for a week. Solicitor Brian McGrane representing him did not attempt to seek bail. Shortly after, Mr Franklin was led to a waiting police car and speedily driven away. A vociferous crowd alerted to the early morning hearing arrived in the town and had to be calmed and ushered homeward by a reinforcement of Gardaí, obviously summoned in expectation of trouble. Some of this crowd, relatives and family friends of Barry Breen, were very angry at having missed the hearing and strong in their condemnation of the accused. Also seen in the early morning gathering were Mr James Fitzpatrick and Mr and Mrs Creamer, parents of two other missing boys, believed dead, over the past five years. They stood quietly aside from the main body of the crowd and would only confirm to our reporter that they were hopeful that the arrest and remand of John Franklin might somehow throw light on the mysterious disappearance of their own sons. Prior to Mr Franklin's arrest, the police team investigating the murder was, we understand, working on the premise that the three cases were possibly linked. The Gardaí were, however, reticent when asked whether they expected that further charges would be brought against John Franklin in relation to the two other missing teenagers. They would only comment that they were continuing to pursue their investigations into those cases.

John Franklin, 37 years old, married with two teenage children, a boy and a girl, is a self-employed electrician. He is well known and respected in his local area. He is currently vice chairman of the Colestown football club and is in fact a former county footballer. One local person confirmed that he was a quiet, affable, well-respected member of this small country town and it seemed inconceivable that his name could be linked with the ghastly murder and sexual abuse of young Barry Breen. Local people are frozen in disbelief that such a grisly crime, or series of crimes as is suspected, could be laid at the door of such a respected pillar of this quiet community.

Beyond saying that John Franklin would be coming before Wicklow Court in one week's time, the Gardaí would make no further comment.

The paper hadn't got the name wrong. It wasn't a typographical error and it seemed unlikely that the Gardaí had acted without definite information. So the shock and sadness of such a tragedy invading our community was going to have to be faced – faced and dealt with by all of us whose lives were touched by John's. For most people in the town of Wicklow it was a grim reminder of the proximity of tragedy. For those of us living in the small village of Colestown, a short mile or so distant and thus closer to his orbit, it was a numbing, mind-blowing, paralysing shock.

CHAPTER 5

Joan

The numbing paralysis lasted for me through the morning and the non-eaten lunch. My colleagues were sympathetic. Knowing how close John and his family were to me, they steered a respectable distance and left me very much alone in my useless, distracted state. That day I was of no value to myself, my co-workers or the bank that employed me. Slowly, however, I roused from my reverie when I became aware that the noise and subdued bustle of the bank's activity had changed to a screaming silence. It was an unreal quiet that permeated even my disassociated being. Looking up, I quickly realised what had caused the silence to descend. Ann, my friend and wife to one of my oldest and best friends, was standing mutely in the middle of the bank, a frozen look on her face and supplication for relief jumping out of her eyes. She looked distressed, and it was clear that she neither really knew where she was nor why she was there. Some instinct had propelled her into this bank!

I can't remember moving towards her, but I found we were hugging. We were drawing strength from each other, which was very strange, as neither of us had any to give. Slowly we lurched, holding tight to each other as if the loss of positive contact would lead us to lose the strength somehow garnered. We found ourselves sitting in the manager's office, deep in the cushioned seats. Tea and biscuits appeared on the table before us as Jim, the bank manager, in his usual kind way ensured we were looked after and were allowed the privacy to handle our grief.

We mumbled, making conversation yet not connecting. Four separate conversations were going on at once. Ann was talking, though her sounds were not connecting with the thoughts floating around in her head. I spoke.

I asked how John was, how the kids were. In reality all I wanted to hear was that a terrible mistake had been made. The police surely had called to the wrong door. Perhaps they had arrested by mistake the wrong John Franklin, or at the very least identified the wrong van. Ann said she was okay, which she wasn't. She said the children – Maura, fourteen, and Brendan, my godson, thirteen – were all right, which they couldn't have been. She said everyone was so sympathetic, which I was certain was true. The tea, barely sipped, had gone cold; the biscuits still lay untouched when we finally coordinated sufficiently to actually have a semblance of a conversation.

Ann gave me a sense of the sequence of events in a muddled fashion that took a while to piece together into my own organised form. The Gardaí had rung the bell at 10.30 two nights previously. The children were in their rooms at the time. John and Ann were sitting, as normal, watching television while having supper in the kitchen. Ann answered the door and admitted three imposing plain-clothes detectives who said they wanted to see John. She ushered them into the sitting room and called him. He went pale and shock visibly set in as she told him police were awaiting him in the other room. Stumbling from the kitchen, he suddenly stopped, turned and muttered, 'Thank God it's over. I'm sorry, I'm sorry. I love you, Ann.'

After saying that, John left her and walked into the sitting room, closing the door behind him. Ann was left alone, excluded from the proceedings, in a state of panic, imagining all sorts of horrors, not one of which even came close to the real one unfolding. Less than five minutes later the detectives emerged to tell her that John was going down to the station to help them with their enquiries. As he left, escorted by the visitors, four other gardaí entered and searched the house and the garage for up to an hour before taking away John's van for 'forensic testing'.

Listening to Ann's recounting, I only heard the 'Thank God it's over. I'm sorry' bit, as the implication of those words heaped disaster on disaster. It was at that point I think that I realised that John was not only arrested for, but also very probably guilty of, a horrendous crime. How could that be? How could my friend, companion of my youth, one whom I had even trusted to care for my own son, have raped and murdered a young boy? Certainty of his guilt invaded me. I was so wrapped in my own guilt, even if just guilt by association; wrapped in my feelings of despair, of disintegration, that I barely heard Ann ask me if I would try to find out for her what had happened. Above all she wanted me to help her to understand how her husband could be associated in any way with such a horrible act.

Jolted back to reality at the enormity of my friend's request, I hastily demurred. What could I do? Weren't the police on top of it and didn't they seem to know everything? Why, Ann kept asking, why had John, her husband, done this? How could someone who for fifteen years had shared her life, her body, her love, her children, go and do what he had done to some poor innocent child? There had to be a reason, and Ann in her grief had elected me to find it.

Leave it to the police, I urged. But she insisted that they would only be interested in whether he did it or not. Ann couldn't move past *why* he did it. What was it that caused her husband to commit such a crime? She had to know, and I was elected as the oracle.

'I work in a bank, for goodness sake, Ann,' I protested.

'You trained as a psychologist before joining the bank, didn't you?' Ann said.

'Well, yes, sort of, but that was a long time ago and I never practised,' I replied.

'It doesn't matter,' she said. 'You are bright, clear thinking, very determined and above all you knew him like a sister for all those years. If there is anything to find out, you can do it.'

When my protestations had finally petered out in the face of her dogged determination, Ann slowly rose and quietly left to make her way home to two children and more despair while I sat on in the manager's chair. I was too stunned by the developments to raise the energy to move.

I needed to clarify for myself what I had agreed to and why. At a time of tragedy such as this it would be almost impossible not to agree to the request of a friend. One tormented by grief and the bereavement of this kind of death. John wasn't dead. He was living, but it was a nightmare surely much harder to bear than that of death. Even random accidental death has a basis in reality. This kind of living hell had no preconceived way of coping with it. I knew that if I were Ann, it would be vitally important for me to find out the 'why'. I wasn't Ann, but I did owe her. I owed in friendship, in love, in years of linked living. Above all I owed John, the boy who was the constant companion of my youth. I owed to the group identity of the four musketeers and their gangster moll, to wit me, to find out why one of us had so gravely moved away from the fine line between acceptable and unacceptable behaviour; a line that the five of us had happily and companionably walked together through our growing years.

The memories of the boy John flooded into my mind. Inevitably those of Ray, Cormac and Franner joined in, as the obligations of my adult friendship with John's wife mirrored those of our happy, carefree youth.

CHAPTER 6

Joan

That night, while still in shock, I went through the motions of parenting my son, Ronan. Not that he needed much. He got himself a pizza, got himself to his room and deployed his fifteen-year-old body to studying for the Junior Cert. Examinations were just three months away. Where I got such a together kid from I don't know. He looks like me but in temperament and discipline is the very antithesis of all that I am or certainly was at his age. At that stage of adolescence I would have been out with my friends getting into some devilment or other, and studying to me then was an obscene word.

I only watched television to hear what turned out to be just a brief update on John, as the nationwide news had moved on from the local trauma of yesterday. It still left me empty, dull and depressed, as I was still totally caught into the rawness of our local tragedy.

Sleep didn't come. Memories did, though. John Franklin, my friend, had sexually molested and murdered a young boy. The same John Franklin could have been, and indeed at one time wanted to be, my husband. I was remembering that at some time or other all four lads did suggest marriage.

Up to now I had thought that I had stupidly picked the worst of the four to become my spouse. Now perhaps I hadn't been as unlucky as I had always believed.

Growing up around the town of Wicklow, it was traditional for the boys to play with the boys and the girls with the girls. Not me, though. At some stage around nine or ten years old, I linked in with John, Ray, Franner and Cormac and we formed a cohesive, mutually supportive group, all five of us. This unity saw us through adolescence, youthful rebellion and school, with its successes and failures, as a united group, inseparable and functioning as one. My mother despaired. Dresses and skirts were alien to me, and why not?

My friends certainly didn't wear them, so why should I?

It all started because of my brother, Dónal. He was a year older than me. He was also a quiet, sensitive, intelligent soul who tended to be a loner. While I sort of hung around with the girls playing house and dolls, I also instinctively kept a wary eye out to mind my big brother. There were only the two of us and, as the more socially adept, I felt obliged to look out for him.

Thomas Mooney was a bully. Big, stupid and aggressive for his eleven or so years, he found in my brother a ready target for his dominance. One day on the way home from school with my friends, no doubt on our way to play in one of their houses, we came across Thomas Mooney pushing my brother to the ground and demanding money from him. Dónal, gentle soul, was taking a beating, though, I was pleased to note, not handing over any money. Thomas Mooney, big and strong, suddenly found himself on the ground, as a tigerish nine-year-old girl screamed invective from on top of him. Had Thomas Mooney picked on me instead of Dónal he might have been able to intimidate me, but the flaring anger at the assault on my brother had me in the middle of a fight before I had time to contemplate the wisdom of my action.

As Thomas Mooney got up from my first, sudden attack he was joined by cronies I hadn't been aware were with him. They all began advancing menacingly on me as I stood guard over my prone big brother. I stood defiant but trembling as the seriousness of the predicament I was in dawned on me. Anger still held sway over fear as my dominant emotion. I wasn't going down without resistance.

Suddenly the scene changed. The cronies were isolated and young Ray Traynor was telling Thomas Mooney that he had to handle the situation on his own without the back-up of his friends. Three others with Ray, boys I hardly knew, then created a cordon around us, leaving me to deal with just Thomas Mooney. I didn't have Thomas's brute strength, but I had wits. Above all, though, I was very angry and willing to fight dirty. Rather like a contest between a cornered cat and a dog, the raking and clawing was done by this tigerish feline with a speed and ferociousness unexpected by poor Thomas. It left him retreating, bloodied and bowed, before the contest had even properly begun.

My brother Dónal, dusted down, went off home protesting his ability to look after himself. Thomas Mooney's cronies wisely melted away quickly. My girl companions, long gone, were probably setting up a game of house in the front parlour of one of their comfortable homes. Me, I was borne away like a trophy by Ray and his friends to glory in the victory of a battle that in fairness had lasted but a few short seconds. My metamorphosis into a tomboy had taken place, and from that time on I became just one of the boys. Their foursome had irrevocably become five.

The next day they were waiting at my school gate as I came out and I joined them, thus setting the pattern for the rest of my youth. I loved their devilment, their disregard for convention and their casual, cynical view of the world and its inhabitants. In many ways their outlook was summed up in the fact that they isolated Thomas from his support network yet didn't interfere in the main game that was afoot. They left me, even as a girl younger and smaller than my protagonist, to fight my own unequal battle alone. Judging by the outcome of the confrontation, the inequality lay with the bully Thomas Mooney, who interestingly never again bothered my big brother and warily strode a wide path around me and my new friends.

I quickly became adept at the wrestling, pulling and punching games that boys use as their primary means of communication. I became assimilated into their group, just one of them, and the burgeoning bulges that differentiated me from them in the process of our moving through adolescence made no real difference to the five of us. They were just a bit more careful where they pulled at and punched me than I had to be in my reciprocation. Needless to add, I used this advantage shamelessly!

We were different, non-conformist and individualistic. Teachers despaired of us. They complained of our lack of application, yet we all comfortably sailed through our exams. In transferring to a mixed secondary school, I moved into the same class as the four lads, and in spite of many attempts to separate us, we always gravitated back together. We were the same yet different. We fused into one unit for functioning purposes, yet were very individual in our contributions to the group process.

Ray was the natural leader. He was bright, good-looking, a good talker and thinker. John was athletic and a good mover. He climbed and did the risky things. He was also very good with his hands and could make or mend anything. Franner was the bull. He had no sense of pain or danger and was always to the forefront when the chancy or slightly illegal thing had to be done. Cormac was a stranger mix. He was bright and sensitive and he generally tried to give us a broad perspective on things. He also had a lovely sense of humour. Individually we were different, yet when any threat to our group solidarity emerged, we all fused together.

I was probably closer to John in temperament than to any of the others. I was naturally athletic, outgoing and certainly always on the look-out for something new or dangerous to explore. Living as we did close to the sea and with a vast rural backdrop to our lives, the opportunities to lose ourselves in the reality of the beauty of the world around us and to create magical fantasies of it were boundless. The Murrough and beyond it Broad Lough wetlands became a hunting, fishing, swimming and boating paradise for the five of us. When not in school, we would leave our respective houses in the early morning and return at or often after dusk, heady with the excitement of our escapades. By nightfall we would invariably be tired and fulfilled by our real and imagined adventures.

The Murrough, an area stretching along the coast with its miles of spacious shoreline outside Wicklow town, was a wonderland for us children and now, in adulthood, is still the place I always take myself to for walking, thinking and calming my tangled adult emotions.

The five of us had a wonderful childhood and teenage growing years together. With tremendous mutual friendship and support we comfortably survived and, we believed, defeated the jungle of our parents, teachers and peers. Little ever happened to one of us that didn't involve all five in some form or other! Nobody got invited anywhere without the others.

Parting of the ways was inevitable as we moved into adulthood. It came surreptitiously over a period of months, even years perhaps. The slow ebbing of inseparable friends could not be measured. It could not be identified. Work intervened first, as Franner went off before doing his final school exams to earn a few shillings. John did the exams, then immediately went into apprenticeship with a local electrician. Ray got a good Leaving Certificate and went on to university, commuting daily by train to Dublin. Meanwhile, Cormac went to work as a clerical officer with Wicklow County Council and was assigned to the local authority motor tax office.

Life and the emerging pressures on each of us individually created a natural pattern of separation. Perhaps it was the very closeness which held us together that caused us to drift apart as gradually fewer and fewer of our activities were shared ones. None of us, as far as I can remember, ever took a decision to go our separate ways. The demands and dictates of adulthood just inexorably took over.

Me, I grew up and became a woman. Dresses suddenly suited me. As the five of us drifted apart, each of the lads as an individual moved towards a one-to-one identity with me. Each asked me out, kissed me, a very strange experience after so many years of asexual friendships, and each wanted to continue a one-to-one relationship with me. I couldn't feel at ease emotionally with any of them, so I went off exploring other territories. Amazingly, to me anyway, once the skirts, blouses and dresses replaced the brown jeans I had always worn, interest in me as a person and as a sexual being seemed to be very positive. I never had any difficulty in getting asked out. Mind you, on more than one occasion I would have needed to be a lot more desperate than I ever was to accept the invitations that were proffered. I went out for a two-year period with a nice lad from Bray, but the so-and-so got an invite to join his uncle in America and went happily off to his future, leaving me behind. He promised to keep in touch and a lot more besides, but I never heard from him again. Not even a bloody card at Christmas! Got one birthday card, and it was weeks late …

I married Ray soon after, more fool me. Whereas the musketeers were my youth, my adolescence, my essence, marrying Ray was my disaster.

CHAPTER 7

Joan

Work after a restless night is never easy. My problem was that in the brief periods during the night when I had snatched some sleep, my dreams didn't help. I got up as uneasily as I had lain all night. Finally at about twelve o'clock I shook myself out of my lassitude long enough to make a decision, one I frequently regretted over the next few weeks.

Jim was, as ever, accommodating, so I had the afternoon off and a definite plan as to how to use it. I set off on the road to Dublin, to Mountjoy prison to be exact. I was going to visit John and, beyond the possibility that it was a decision taken out of an excess of tiredness or a perverse sense of responsibility for his actions, I really didn't know why I was going. Was I putting myself out to help my friend Ann? Was I on some crusade of my own? I didn't know and it probably didn't matter really. It was enough that I was going.

Surprisingly, though, I came alive on the journey to Dublin. The lassitude and tiredness that had dominated my morning seemed to evaporate. I began to feel quite energised at the prospect of immersing myself in John and his troubles. Naturally I had a presumption that he would be pleased to see me and that he would readily clear up the issues that were troubling Ann.

I began to convince myself that I was on my way to be the conduit of enlightenment. Some hope!

As I was driving, my thoughts turned to the John I knew as a child. As a group we didn't tend to play in each other's houses. We were much more interested in keeping ourselves and our activities away from our parents than in involving them. Our agreed policy was 'the less they knew about what we did, the better'. However, on occasion we inevitably would spend short periods in each other's homes, except John's. He never invited us and never ever talked of his family. We were all very well aware that John hated his father, who, though he had a good job driving an oil tanker, was known to be a bully and a very short-tempered one at that. Our belief was that John was the only one in his household who stood up to his father and, because of that, was at the wrong end of some beatings in the early years. The only time I remember going into the house, I got a horrible feeling of unease about the place. John's mother was quiet and kind in a guarded sort of way. The other children – John had two brothers and a sister – were all unnaturally quiet and subdued. Mr Franklin, though, was something else. He gave me the creeps. As he spoke to me there was something nasty about him even when he was being, in his terms, nice. I got a horrible feeling of Mr Franklin eyeing my twelve-year-old body up and down and he made me feel really uncomfortable. I was glad to get out of there and, interestingly, John made no comments about his home as we walked off down the street. I never called for him again. We heard, predictably not from John, that his father had been arrested for, though not charged with, an assault on his wife a year or two later. John's two brothers and sister emigrated as soon as they grew up and, apart from their father's funeral, I never saw them again. John, I always felt, stayed to protect his mother and to act as a deterrent to the worst of his father's outbursts. More than any of us, he depended on us as a group to be the centre of his existence. He had anger in him, but we never saw it. With us he was bright and inventive, a nice kid … Now he was an adult and in prison on a charge of murder.

The prison was a big disappointment. It was huge, imposing, old and quite frightening. John was an even bigger downer. I saw him in a small, dirty room smelling of old cigarettes, a chipped table dividing two uncomfortable chairs. A prison officer stood behind him throughout the visit. At least I got in, which for a while seemed unlikely. I wasn't a relative, a wife or an in-law, but finally after submitting to a thorough search I breached the prison defences.

John wasn't as I'd imagined. He wasn't open to confiding. He was just angry at my coming. He didn't really want to see me and certainly wouldn't communicate much with me. Yes, I assured him, Ann was okay; so were the kids and I was keeping an eye on them; after all, wasn't Brendan my godson? Beyond that John wouldn't go.

He was fine, eating well, they were treating him well and he needed nothing. Did he want to talk about it? No. Did he need anything? No. My plea that Ann had asked me to see if I could help was met with a blank silence. Some detective, some investigator I was. I know: try friendly; try the old pals' act. I did, but got the same response.

'Come on, John,' I said in desperation. 'You and I were inseparable growing up. We have so much of a history together. You know I would do what I can to help. Why don't you let me?'

Silence stretched out while he looked through me with an indecipherable expression on his face. All the same, it was the first time I saw something other than anger or blandness in it. Pain, perhaps, was what I saw, but I couldn't be sure. The result of my prodding was not what I expected, though. I didn't elicit from him a true confession. I didn't get a pouring out of the rationale for his actions. What I got I didn't expect or want. What I got came suddenly and sharply after a prolonged period of tense silence. It came as a vitriolic, angry outpouring that John almost spat at me.

'You wouldn't marry me. You should have married me. I only ever wanted you, but no, I wasn't good enough for you. Had I married you everything would have been fine. None of this would have happened. I would have been all right. I know I would. But no, you wouldn't marry me. Off you went with that prat from Bray and then when he dumped you, did you turn to me? No, of course not. You married that bastard Ray. Fat lot of good it did either of you. Serves you right anyway.'

Startled, I tried to interject. Tried to think and then to clarify the time scale. When I was dumped – I resented and objected to that description, but this wasn't the time to say so – John was engaged, due to marry Ann. I told John that.

'So what? What difference would that have made? You knew I loved you and would have married you. I needed you. But no, off to fucking Ray you went. Now you come here all sweetness with … with your "can I help you?" act. "Tell me your problems and I will make them better." Well, precious Joan, why don't you just fuck off? You wouldn't help me, wouldn't marry me when I wanted you to, so it's too late now. Go away. Leave me alone. Just … just fuck off.'

With that John stood up, pushing his chair behind him, then suddenly he overturned the table, causing me to quickly rise and back off to avoid it landing on me. John raised his voice even more, screaming 'Fuck off!' into my startled face. Before I could gather my scrambling wits he turned to the prison officer and indicated that the interview was terminated. He left without a backward glance in my direction. I had no option but to take my startled ego off slowly, thoughtfully, home.

While driving back to Wicklow I tried to remember that time. Funny how years just blur into each other and the events or emotional traumas of them are hard to isolate into their true time frame. Sure I was hurt when that prat – John at least got that bit right – went off to America. I was an easy mark for Ray at that time, but I could recall no memory at all of John making any approach to me. Perhaps he just assumed that I would know he still loved me. How strange life is.

CHAPTER 7 - JOAN

As teenagers John and I went to the school debs together. He kissed me that night and asked me to marry him. It was just a child's game, I thought. We did go out two or three times after that, but I never for a second believed he was in love with me. I just presumed it was a sort of continuation of our long-term friendship. Anyway, I remembered that kissing him made me feel very uncomfortable, almost as if I was committing incest. It somehow felt as though in kissing him I was kissing my own brother. Surely he must have felt the same!

I remembered that John did call around to my house a few times after my break-up. But he was engaged to Ann at the time and I never thought anything of it. I just presumed that on the basis of our long-term friendship he was supporting me in my time of rejection. I'm certain he didn't say anything at the time … definitely he didn't.

Before I reached home I had made up my mind to abandon this stupid task. It was beyond me anyway. All I had achieved was, in some peculiar way that was totally beyond my understanding, to get myself blamed for the murder of that poor boy. Somehow in John's strange, warped mind, my not marrying him was a factor in leading him to commit such a horrible crime. Forget it, Joan. You are out of your depth. 'Leave it be,' I said aloud to myself as I neared my house.

However, before going in I briefly detoured.

I told Ann that John had refused to talk with me. I said that all I got from him was a brick wall, so it was pointless to continue.

'See the others,' she urged. 'See Ray, Franner and Cormac. Find out if they know anything.' I argued that they, like John, wouldn't talk to me, wouldn't tell me anything (if there was anything to tell in the first place). So, I was going to forget it. When I finally left Ann's house to go home, I felt sad for her and angry with myself for not being of any help at all. Again, I couldn't sleep. My mind was racing, so I tossed and turned a lot of the night. No inspiration came except a determination to stay a safe distance away from John and his murder. Sadly, the one thing to come out of my abortive prison visit had been the removal of any lingering hope I might have had that John was innocent.

A great day's work indeed! All I had achieved was to confirm for me what everyone else already knew. One of my best friends, John Franklin, was in prison facing a murder charge.

CHAPTER 8

Joan

The following evening after dinner, Ronan had gone upstairs to study or watch television or both, as fifteen-year-olds do, and I still couldn't settle. I felt restless, edgy and guilty. Guilt at so readily jettisoning my friend's request for help kept nagging at me. She was unreasonable, unrealistic in asking it of me, I rationalised. What she needed was a professional police officer or psychiatrist or both, and certainly not a bank clerk. How could my friend Ann think I was equipped for the role she asked of me? What could she see in me to give her the idea that I could do anything to help her or her husband in the mess they were in?

I grew up in Colestown and have moved house only once in my life, and even that was only a few hundred yards around the corner from the house in which I was born. My whole life has been lived inside the rural perimeters of a little village within a short distance of the small town of Wicklow. My mother worked as a cleaner, for God's sake. Did that equip me to be Ann's saviour?

I sat drinking tea in the kitchen with a pop station blaring from the radio as my mind moved back to thoughts of my mam. It would certainly be unfair to describe her as just a cleaner. There were four of us in our council house: Mam, Dad, Dónal my older brother and myself. Life should have been, and no doubt would have been, very good for us had it not been for the accident that happened to my dad when I was only three or four. He worked for Wicklow County Council as part of their maintenance crew and my early memories are of a quiet, soft, lovable man. Sadly, while doing a 'nixer' for a friend who was building his own house, Dad fell and seriously injured his back. From that time on, a wheelchair dominated our sitting room. He could walk, but only a few steps from his static chair to his mobile chair. Though it meant we got a second bathroom downstairs, with a wide door, we lost our living room to Dad's need for a ground-floor bedroom. It's not that he made demands on us. He was as independent as he could be. He even suffered a lot of pain in silence, but the bread-winning role had by necessity shifted to Ma. She took not one but two cleaning jobs in an attempt to give us a standard of living that was just about equal to the fairly basic level of our neighbours.

Dónal coped by becoming very introspective and stayed indoors a lot, studying hard and becoming academically successful. He, of course, then left home as soon as he finished university and got a job, a wife, a family and a life of his own across the water in England. His wife is as quiet and self-contained as he is, and I rarely see them now. I coped by staying out all the time, spending every free minute with my four friends and using home as a bed, breakfast and dinner establishment that also did my laundry.

I was happy growing up. There was love in my home, though neither parent had the energy to be too overt about it, and my friends Ray, John, Franner and Cormac gave me an identity, a sense of belonging and a very masculine-dominated logic.

When I finished my Leaving Cert, it was obvious that third level was a very difficult option. Dónal was attending university and it was clear that, with Dad dependent and Mam working two jobs, my choices were limited. I would have liked to do a psychology degree but settled to do a two-year diploma in the psychology of humanities and worked weekends and a few nights a week in the local supermarket to fund it.

Two years later I tried to get a job as a psychologist but found out I had been very naïve. My hard-earned diploma was interesting and had been stimulating, sure, but it was nowhere near good enough to even get me an interview, not to mind a job. After two years of effort all I was equipped for was to continue in the supermarket … Bummer!

Ma, however, sorted it. I went, at her request, to see Jim, the manager of the local bank: the one that my mother had cleaned every evening for the previous thirteen years. He was a big, cuddly man who liked and respected my mother greatly, so on the strength of her character and a psychology diploma I couldn't really use, Joan the tomboy daughter got a job as a temporary cashier in a bank that expected her to wear a respectable uniform.

Actually, I took to it like a duck to water. I found I had a natural aptitude for figures and a way with customers that seemed to please everyone. Jim naturally claimed that his vision in seeing the advantage of bringing in a psychology graduate, which I'm not – well, only sort of – to focus on the customer relations part of the job showed his true genius. I also discovered that dresses suited me and that men noticed me in them. Slowly, inexorably, the tomboy youth evolved into the staid businesswoman … on the outside at least.

Banks being big bureaucratic structures, I eventually had to take an exam and attend an interview in head office to be made permanent. I swear Jim, my mentor, sweated over that test a lot more than I did. Anyway, I passed it and became permanent and pensionable. It is hard to believe all that happened seventeen or so years ago and I am still working in the same job. Different role, though, and all thanks to the support, and most probably nagging, of Jim. Traditionally, while most of the bank staff were local, it was the practice to have an assistant manager in place who was learning the finer points of the manager's art, all the while waiting for a promotion to a bank of his own. Some of them were capable, some not. None of them were local and a few of them, particularly the city raised and trained ones, simply didn't understand the individuality required of a personal bank service in a small town. This lack of local perspective could lead to problems. One of those problems changed my role in the bank.

When I had settled in to the job, I discovered that computers were things for which I had a natural affinity. Jim, recognising this, made me undertake courses and gradually I became the local computer guru. This was very beneficial to my manager, who described himself as computer 'illegitimate'. My efforts to 'legitimise' him floundered on his fear of the 'bloody things', as he called them. This meant that gradually I was spending less and less time as a cashier and more and more time monitoring the accounts. Then one day an enthusiastic assistant manager refused to honour the salary cheque of an employee of one of the large local firms and all hell broke loose. Imagine the scene. Friday lunchtime and rumours flying around, as they do in a small town, that the firm was bankrupt and closing. Jim was trying desperately to effect damage limitation at the same time as controlling his language at the defiant, self-righteous assistant manager. When things had settled and the rising community panic had abated, I suggested that perhaps Jim should go to the firm, talk to the managing director and accountant and try to help them plan their finances in a more structured way to avoid this sort of crisis happening again. Jim, desperate for a solution, said 'Yes, why not?' and promptly sent me, which was not what I had in mind.

'What is the point of having our own psychologist on staff and not using her professional skills to the maximum?' was his refrain. He was deaf to my belief that as manager his intervention would be more effective. So I went, or rather I was sent. Actually I really enjoyed the challenge and ultimately the intervention proved very beneficial for both the firm and the bank.

Arising from that experience, Jim delegated me to deal with company finances. Over the years I have developed some expertise in this area and, as a result, a lot of new business initiatives in the town have been financed through our branch. This was a very exciting innovation and the links with the country's business and employment agencies, IDA and FÁS, all helped to improve the bank's profile in the area. They didn't harm our profits either. Our innovations were very well received in Head Office and Jim used this to have me allocated a senior post within the bank. I couldn't be called it because I didn't have the approved banking qualification, but I became in effect the permanent assistant manager.

This I have done now for ten years, and I like it very much except that Jim keeps at me and at me about doing the bank's two-year internal training course so that I can be formally appointed. I tell Jim that what he wants is for me to take over as manager when he retires so that all his mistakes can continue to be hidden from Head Office. In truth I know that I should have done that course years ago and probably would have had my personal life not been such a mess. I like the bank. I am good, very good at my job and, I think, well liked and respected in it. But outside of work my emotional life has been a disaster.

Dad died shortly after Dónal went to take up a post in England. He got an infection and didn't recover, and Ma and I settled down together. Strange how the conflicts of my teen years disappeared in a very short time! Actually we found a tremendous compatibility together as adults. Sad it only lasted a few short years. She was so proud of me. The only downside to all this was that Jim and herself spent hours gloating at their joint success in converting the local tomboy into the town's psychologist and business guru. You would swear to hear them talk that I had no hand, act or part in this metamorphosis.

To be honest I was delighted at the pleasure it gave Ma to talk of how the daughter of the bank's cleaner had become the bank's 'person' expert. Those few years, after my relationship had finished, spent with my mam and with an active sports life, were probably the most contented I had been in my life. Her sudden death robbed me of my best friend and possibly caused me to make the worst mistake of my life. Perhaps I would have done what I did regardless, and her death is just a convenient excuse to rationalise the mess I made of my personal life.

AN ENEMY WITHIN

I was going out with this apparently nice guy from Bray and at that time it seemed as if I was all he needed. Sadly, he was ambitious and when he got a chance to go to America, off he went and left me with hardly a backward glance. Two years of dating and all it warranted was one lousy birthday card a few months after he left, and even that arrived late. To think I gave my virginity to him only a few months before that as well.

I swapped one ambitious guy for a well-known local one with good prospects: a friend whose drinking habits I could change! Of course I could change his drinking, but it changed for the worse, not the better. It took me ten years to give up on that unequal struggle. Ray, my childhood friend, my love, or was it my rebound? Whatever … it certainly was my disaster. Dumped, Ma dying, then a quick marriage!

On reflection I doubt if my mam could have stopped me from the mistake of marrying Ray, but she certainly would have supported me through it. Her death robbed me of so much.

I liked sport and from my teens played a lot. I was good at hockey and played at school and after. Because of the years spent with the lads, I was instinctively tough and aggressive so I had some success. Through one of the girls in the bank I started to play squash, another competitive game, and by dint of hard work and great stamina I became the top player in the county, which I have remained for twelve years now. Mind you, as not too many play squash and very few girls are now taking to it, the threat to my dominance isn't too great. It is only when I travel to the city of Dublin to play matches that I come back to earth with my regular defeats. Over the years this sport has been a great antidote to the struggles I have had in coping with my husband. Actually, sitting here ruminating, it occurs to me how amazing it is that here I am, successful to a degree in sport, successful in work, yet due to the failure of my personal life I have no sense of myself as a capable being. This of course makes it easier to walk away from a promise to a friend.

Mind you, it doesn't make it easier to live with myself.

CHAPTER 9

Kevin

I stood in the interview room waiting for John Franklin to be brought down from the cells. Frustration was, I'm sure, etched all over my body and face. The excitement of getting my man had gradually been eroded over three previous fruitless interviews, not that I was the only one hitting that brick wall. My hopes for this, the fourth, were only slightly higher.

We had had three 'interviews' of almost total silence. No request for a solicitor; not even acknowledgement of his name. Three interviews, three hours of totally one-sided conversation: whether I was soft and sympathetic or deliberately aggressive, John Franklin just sat staring at a seemingly fixed point in the grey wall. His face and eyes remained expressionless and depressively blank. He shuffled into the room behind a prison officer, sat where indicated and an hour later stood up and shuffled off in the same way.

The prison psychiatrist suffered the same unresponsive treatment. Depression was his unconvincing diagnosis. Franklin had refused medication. He talked to nobody, didn't read, didn't look at television, just perfunctorily ate food provided and sat staring blankly at nothing.

The fourth interview was likely to be a mirror to the other three. I had one small hope. The previous day John had spoken, had reacted, to a female visitor. Perhaps this was a catalyst for a breakthrough. Con always claims I am an optimist, so it was natural for hope to spring eternal in me. This hope was frustratingly dashed an hour later. An hour of cajoling, pleading, questioning, even at times haranguing had borne the same result as the previous three interviews.

I was left sitting alone in the bleak interview room, frustrated and angry. I had arrested John Franklin and was confident of being able to secure a conviction, but the hoped-for breakthrough in my search for the missing boys had not had the desired result.

I knew that Mrs Creamer was not going to leave me alone. She was going to ring and/or present herself at my workplace, and I could neither ignore nor blame her. The only one I could really blame was myself. And, of course, bloody John Franklin.

Desperation can lead any of us up desperate paths. Mine drove me to the prison visitor record section and, armed with the information I found there, it led me up the path to Joan Traynor's door.

CHAPTER 10

Joan

Time passed. Life moved on. Normality had resumed its staid process. John and his murder had, or at least seemed to have, receded slightly. Rather like the death and loss of a loved one, it moved from the dominant life force to a quiet shadow, though one that still hung a pall of lassitude over all my activities. Nonetheless, as normal, I went to work, cooked, cleaned and nagged Ronan to go out a bit and ease up on his studies. I even resumed my squash playing. My failure to act on the request from Ann still bothered me. Rationally I knew there was nothing I could do to meet her need. So why torture myself, I reasoned. Why follow up on a fruitless chase? Why put myself further into the mire of that sad, horrible tragedy? I still felt guilty at abandoning Ann's quest so easily. But rationalisation is a very sound mechanism, and why shouldn't I use it to good effect? See, my diploma in psychology wasn't totally wasted, was it!

I also took to walking along the Murrough for an hour or so after work most evenings: the fact that I was doing it so regularly probably reflected the sense of unease I still felt within myself. Walking along the beach with the sea murmuring its arrival on the pebble-strewn shore somehow always seemed to calm me. It also enabled me to think: often great, wondrous thoughts. Sadly, I would invariably have forgotten them before I reached my car to drive the two miles back to my home. On that walk, whenever time allowed, I liked to cross the railway line and go to Broad Lough. This is a beautiful area, where memories of so many childhood sunny days and calm evenings would invariably flutter through my mind. The swans, ducks, gulls and herons that inhabit it add to the ever-changing, ever-wondrous isolation of the area. It always amazed me how my problems or my emotional traumas were never changed by taking this walk, yet on the return to my car and to my reality, they always seemed somehow easier to bear, or at least to be more manageable. I can never get Ronan to join me on my walks now that he is grown up, though as a child he loved visiting this place with me. Mind you, the beauty of an area like Broad Lough didn't create the same images of peace and contentment in my childhood as it now does in my adulthood. To my youth this area was a source of excitement, opportunity and exploration. Now it was a cocoon against life's vicissitudes.

'Ma, there is a big fellow says he is a detective and wants to see you. I put him in the sitting room,' Ronan said, interrupting my memories as I was clearing up after our dinner one evening.

'Who is he? What does he want? I didn't hear the doorbell,' I said in a barrage of questions and comments to Ronan.

He, teenager to his fingertips, shrugged as he replied. 'Don't know, don't know, and if you didn't have the radio on so loud you would hear the door bell.' With that he walked down the hall and climbed the stairs to his room, leaving me to the social process of dealing with my visitor. One strange thing about Ronan, and very individual, from what I hear from other parents of teenagers, is that it is he who turns down my radio and complains of it being too loud, not, as it should be, the other way round.

Big the visitor sure was, six two or three and strongly built as well. I didn't have to be told that he was a policeman.

CHAPTER 10 - JOAN

'Kevin Brady, detective with a special task force based in Dublin,' says he, holding out his hand for a handshake. I consented to respond, fearful for the future of my fingers, but his handshake was only a moderately firm one.

'Joan Traynor,' I said, motioning him to sit back down. 'What can I do for you?' I stayed standing just to give me a sense of control. After all, I was in my own house and a quick inventory of my recent actions sort of assured me that I had nothing to fear from an officer of the law.

Kevin Brady sat down and, after a brief silence, he said 'You paid a visit to John Franklin last Wednesday afternoon. Can you tell me why?'

He asked this in a very serious, slightly aggressive tone and one that, I have to admit, grated on me. As I was still feeling guilty about abandoning Ann's request, I reacted by getting more irritated than was perhaps justified and snapped back at him. I asked how he knew I had visited John, what it had got to do with him, and added that surely I didn't need to answer these questions. Mr Brady wasn't pleased at my non-capitulation. He launched into a degree of waffle about the police and its need to be assisted in its enquiries and ended by wondering why I was so defensive about a simple question. With that he stood up, an action that I construed as his trying to dominate me and one which, given my personality, made me even more determined not to be intimidated by him.

'My visit to Mr Franklin was personal and private. As I can't see how it is any business of yours, you might like to leave,' I said, stretching up to my full five foot six inches, all the while regretting that I was in house slippers and not heels.

'You mean I am not even going to be offered a cup of tea? I always understood that these small villages were famous for their hospitality,' he said, a smile softening his solid features.

He must have thought I was an awful gobshite to be conned by a move like that. I had worked in a bank for years and such tactics were second nature to me. So I ignored his overture, indicated the door and gestured for him to depart.

Seeing the stiff, determined position I had adopted, Mr Brady sighed, then changed tack.

'Look, I'm sorry,' he said. 'I obviously got off on the wrong foot with you, Mrs Traynor. You see, I came here hoping you might be of help to me. God knows I need it. So could we perhaps sit for a few minutes while I outline my problem … please?'

Bullying didn't work. Smarm didn't. Now he was trying to use the sympathy approach. Ah well, I was only going to look at television anyway and he did look much less in control in this mode. So I indicated for him to sit back down and then, as he was about to start talking, I suggested that perhaps I could make tea and maintain the town's reputation.

My kitchen isn't small, but he certainly made it seem so. It wasn't so much his height, it was the solid square frame that gave him the illusion of being huge. I was grateful that I had some tea brack, a passion of Ronan's, still uneaten to accompany the tea. While I prepared the tray, Kevin picked up the tea towel and without comment finished the drying up I had been doing. He also found the cutlery drawer and the crockery press without any help or direction from me. When the tea was made and on the tray, we went back into the sitting room, where I sat opposite him. As I was pouring the tea, I began, with unaccustomed formality.

'Mr Brady, you have a problem, I think you said.'

'Kevin to my mother, but to everyone else it is Kev, please.' Nodding impassively to indicate my receipt of this jewel of information, I waited for him to continue. After a momentary pause during which I could see that he was evaluating me and trying to decide on his approach, he began by outlining his job and his dilemma.

According to himself, he worked in a special serious crime unit based in the Garda headquarters in Dublin. His unit had special responsibility for dealing with crimes that were not local to a given area but had broader countrywide dimensions. They dealt with bank robberies, crimes against isolated farmhouses, of which there had been a spate recently, or individual

CHAPTER 10 - JOAN

murders that seemed to have national rather than local dimensions to them. For the past four years or so he, Kevin Brady, had been investigating a case of a missing teenage boy named Frank Creamer. A few years later, he told me, another boy, eleven-year-old Terence Fitzpatrick, went missing in unexplained circumstances and Kevin was also looking into that one. Over the past few years he had got to know the families of the two missing boys very well, and to see and feel in a personal way the pain they were suffering. He explained their need for any news, however bad, of their beloved children. Kevin was working on the premise that though they happened in different counties, the two cases were in some way linked.

He went on to explain that he had very much hoped that the finding of Barry Breen's body might give him the breakthrough he needed in the search for the two boys. He hoped that if he could establish a link between the three, this might lead to the discovery of the two missing bodies. It was obvious listening to Kevin that he was very involved in the other cases and that he felt for the poor parents of the missing boys. He explained that the Creamers and Fitzpatricks needed to find the bodies of their children so that they could begin a process of grieving. A process of facing a reality which, no matter how horrible, had to be preferable to the vacuum they had been in for the past few years. The Creamer and Fitzpatrick families had their lives on hold and needed a resolution, even if it was the discovery of their children's bodies, to help them move on. Kevin was passionate and obviously committed, but I couldn't see what all this had to do with me.

'Fine,' I replied when Kevin had slowed down. 'But why did you come to see me? Surely it is John Franklin you need to see.'

'Oh, I have seen John Franklin … four times, in fact. I have talked to him or tried to. But I have hit a brick wall. He says he has never seen the boys, doesn't know anything about them and doesn't have anything more to say to me.'

So why, I asked, did he come to see me? Kevin looked intently at me, and for the first time I began to realise just how totally driven he was by this case.

'You went to see John Franklin. You might know something that could help. Or maybe you could get him to talk to you,' he answered intently.

'Sorry,' I replied. 'He wouldn't talk to me at all either. I got nothing from him.'

'Tell me, why did you visit him? How are you connected to him? You're not related,' Kevin then asked, relaxing somewhat in his intensity.

Thinking it out a bit, I decided that it couldn't do any harm to share with Kevin the reason for my visit. So I talked to him of my long-term friendship with John and of my being a godparent to his son Brendan. I explained about Ann's request that I find out how her husband could have come to be involved in the death of that young boy. I finished by reiterating my failure to get anywhere and the realisation of the futility of even trying.

'You do believe John Franklin killed poor young Barry Breen, though?' Kevin asked.

'Yes, I am certain that he did kill that poor boy, but I don't have any idea why. I don't know anything about the other two children and certainly John didn't talk to me about them.'

After mulling over the situation together and my replying to Kevin's many questions about my history with John, we finally lapsed into silence. My silence was dictated by the need to come to terms with the probability of the other missing boys also having been killed by John. In spite of the references to them in the newspaper reports, I had totally ignored the possibility of John's involvement in their being missing.

Presumably Kevin was pondering another dead end in his quest for information on his outstanding cases. We had more tea, still in silence, while the tea brack disappeared rapidly. Ronan won't be pleased, I idly thought. Finally Kevin asked me if I would continue my enquiries as per Ann's request, in the hope, he explained, that somehow something else might break and more information would come to light. He overrode my protestations. He insisted that while it seemed to him that he was not going to get anywhere with John no matter how often or long he tried, it was just possible that on the basis of my long-standing friendship, John might talk to me. He argued that John reacting so strongly to me and then tipping over the table while getting very angry showed that I could perhaps get him to open up. Not one of the officers that had interviewed him got a reaction of any sort. Maybe, just maybe, he suggested, I was the best hope of reaching him. Kevin offered to support me in it and promised to give me any help he could.

Reluctantly I agreed to think about it after being reassured again that it was almost certain, in Kevin's view, that the cases were linked and that he strongly believed John had been involved in the probable death of all three boys. Promising nothing, I showed him to the front door. I took his card and assured him that I would think hard about his request. Kevin left quickly, but then, when he was ten feet away from the front door and just as I was about to close it, he turned and walked back with a purposeful look on his face. He came up to me, kissed me briefly on my lips and strode off again, leaving me nonplussed, rubbing my face, all the while gazing at his broad retreating back.

Now what the hell was that about? The cheek of him, and me a married woman, I thought. He didn't know that I was separated! But then I realised that, being a detective, he would have done his homework before visiting me. He almost certainly knew a lot more about me than I could imagine. The odd thought that he probably knew the colour of my knickers and that I bought them in the local supermarket jumped unwittingly into my mind. Keep out of this, Mr Freud, your interpretations are not wanted!

I should have been thinking of John, of Ann's needs or at least about Kevin's proposition. I wasn't. Strange disturbing thoughts and feelings long buried and forgotten took over as a sense of the brief contact continued to tingle on my lips.

CHAPTER 11

Joan

A sleepless night followed: well, a restless one anyway. Many thoughts flooded through my vibrating head. The kiss and what it was all about dominated in spite of the more important issues arising from Kevin's visit. Strange, it evoked for me an awareness of the dearth of sensuousness in my life over the past ten or so years. Ever since I got fed up with the unequal contest between the bottle and myself for Ray's attention and affection, I had been living a very quiet, emotionally bland existence.

The images of the poor parents of the missing teenagers so graphically described by Kevin also kept invading my sleep. Somehow the torment of the unknown seems so much harder to bear than facing up to the death and loss of a loved one. Surely, I thought, the clinging to a hope that you know logically doesn't exist has to be totally destructive. It has to be detrimental to our bodies' need to explode in grief before gradually beginning the process of rebuilding our lives. I thought about those two families. Their lives were on hold. They were waiting, almost praying for the deliverance that even the worst news possible could bring. This continual torture impacted strongly on the struggle within me as I tried to convince myself that I could play the game of being a detached onlooker.

I lost. How could I, no matter how hopeless the task, ignore the pain and suffering of those poor people while I got on with my own safe life cosseted in the quiet backwater of Colestown?

In the morning while making breakfast, it occurred to me that last night's visiting detective wouldn't want to kiss me in my present ravaged, sleep-deprived state. While I was going through the motions of juice, cereal, tea and toast on autopilot, my conscience kept up its invasion into my defensive process. Logic urged me to stay a bystander and not get involved in assisting, if that was what it could be called, this particular policeman in his enquiries. My conscience, however, reminded me of my debt to my godson Brendan and his family.

'Ronan,' I said to my sleepy son as he silently grabbed at his morning repast. 'Will you be calling into your granny's house on the way home from school?'

'Can do,' was his brief reply.

'Will you ask your dad, or get your gran to ask him if he isn't around, to call up and see me please?'

'You want to see him period or only if he is in a sober state?'

Stifling my instinct to correct the reference to his father's propensity towards drink I asked him to pass on the message only if his dad was in a state to hold a reasonable conversation.

'Will do,' Ronan said before kissing me on my cheek, hastily grabbing his school bag and departing. As I listened to the bike being unceremoniously dragged, as usual, from the back porch and the gate clattering closed behind him, I idly thought that it wasn't bad to be in receipt of even a sketch of a kiss from a teenager of his years. Kiss … that word again! I think I am developing a fetish!

I went to work. Extra care was needed with the make-up to hide the remnants of the storm-tossed night. I then went home to prepare dinner and build myself up for a session with my former husband. Ronan was right: Ray could only be faced if his day's drinking was still ahead of him.

'To hell with this,' I called out to the empty house. I should be out walking on the beach, reinvigorating myself, not hopping around from one foot to the other, anxious at the impending visit of the man I once promised to spend my life with.

Ray did arrive, but not that evening. Too much to expect, I suppose! He came the following one. Before that, however, I had a different and a very unexpected visitor to the bank.

I was serving a customer at the foreign exchange counter when I looked up and saw him standing there. Going through the well-practised motions of checking the rates and resolving the exchange gave me time to compose myself. It was coming up to the busy lunchtime, which is why I was helping the counter staff. After I had been relieved I, with a detached, indifferent air, brought Kevin through to the interview room and indicated for him to sit. As he settled himself, I slowly closed the door and joined him. All the while my mind and my emotions were running in all sorts of directions. I was surprised to realise just how pleased I was to see him. I was also anxious that he might be bringing bad news about John. Above all, though, the strange feeling in my stomach, while it could have been the result of anxiety, had about it another, more personal feel. It was an emotion, or more accurately a cluster of emotions, that I was unable or perhaps just not yet ready to face.

Kevin himself seemed to be having trouble in getting started on the purpose of his call. Eventually, after much humming and hawing, he blurted out, 'Look, first of all I want to apologise to you for my, eh, eh, forward behaviour the night before last. I don't know what came over me. Most unprofessional … I … I do apologise.'

So that was it. He was fearful that I might have somehow misunderstood his act and would be – what, reporting him? … For what – aggravated assault on my person, to wit, my lips? Did he think that the kiss had upset me? Well, I could play things cool; after all, this was the bank, where I was the one with authority and power, so I was in control.

'Oh … the strange way you had of saying goodbye? Don't worry about it. I didn't give it another thought. I just presumed you did that every time you left a stranger's house late in the evening. I just imagined it had to be a little, eh … idiosyncrasy of yours.'

Shut up, Joan, or you will give the lie to the 'I didn't give it another thought' line, I inwardly urged myself.

'No of course I don't do it … ever. I have never done anything like that before. I don't know what came over me. I just, well, wanted to. Once or twice when I was in your kitchen I wanted to take you in my arms and well it … it just happened.'

For such a big fellow, Kevin was certainly squirming.

'Forget it. I have,' I said emphatically as I sat back. I was feeling very much more in control of this little scene now.

Kevin was still decidedly uncomfortable as, with a vague wave of his big hand, he continued. 'I'm really sorry. I did it because I liked you and wanted to, but it was very unprofessional.'

'I said forget it. I have,' I interjected quickly. Then, as I was anxious to change the direction of the conversation, I hastily asked, 'How is John Franklin?'

'Oh,' said Kevin. 'Yes, eh, John. Well, he was up before the court again this morning. The judge adjourned the case for a further few weeks to give us more time to complete our investigations. John's solicitor didn't ask for bail, so he will have to stay in prison.'

'Was there any trouble?'

'No,' Kevin replied. 'We brought him in through the back entrance and straight out again. The whole thing didn't last more than ten minutes. I was involved in smuggling him back out again, so I didn't see who was in the court room and I don't know if the Creamers or Fitzpatricks were present for the hearing.'

'So you have bought yourself more time, then?' I asked.

CHAPTER 11 - JOAN

'Yes,' said Kevin, adding, 'You will continue on with your own enquiries, won't you?'

So that is what this visit is really about. He was scared that the insignificant little incident at my front door would cause me to pull out of my promise to at least think about talking to the other lads. As if I cared enough about him and his stupid kiss. The bloody cheek of him!

'I have asked my husband to call in and see me and I intend to ask him about his past history and John Franklin. You needn't fret. I can certainly assure you that I wasn't upset enough not to at least ask Ray a few questions. As I said, I didn't give your unorthodox parting another thought.'

With that I stood up and Kevin, with a sheepish nod and a hesitant step, left the room and the bank without another word. I escorted him out rather in the manner of a security man ushering an undesirable from the premises. We parted formally. I just nodded before turning and walking back to my office without a backward glance. Thinking about it afterwards, as I may have done once or twice during the afternoon, I was inordinately pleased with myself at how I had handled that little interview. Kevin Brady had been neatly put in his box.

That evening, after Ronan had gone off to play a football match, I was again reliving in my head the lunchtime interview. By this time, though, I wasn't as sure that I had been as masterful as I'd originally thought. However, my reverie was interrupted as Ray walked in.

Ray was dressed in the style of the accountant he was, not that he had functioned much as one for the past few years. He was sober, his mother's influence no doubt. Naturally he tried to remedy that first. He went straight to the liquor cabinet on his arrival. To his disgust, the options were very limited: 7-Up and orange juice, to be precise. Banging the cupboard door shut, he asked to what did he owe the pleasure of this summons.

Avoiding the issue, I enquired about himself, his work, his life, his drinking. He, as usual, said that he had a few good mates and that doing their books kept him fully busy. He was hardly drinking at all now, he added.

Then, to distract quickly from that obvious inaccuracy, he asked how come Ronan didn't seem to be doing any work and the exams only a few months away. I wasn't about to be fooled by that oft-used technique of Ray's. Living in a small village, I knew the reality of his drinking much better than that. Ray by now had only two friends whose books he did, and they were one-man businesses. The work on their accounts could be done in ten minutes each week. As I well knew, Ray drank all the money he had and just drifted from drink to drink. The trouble with a small country place is that every individual's life patterns are well known to the rest of us. It was a point of sad amusement to me that at any time of the evening I could unerringly find Ray. Seven thirty he would be standing at the bar of the pub at the top of the main street. Eight fifty would see him traversing the seventy or so yards to the next pub. Come ten fifteen he was invariably to be found in the third and last pub in the town, sitting closeted with his mates in the men's nook. There, as far as I could work out, they spent their time recycling the same stories night after night. I could never figure why Ray moved around like that. Maybe it was just a sense of responsibility he had to the publicans in the town to balance his custom between them all.

Interestingly, his drinking cronies didn't follow the same pattern of movement as my ex-husband. Most of them had a regular pub and were loyal to it and their own space within it. They located in one place and stayed put for the evening. It might have been that Ray had a need to share his company with a broader group of people for his evening's entertainment, a need not shared by the other regular drinkers of the town. It might have been more difficult to come to understand the logic of my husband's drinking pattern than it would be to unravel the mystery of John Franklin's criminal behaviour. A mystery that I was busily avoiding discussing with Ray now that he was here!

Over a cup of tea that he didn't want, I finally plunged in and asked him what he thought of the horrific thing John had done. Ray was, as I should have predicted, his usual caustic, dismissive self. John Franklin was a bastard, driving around in his silly van, his name splashed across it, full of his own importance. When was he ever any different? Ray was launched.

'That fucker,' he continued. 'He took away the business of doing his books from me without a by-your-leave and he encouraged everyone else to do the same. He did it vindictively and deserves anything he gets.'

My memory was that John spent weeks if not months chasing Ray to do the books. Finally, one night in desperation he came to our house. He took his accounts from Ray's office and sent them elsewhere to be audited before, as he said, the tax people put him out of business. However, I decided it was more convenient not to mention those facts at this juncture.

I had started and as I had to continue I asked, 'You were great friends; we all were as kids. Did you notice anything that could explain how John would do this?'

'No, and we weren't all that great friends.'

'Come on, Ray,' I said, exasperation showing in my response to him as it so easily did. 'Franner, Cormac, John, myself and yourself were the best friends we could have been. How can you say different?'

'We were only friends as kids. When we started to grow up we split up quickly,' Ray answered dismissively.

'That's not true. Right through our secondary school years we were never apart. We did everything together, the five of us.'

Ray fixed a dismissive look on me. This look was a regular feature of our years together and one that I am now delighted to be rid of.

'How stupid can you be? We weren't like that. The four of us only ever went around together at that time when you were on the scene. It was you we all wanted to be with.'

'Ray, that's a load of bull and you know it,' I said, beginning to show my exasperation.

'No, it isn't, all those three fuckers were in love with you. They only ever wanted to get their hands into your knickers, that's all,' Ray said and then, with a disgusting leer, which I think he considered to be his version of a gamey look, he added, 'Of course I wiped all their eyes on that, didn't I?'

'Just because you were the one I married – and what a stupid mistake that was – doesn't mean you were the only one of the lads who, as you so delicately put it, got his hand into my knickers, you know, smart alec.'

God, I can be such a bitch, can't I? But then ten years of stupid pointless marriage, one of getting him out of the house and then the last five avoiding the reality of the mess I made of my life can lead a person to be like that!

Ray, of course, wasn't going to let that sort of opportunity go to waste, so he quickly countered: 'It wouldn't fucking surprise me what you let them or anyone else do. I always knew you weren't to be trusted.'

'Come on, Ray,' I said, trying to get a grip. 'Let's leave our own sorry personal history out of this. You knew John as well as anyone. Think about it. Is there anything you can remember that might explain how John could commit such a crime?'

'No, there fucking isn't, and why are you asking anyway? Why don't you mind your own business?'

In a pleading tone I said 'Ray, Ann has come to me. She asked me to find out why John could have done this. I promised to try and see if I could help.'

Giving me a withering look, Ray turned his back on me and over his shoulder half shouted: 'You, help ... some joke. All you are is a bloody office girl. Just because you wear a fancy uniform in that bank you think you are something. All you are good for is to make tea for that fat fool of a bank manager and to count money. Unless of course you let him have it away with you like you did with your sad childhood friend John Franklin. Is that how you got your promotion then?'

With that he moved to the door and opened it. Before finally leaving he spat at me derisively: 'If that's all you called me here for, you can go and fuck yourself. I'm out of here. I'm busy. I have things to do.'

'Ray,' I said in desperation, 'Stop, wait. Look, the police called as well. They interviewed me and asked that I talk to Franner, Cormac and yourself. They think that there might be something in the past that can explain John's behaviour.' With that I reached out and caught him by his shoulder. 'Please, Ray, help me. Help Ann. If there is anything that might explain John's behaviour, you have to tell me,' I pleaded.

Suddenly Ray turned around and slapped me sharply across the face. For a few seconds we faced each other. Shock was visible on both our faces. Mine because in all the horror times that we had had, with all the horrible things we said or shouted at or about each other, Ray had never once laid a hand on me before this night.

Ray himself was clearly taken aback at his own action. But knowing him as I do, an apology was not something I was expecting. He never ever apologised for anything.

'Stay out of my personal business. You have done enough already to ruin my life. Just stay out of my business,' he hissed at me before turning and quickly leaving the house.

I stood there almost immobilised for a long time while the sensation of the slap lingered. It tingled it seemed forever on my face. I was in total shock at Ray's violence and confused as to what could possibly have given rise to such an outburst from him. All the times past when we had been so angry with each other, he had never even come close to striking out at me. I must have touched a very raw nerve for him to hit me like that. The thing that really scared me was that I didn't have an earthly idea what nerve it was that I had touched.

It had been a pointless, fruitless meeting, as I should bloody well have known it would be. All I achieved was a meaningless row and a reaction that would drive Ray even further away from me. It would also give him more reason, not that he needed it, to wallow in the depths of his destructive alcohol habit. Blast Ann and particularly bloody Kevin Brady for getting me back into this stupid quest, a task in which I was totally out of my depth.

CHAPTER 12

Joan

If you make a mess, compound it. I seemed to be living my life by this dictum those days. Ray's angry departure had left me in a state of suppressed desperation. I had made a total mess of the meeting with him, and it left me upset and angry with myself. I was out … way out … of my comfort zone and knew it. The thing to do, as I told myself over and over, was to forget the whole scenario. Forget John; forget Ann and especially that bloody detective. The thing to do was to retreat into my safe existence.

But did I do that? Of course not! Instead I got into my car and drove the four or so miles out the road to visit Franner, one of the best friends of my childhood. I'm not sure why I did it, as I certainly didn't want to. It was probably one of those times when doing something, anything, was better than sitting thinking and feeling sorry for myself. Perhaps I should have sat and thought, even if they were miserable, uncomfortable thoughts.

On the way to his house my mind drifted to the memory of Franner, or at least the young Franner of my childhood. We grew up in different parts of the town and our family structures were totally different. His father was a prominent local solicitor and his mother a member of the tennis set. My parents were working class and proud of it. His family had hopes and high ambitions for him, whereas my mother's real wish, as she had frequently said, was to see me wear a skirt and begin to act like a proper girl. All things considered, I wouldn't have swapped places with him for anything, because although we didn't have luxuries, space or a big house, we had love and a parent who was always there for us. Franner's dad was very busy with his practice and his mother, when she wasn't helping in the office, lived for her tennis and social circle.

Franner enjoyed getting himself wet, dirty or generally messed up by diving head first into whatever activity or hobby appealed to him at the time. We were both impulsive, so it was one or the other of us who usually started the most hare-brained schemes the group got involved in. I smiled as I remembered the summer that we found the bird's eggs. They were left in a nest abandoned by the parents. We reckoned that the parents had probably been victims of a predatory fox. Franner decided that we could take over the parental role of hatching and then rearing them. A series of early morning and late evening feeds commenced as they hatched. We jointly and separately performed the mothering role. How we rejoiced as the fledglings grew, and how we cried together as two of them died under our inexpert care. Franner as a child had a hard, determined shell but a soft, gentle core. No doubt with the successful growth of his business he had learned to protect and probably hide the soft part.

We were so alike that it was impossible to believe that we had grown so far apart. It must have been over ten years since we had even spoken. Oh sure, we waved and smiled as we occasionally drove past each other, but neither of us seemed to have had a need to reconnect. It would have been inconceivable to us in our teens that we would live just a few miles distant and not be in regular contact. I think that we all took the friendship of the five of us so much for granted that as it began to slide, none of us made an effort to hold it together.

Franner was married at this point, with four boys, the eldest a year or so younger than Ronan. His middle two were twins. Breda, his wife, was not local. She was nursing in Dublin when they met. The first time I was introduced to her was at their wedding. I must say I really liked her. However, in spite of promising myself that I would make a point of getting to know Breda in the following months, I didn't follow up on it. By then the cracks in my own marriage and the drinking of my husband had become real issues and I didn't have much energy left for developing social contacts.

The wedding itself presented an interesting dilemma for me. When the invite came I was sort of surprised, though delighted to get it. Then Ray realised that he wasn't included. Actually, neither John nor Cormac was invited either. Anyway, Ray exploded. He called Franner all the names he could think of and then dramatically instructed me that I was not to attend. Needless to say, given the perversity of my nature, it was the fact of being instructed that was the catalyst that actually decided for me that I was going. I have to admit that in the end, while I went to the wedding mostly out of contrariness, curiosity was also a determining factor. I was dying to see and meet the girl that Franner had decided on marrying.

Franner left school a few months before he did his final exams. He wasn't academic by inclination and certainly didn't want to follow the path drawn up for him by his parents. Law and ultimately taking over the family practice wasn't for him. For weeks before he made his decision known to his parents he talked it out with me. Those few months, before he left home and just after he started work in the warehouse of a local electrical store, was probably the last time we were really close.

Now, all these years later, he owned his own thriving company. He could probably have bought his father's practice and not felt the strain.

And I was going to see him to reawaken long-buried history!

By the time I turned into the entrance to his house I was reconnected and looking forward to seeing him again.

The house was large and impressive, set in its own grounds with a horse paddock at the rear. I got a shock when the door was opened in answer to my ring. The young lad that answered had a bright, open, friendly smile set off by tousled fair hair. I found myself almost hoping that this mirror of the Franner of my youth would suggest that we go, as we so often had done, down to Broad Lough and spend a few hours fishing in the near dark. No such luck! Instead, he said that he was sorry, his dad wasn't in, but I was welcome to come in and see his mam. Having politely settled me in the opulent sitting room, he smiled and promised to send his mam in directly. Just as the door closed behind him I heard a loud roar of 'Ma, someone for you!' and then quick retreating steps that indicated he had moved on to more pressing tasks, an act so reminiscent of my own son.

Breda looked assured and composed as she came in brushing her hands busily on her skirt. I recognised her from the wedding, but then I knew who to expect. It took some time before realisation dawned and she uttered, 'Joan, how nice to see you.'

I apologised for calling unannounced and explained that I just wanted a quick word with her husband. She brushed my apology aside, saying that I would always be welcome, and indeed her demeanour indicated this. Then, as alarm bells began to ring for her, she asked if anything was wrong.

'No,' I assured her. I hastily added that I just wanted to talk to Franner about John Franklin, so there was no need for alarm.

'Terrible business,' Breda said, relaxing again, 'so horrible for his wife and children.'

I explained that they were having great difficulty in coming to terms with John's arrest and I had called to see if Franner could be of some help.

'Well, I hope so,' Breda answered. 'But I have to tell you that when he came in from work on the day of John's arrest he hadn't heard anything about it, so I showed him the paper. Franner read it and seemed to go a bit pale, then he threw the paper in the bin and hasn't mentioned a word about the case to me since.'

'Maybe I shouldn't talk to him about John. I should go,' I said as fear rose in me.

CHAPTER 12 - JOAN

'Nonsense,' Breda interrupted. 'If you want to talk to him, do. Anyway, I'm delighted you called as I have been meaning to talk – to have a chat or, well … at least to apologise – to you for a long time.'

This startled me, but before I could react she muttered 'tea' and left the room. I heard her negotiating with one of the children before she returned and sat down again opposite me. With a smile she said, 'They're great kids. They just need handling when you want them to do something for you.'

'Apologise?' I said. 'What do you have to apologise to me for?'

'Well,' she answered, sitting more erect in the chair. 'When I heard that Ray and you had separated, I told Franner that he should call to make sure you were all right. Then when he didn't or wouldn't, I kept intending to call myself, but I … I just feel guilty at not having done so.'

'Are you sorry you missed hearing all the gory details first hand?' I asked, though I was smiling as I said it.

'Exactly, you got it in one. I do so enjoy everyone else's misery.'

'You should have called, then. You sure missed a basinful in my case.'

We smiled at one another, and I was taken aback at how much I was beginning to like Franner's wife.

'Actually I owe you an apology as well.'

'Oh?' Breda said, still smiling. 'Well … apologise away!'

'When you were first married I sort of meant to give you a call and invite you over. But … eh … things weren't great with Ray even then. I spent years trying to hold on to something that didn't exist and I never did get around to inviting the two of you over.'

Breda shrugged in acknowledgement of the realities of my life, then, reaching into her pocket, she took out a packet of cigarettes. She placed one in her mouth; having lit it and as she blew out the smoke she sighed and said, 'I reckon I was probably lucky. If what I hear is true you would probably have tried to drag me down to that squash club of yours for some disgusting exercise.'

Before I could form a suitable response to her quip, the front door opened and banged shut. Seconds later Franner, heavier and older looking than I expected, strode into the room. The smile he directed at his wife froze as he saw me out of the corner of his eye. I stood up while he did a double take and then, feigning shock, asked in a brusque, sarcastic tone, 'Who's dead?'

This was said, I noticed, without any greeting or sign of welcome to me.

Taking up his clipped tone, I answered in like manner. 'A young boy, killed by an old friend of yours. I came over to see if you might help me to understand how it could have happened.'

Franner stared through me for a few seconds, then, in a slightly raised tone, asked, 'How the hell do you think I can help? I haven't seen that bastard for years, nor do I want to either.'

Trying to be conciliatory, I gently, if a bit late, said, 'Come on, Franner, we were all close friends. We went around together for years and years. Someone somewhere must have known or seen something. Is there anything that could give us a clue as to what could have made John do something as horrible as murdering a young boy? Nobody, and certainly nobody we knew so well, could have done this just out of the blue. There must be a trigger somewhere. We were all the best of friends. Surely we should try to find out why … what made him do it.'

My attempt at conciliation didn't work. With a sudden burst of anger, albeit controlled anger, Franner said in a rush, 'Friends, sure ... we were the best of friends, Joan, of course we were. So good that you haven't bothered your arse to visit me or my wife here in how many years, even though I only live a few miles from you. Now when you do, it's to try to find out if I am somehow to blame for something John Franklin did. You want a trigger? I'll tell you what, get a gun and I'll gladly pull the trigger to rid the world of that bastard. Now leave me alone. Go … go … get out of my house.'

While I struggled to absorb the suddenness of this – no doubt I was standing stupidly with my mouth open – Franner walked over to the drinks cabinet, where he poured himself a stiff Scotch. Having filled his glass and without offering either of us a drink, he left the room and could be heard climbing the stairs. Breda, I think shocked at Franner's sudden explosion of anger, started to apologise, but I stifled it while making motions towards leaving. Actually all I wanted to do was to go before I lost control and started to cry. At the front door we stood looking at each other, words not coming, as we separately tried to deal with the suddenness of Franner's outburst. Neither of us knew how to take our leave properly in its aftermath. Suddenly Breda hugged and held me, giving and getting support. Moving apart, we smiled at each other: my smile, I'm sure, was very forced, cementing an unexpected friendship as the tension created by Franner's anger eased. On that positive note – and God knows, the rest of the evening had been a miserable catalogue of fruitlessness for me – I left, promising to ring her very soon.

As I was driving home, all I could think of was the stupid blundering about I was doing. My ex-husband had hit me for the first time in all our years of knowing each other. One of my best old friends had more or less told me to fuck off out of his house. I was miles out of my depth. I drove in anger and despair. I was angry at myself and at Kevin, who had suckered me into trying to do something I was totally incapable of. I turned up the music in the car and, as one of my tapes blared out, I began to calm a little.

Slowly I settled and thought. Surely Franner's sudden anger and his reaction to my albeit unsubtle questions about John had an element of something else: possibly even a kind of panic that didn't seem to fit with a rich, successful businessman? Surely, I reasoned, Franner's outburst on top of Ray's angry response had to add up to something? But then what the hell did I know? I was just blundering about in the bloody dark trying to meet the needs of – who? Ann … Kevin … the parents of those missing boys? Or was I just trying to prove something else? Was I trying to convince myself that the friendship, that inseparability that was the existence of my youth and the mainstay of my growing-up years, was a reality and not just a figment of only my memory?

Clearly my view of our childhood friendship was seriously at variance with that of at least two of my youthful comrades.

Mind you, it occurred to me as I came close to home that I did get a genuine hug, and it was a long time since anyone but Ronan had given me one of them. I had also got a kiss of sorts the other night, and from a man. So, some things might be changing in my life. Of course I also got slapped and told to fuck off out of an old friend's house.

A roller coaster of highs and lows!

But who the hell was at the controls?

And where was it leading?

CHAPTER 13

Joan

Sleep came eventually, but it was a night of vivid recurring dreams. No doubt they were strong in their metaphors, but not a vestige of one of them could I remember as I gazed at my ravaged morning face in the mirror. I could have grown tomatoes in the bags under my eyes. But I could also by then be sure that I had hit a chord in Franner. Something had been triggered and then buried by him in anger. The question was, what had I touched? But then what the hell did I know about any of this?

Eventually I rounded up the energy to blunder downstairs in a bleary-eyed state to begin the process of attending to the preparation of my son's breakfast.

I saw Kevin Brady twice that day. Lucky me! The first time was during my lunch break at the bank. I was having my tea and sandwich: thank you, Ronan, for making it, but you should by now know I don't like as much salt as you. While I was idly watching one of the girls reading the paper, suddenly and startlingly a familiar face gazed at me from its back page. Biding my time, I borrowed the paper from her and in the privacy of my office I read the caption:

VETERAN MIDFIELDER IN NEXT SUNDAY'S CHAMPIONSHIP MATCH

It shouldn't have surprised me to find that he was an athlete or a good footballer. What strangely pleased me was the 'veteran' bit. Thinking about it, it was difficult to place his age. I had actually reckoned that, all things considered, he was really quite young and that he couldn't have hit thirty yet. This was of course a reassurance, as it put him outside the realms of my thirty-plus years. It also dismissed his kiss as a sort of strange handshake. Maybe his way of saying goodbye was just a custom peculiar to some odd part of the county Laois where he grew up. His being a veteran, however, put him into a slightly older category. In sporting journalistic terms, it was unlikely that anyone would be described as a veteran if they weren't at least a few years over the thirty mark. Joe, one of the tellers, who I knew was into sport in a big way, confirmed this for me. Needless to say, my question to him was in no way specific to any individual inter-county player.

On arriving home, I was surprised to find the same Kevin sitting down at my kitchen table with Ronan. They were engrossed in making tea and in deciding on which of the freezer pizzas they would share.

'Make yourself at home, why don't you?' I commented on entering with a heavy dose of sarcasm in my voice.

'Hi, Ma,' said Ronan. 'Kev here called to see you and as I was just about to put on a pizza, he agreed to share it with me.'

My sarcasm directed at Kevin had obviously bypassed my lovely son. He was totally engrossed in getting some food together for the two of them. 'Fine, how was school?' I asked. After all, I had to be seen to be the caring mother, didn't I?

CHAPTER 13 - JOAN

When I came down from changing out of my work clothes and tidying some of the day's ravages, Ronan was halving the microwaved pizza. Knowing my antipathy to them, he didn't even enquire as to whether I would like some. He then took himself off to his room, leaving Kevin sitting at the kitchen table grinning up at me as he tucked into his share of the repast.

'Do make free of my home,' I said, regaining my sarcastic ground.

Kevin's face broke into a full smile and then, exhibiting half-masticated pizza, he answered 'I will, thanks. How are you?'

'Fine,' I replied. 'What is it now? Do the Garda Síochána need my help in finding the gang who robbed the bank in Galway yesterday? They sent you to try and recruit me for that job, is that it?'

'No,' he replied lightly. 'But you know we're always grateful for the help of Joe or even Joan Public. So if you can assist us with our enquiries into that case I promise to be grateful.'

With a superior leer and a good impression of sudden inspiration, I said 'I get it. You are just hiding out to escape all the adoring public who are clamouring for your autograph after today's newspaper exposure. You're looking for temporary sanctuary in my humble house. How nice for us. Well, okay, you can have it, but when it's dark please leave quietly and don't bang the door. Do tidy up first, though, won't you, as we aren't too star-struck around here.'

With that I turned to make fresh tea for myself, feeling in control of the conversation.

'You saw my picture, then, did you? Personally I thought it didn't do me full justice. I look better in profile that I do full face, don't you think?' he said, posturing and turning his face to the light.

I ignored that, naturally.

'"Veteran" – that means "past it – should hang up his boots", doesn't it?' I enquired innocently.

'Still younger than you all the same,' he replied with a grin.

'How do you know?' I asked haughtily.

'I'm a detective, so I detected.'

I decided that this was not a topic I should stay on, so I brusquely changed the subject and asked what I could do for him.

Levity instantly dropped from Kevin as a shadow darkened his face.

'John Franklin attempted suicide this morning. He tried to hang himself. He was taken from the prison to the Mater Hospital and is being kept in a private room under guard.'

He held up his huge hand to stave off my obvious question and continued. 'He is okay. He didn't do much damage, only slight bruising around his neck. But the prison authorities took him to the hospital for observation and, well … to monitor John carefully, as it wouldn't do to lose him that way, now, would it?'

As the frustration of the previous day burst out of me, I snappily said, 'It would be better for all of us if he did top himself, if you ask me.'

'No, it wouldn't,' Kevin said sharply. 'Maybe then I would never find out about the other missing boys, and that wouldn't be very good.'

'Have you made any progress?' he continued.

I ignored his question. 'Has anyone told Ann about the attempt this morning?'

With a sort of sheepish grin, Kevin answered 'Well, no – not yet. I sort of hoped you might tell her for me.'

'Of course, of course, I am to do your detecting for you, so why not get me to do the rest of your job? Any poor people killed in accidents that you would like me to break the bad news to their nearest and dearest while I am at it, eh?'

Grimly, Kevin said, 'Not at the moment, but I sure would prefer you to give me bad news than me, if you know what I mean. That is if you were ever to drop the sarcastic bit out of your repertoire. Seriously, Joan, I am happy to tell Mrs Franklin. But I thought you might tell his poor wife and maybe bring her in to visit him in hospital. It will certainly come a lot better from you than from me.'

CHAPTER 13 - JOAN

For the first time since I came home and found Kevin ensconced in my kitchen, there was silence. He continued quietly finishing off the pizza while I poured out the fresh tea and included a new cup for him. As I placed it before him, he nodded his silent thanks … very bloody domestic … quite nice, actually.

'All right, all right,' I finally said into the silence. 'I will go over to Ann and tell her. You would only trample all over the poor woman's house and probably raid her larder as well. So it will be better for her and cheaper if I go.'

Softening, I added, 'I'll bring her in to see John as well.'

'Good … thanks,' Kevin muttered, adding, 'You might get a chance of a quiet word with him while you are there. I'll clear it for you both to be left alone with him, okay?'

I looked seriously at Kevin for a short moment before asking, with a slight smile playing around my mouth, 'I suppose you will pay for my petrol money?'

'No, but I will buy you a meal to make up for it,' Kevin answered in a tone that was more of a question than a statement.

'Always supposing I might be in the slightest degree interested in eating out with you in the first place, Mr Veteran Detective. Now I'd better get ready and go over to Ann,' I said as I motioned him towards the door.

'I don't suppose you have anything to report on your other enquiries, do you?' he asked innocently.

'No, I don't. Now out with you. Go and let me get on with doing your bloody job.'

After he left the house he paused at the gate and turned.

'Stop,' I said. 'Keep your peculiar practices to yourself and turn back around and keep going.'

He opened his mouth to say something but stopped, gave me a wide, bright smile and, while still waving, proceeded to his car.

I closed the door with a lightened heart and a smile on my face. The reality of what was ahead of me for the evening soon changed that. In a more sombre mood I went upstairs to tell Ronan what had happened and to remind him to clear up his and Kevin's mess in the kitchen before I started to get ready for what promised to be a very trying night.

CHAPTER 14

Joan

I had been in Ann and John's house three times since his arrest and it hadn't changed at all. The pallor of a house in the throes of a recent bereavement still hung over it and all that dwelt in it. The big difference between them and those suffering actual bereavement was of course the fact that this family didn't have a stream of neighbours and friends identifying with and sharing in their grief. They were isolated in a cocoon of their own tragedy: a tragedy in which Ann, Brendan and Maura were as much victims as were the family of poor Barry Breen. Because of their association with the perpetrator of this ghastly act, they were caught in a trap of grief. The difference was that they didn't have a process of grieving to enable them to cope with and ultimately recover from it. I, a willing visitor, could only tread with uncertain steps around their unusual yet very deep distress. It seemed that guilt pervaded even the fixtures and fittings of this home, one that had so recently vibrated with life, love and vitality.

My beloved godson, Brendan, answered the door and signalled his invitation for me to enter with a mere flicker across his deadened eyes. As he closed the door I hugged him, but his body was stiff and unresponsive. All I got was an almost inaudible 'Auntie Joan' coming out of him as I moved away from his close proximity. The 'Auntie Joan' nearly broke my heart. Brendan was my only godson. He had been a child of amazingly sunny disposition and he held a place in my heart and thoughts close to my own son. How I had treasured and enjoyed the time spent with him. I babysat him and regularly had him to stay over in my house. Because Ann and I spent so much time together when our children were young, it was like I was share-rearing him with his own mother and family. 'Auntie Joan', to which I had no title in common familial relationship structures, was something I gloried in. Sadly, it had been lost some two years previously as he, I presumed, grew out of the dependent child stage. The normal process of growing up and moving towards a peer dependency usually leaves aunts, real or not, behind. Hearing him murmur 'Auntie Joan' now was almost like a regression in him. It sounded like a subconscious statement of his need to retreat to a phase of his life when he could depend on having his emotional needs met by loving parents and 'Auntie Joans'. As Brendan and I walked together into the sitting room, I instinctively held his hand in a light touch: I noticed he didn't demur.

In the past two years Ann and I had often commented on Brendan's move away from physical contact with us and the apparent struggle he was having in making the transition from childhood to early adolescence. The warm, sunny disposition of his childhood had been supplanted by a quieter, sadder, more withdrawn boy. As a young man he tended to avoid the close physical contact under which he previously glowed. Our hope was that he would mature through it into a young adult replicating the adorable young boy of his childhood. What hope for him now with having to deal with his father's arrest as well as his normal teenage confusions, I despairingly thought.

Ann and Maura, Brendan's older sister by a year, were sitting close together. Neither of them seemed to be paying any attention to the television breaking the deadening pattern in the room with its vacuous unheard drivel. My arrival at least changed that. We moved into the kitchen and, on my initiative, made tea. In reality all I was doing was trying to get some movement, some sort of life into the three of them while I was putting off the next step. Here I was bringing even more upset into the desolation of this home. How I hated John Franklin at that moment for what he did, for bringing such torment on three lovely people. I, God forgive me, even hated him for not having the grace to succeed in his suicide attempt. His death would at least have had the effect of giving a focus: a process of resolution from the pervading depression on the home of his supposed loved ones.

My initial intention had been to tell Ann the bad news and then leave her to deal with informing the children. Clearly that was not practicable. It was obvious to me that Ann was not capable of taking on board her own stress, not to mind the children's. So reluctantly I broke the news to them all. Having reassured Brendan and Maura that their Dad was alive and relatively unscathed from his suicide attempt, I bundled the two children out of this depressing house and over to my patient, studious son's adolescent care before I took Ann in to visit her husband.

John was drowsy. His neck was bandaged and his voice was somewhat strained. Nonetheless, we were allowed some space to talk with him – Kevin's intervention, no doubt. A prison officer sat impassively on a chair close to the bed, but throughout the visit neither spoke nor made eye contact with Ann or me.

On entering the hospital room I moved over to the window to allow Ann some privacy with her husband. I noticed they didn't embrace or even talk very much. Wishing I wasn't there, I idly watched through the window the constant movement of illness and accident victims moving in and out of the casualty doors. Reassured of John's stable health, Ann quickly exhausted her conversation pieces with her husband of fourteen or so years, and, without touching him at all, she signalled to me her desire to leave. I escorted her out and then left her sitting over a cup of coffee in the visitors' area while I returned to confront John for the second time.

Whether he was drowsy or not in reality, he used it well to batten down his defences against any questions I tried to ask him. It was a total waste of time. I held his hand, coaxed him, cajoled him and finally spoke out of the anger suppressed since earlier that evening when I visited his home and caught sight of the three people who were suffering so grievously from the debris of his actions. But all my attempts were to no avail as John seemed to sink further and further into an almost catatonic state. Finally, anger spent, I gave up but didn't leave the room. Instead, I went over to the window and looking out of it I recommenced my perusal of the comings and goings around the entrance. Silence seemed to reverberate around the room. John's unmoving body created in me an eerie sense of fear, a terror that seemed to go to the very core of my being!

My instinct was to leave, to take flight. Suppressing the impulse, I forced myself to stand still and let the silence hang. The distant bustle and flurry of activity while so many people went about their lives unconcerned by the drama that dominated me helped me to get a perspective and calmed my tension. An age seemed to pass.

Finally I turned and, looking at his immobile shell, I slowly, quietly, in an unemotional tone began talking of my encounters with Ray and Franner. I talked of my growing belief that there was something, some shared secret that bound them all together yet at the same time seemed to have driven apart the inseparable friends of my youth. I talked from a need to prod, to get a reaction rather than from any absolute belief in the truth of what I was saying. As my rambling words wound down, John's eyes opened and held mine in a searing gaze, though his thoughts were totally unreadable. Then slowly, almost dismissively, he closed his eyes and returned to an inert state that I knew would not shift quickly. I stood there for quite a few more minutes saying nothing, all the while looking at his still form in the bed. Then without further comment I turned, nodded to the deadpan prison officer and left.

As I made my way back to Ann, I pondered on John's response or lack of it. I slowly began to feel that just maybe there was something to be found, some long-held secret to be unearthed. The trouble was that I was unsure of my desire to be the instrument of its releasing. In truth I wasn't at all sure I could release it, not to mind the complication of being able to handle anything that might emerge from it.

CHAPTER 15

Joan

I drove home with Ann. Both of us were so wrapped up in the depression of our own thoughts that even perfunctory conversation was absent. When we arrived at my house we found that the children looked a little less frazzled, thanks to the entertaining of Ronan, who is a real gem. He had them playing some weird games on his computer … games that at least afforded short-term relief from their constant cloud. I made tea and sandwiches that the children ate around the flickering computer screen, though I noticed that while Maura tucked in with enthusiasm, Brendan only picked at his. Ronan naturally had no inhibitions about stuffing himself and was quickly looking for more. I played a game with him about it, but though Maura was amused and even joined in, Brendan remained detached. It was very late before I finally brought them home, but I felt that any interlude that got them out of that sad house could only help. Ronan was not yet in bed when I returned, so we talked for a bit. I told him how much I appreciated his help with the kids. Shrugging this off, he surprised me by asking what was going on between Kev, as he called him, and me.

'Absolutely nothing,' I replied positively. However, his question and the feelings it created within me made me uncomfortable, as if I had told a blatant lie. Unusually for my son, he didn't take advantage of my obvious discomfort. He just nodded his head a few times and then got up to leave. As he walked away I casually enquired whether he would mind my seeing someone else. I held my breath awaiting his reply, but all I got was a shrug from his departing back and a tossed-out 'Your business, nothing to do with me' as he climbed the stairs to sleep in the incoming day.

Sleep again failed to embrace me. At this rate I would have to start redesigning my daytime schedule, as the regular twelve-to-eight sleep pattern I had enjoyed in the past few drink-free years had been thrown totally askew. My tossing and turning had, however, absolutely nothing to do with Kevin Brady. John Franklin's flat, expressionless face and his ability to close off the world and its realities had really freaked me. Yet, given the suicide attempt, he had to be living in a cauldron of guilt. He must have been full of self-loathing and despair. I couldn't get him to talk things out, to divulge the whereabouts of the two missing children or to consider any possible incident in childhood that could have a bearing on the present. His stare was so expressionless. Yet I wondered if there was some sense of fear within him. Was some apprehension hidden deep within that fixed gaze? Was I being fanciful? Did I imagine that fear? Or was I just reflecting within myself a need for something, anything that might explain and compartmentalise an act of such brutality?

Mind you, surely the murder of a young boy could have no real basis in logic.

I went to work the next day like an automaton. Fortunately I was so well established and practised in the bank that it didn't even surprise me when my till cash balanced at the end of the day. The fact that I had hardly emerged from my office retreat all day no doubt helped in that. That evening, after dinner was over I had an unexpected caller to the house. I didn't answer the door. Strange how till this past few weeks Ronan wouldn't answer it even if he were in the hall when the doorbell rang! I heard his hesitant 'hello' from my post drying the dinner dishes, then a 'come in' as he recognised the caller.

This was followed by 'Robert is your son, isn't he? He plays in the same club as me. He's with a younger team, the under fourteens. He's not a bad footballer, you know.'

'That's right, Ronan,' I heard her say. 'According to him you are one of the best bleedin' players in the whole club, you know,' she added in a clear imitation of her son's expression.

A laughing Ronan ushered Breda Crowley into the kitchen and, having done his social duties, he retreated with a smile. She looked around the kitchen while I put on the kettle, and murmured 'very nice', which, considering the opulence of her place, amused me. Nonetheless, I was very pleased to see her again so soon.

'You sure stirred up a hornet's nest in my marriage, you know,' came as her opening salvo. Her tone was not one of criticism; rather it reflected a sense of comment, an opening of a discussion topic.

'A good or bad thing?'

'Hard to say, really,' Breda answered as she sat and lit a cigarette after checking that I didn't object to the habit. 'Beneath that bullish exterior Franner really is a very nice, soft man and a very good father to our children.'

Putting down the tea towel, I sat across from Breda and reinforced her comment with one of my own. 'He was a very nice kid, and he and I had a great time together growing up.'

'He never talks about that period of his life, you know. Apart from Franner being insistent that you were invited to our wedding, the only way I got to know about the friendship of the four lads and yourself was from his mother. She often talked about it and puzzled over Franner's lack of contact with his old friends.'

'I had always believed that we were inseparable growing up, but talking as I have done this past week, John, Ray and Franner don't seem to hold the same view as I do of that time. They insist that they weren't that close to each other. They each held an individual friendship with me but not with each other. It's a view I'm having difficulty in coming to terms with. I am having huge problems in accepting their slant on our childhood. My husband Ray reckons that they all hated each other and only stayed around me because they all wanted to … well, wanted me. I'm sure that's ridiculous.'

'Well,' Breda replied, 'I couldn't say whether it is true or not from Franner's perspective, as he never says anything personal at all. He hardly ever talks about his parents, not to mind friends. I sometimes wonder how we even got married. Mind you, the fact that it was I who did the proposing probably helped.'

Breda smiled at the evoked memory, then, tapping the ash of her cigarette, she continued. 'He never speaks at a feeling level at all. Sorry, Joan, I don't know why I am talking like this to you. Though I suppose you deserve it. You did open the floodgates by calling and asking questions.'

In the silence that followed I got up and made a pot of tea, and after that hiatus Breda went on.

'Don't get me wrong. I am not unhappy in my marriage to Franner. I love him and I know he loves me even if he doesn't often say so. I clearly knew what he was like before we got married and went into it with my eyes wide open. I knew he was driven and that all his time would be spent closing deals and chasing after business. I suppose I just loved him and when I compared him to the other guys I could have married I had no doubts. He is a wonderful provider, generous to the children and myself and often forces me to buy things for myself even when I don't need or want them. He loves the kids and while it would be nice if he would spend more time with them, as I keep telling him, I accept that he has to be as he is. I always knew that I wouldn't change him, so I have never wasted much energy or emotion on trying.'

Breda refused a biscuit with a wistful shrug, then took out another cigarette, lit it and went on.

'Just a few months ago we had a holiday booked together and Franner had to change it for business reasons. I understood and was happy to cancel but no, his mother was organised to care for the children, so he arranged for the travel agent to change the holiday destination from Costa del somewhere to Vienna and insisted I bring my own mother. I'm sorry, Joan, to be going on with this drivel at you. Mind you, calling as you did, you probably deserve a lot worse. You see I … I want you to understand how I feel. It's not that I have any intention of changing Franner. I'm just anxious to make sure he isn't unhappy, and if delving into some past event can help, then I will do it.'

We both sat and she smoked while the summary of her marriage settled on both of us.

Finally I said, 'Look, it's obvious that Franner, being as you have described him, isn't going to tell us anything. That is presuming there is anything to tell in the first place. So don't pressure him. Just, I dunno, you know him better than I do now … just be there for him and if anything breaks with the others, I'll keep you posted.'

Breda grinned and wryly commented, 'My God, the decisive bank official in action … how impressive!'

We both laughed as the tension was broken. On an impulse, as I hadn't particularly intended to go myself, I suggested that we might go for a walk. With a wry look at the cigarette in her hand, Breda nodded, agreeing that it wouldn't do her any harm to have a little exercise, particularly as it was a nice evening. We walked, as I so often did, along the Murrough, where she had been herself, though infrequently, she said, and mostly when the children were smaller. As we strolled we just chatted, cementing our unexpected friendship. In between periods of filling each other in on our respective children, I told her in detail about the previous night, John's suicide attempt and the state of Ann and the children. I spoke, possibly for the first time ever, about Ray. I talked about my marriage, his drinking and his anger at me for asking questions about John and their youth together.

As I hadn't yet come to terms with Ray's striking me across my face, that didn't get a mention. It was still too vivid and just too personal. While talking, I turned as I usually did along the track heading for Broad Lough and Breda was surprised, as she didn't know this area existed. Her surprise turned to delight as she saw the river, the streams and the myriad ducks and swans that inhabit the area. That evening we even saw a few fish jumping out of the water, no doubt in joy at their lovely surroundings. Breda went quiet as she was taking it all in for the first time. I, being a regular visitor, was more intent on my sorry history with Ray. Having been bottled up all these years, I suppose once it got an opening it just gushed out.

Breda listened as she took in the magnificence of the area.

Once I started I couldn't stop, of course. So naturally I told her of Kevin, his visits, his need to find out more about the two missing boys and his sort of interest in me. Telling her of Kevin's sort of pursuit of me was a mistake – a big one. That sure caught Breda's imagination. Her awe at the surroundings was put in abeyance. In no time she was making constructions of what was happening far away from my reality. In her eyes it was only a question of when, not if, he was going to have his way with me. The way Breda talked, I should be encouraging him as much as possible.

To distract her as much as for any other reason, I told her of the day when the five of us – we were probably thirteen or so at the time – came on this spot. Seeing a rowing boat on the far side of the meadow, Franner stripped to his underpants and half waded, half swam across the river cum lake to, as it were, 'borrow' it. Ray, John, Cormac and I went back to the timber yard a few hundred yards away and acquired some wood from which we fashioned oars. The five of us then rowed deep into the lake, making our acquaintance with the inaccessible parts of that lovely river and lakeland area. We spent hours there and when we got back the tide had come in, so we left the boat on our side of the river, as it was more difficult to cross in high tide, before skipping home. We 'borrowed' that boat again quite a few times before John, who was very handy with his hands, decided to build our own craft. Breda was intrigued and puzzled as to why Franner had never brought her down here.

'He moved on, I suppose,' was my fairly lame explanation.

CHAPTER 15 - JOAN

As we slowly wandered back to where we had parked my car, Breda to my discomfort returned her focus to the exciting possibilities opening in my non-existent love life. I was quickly and painfully coming to realise that this girl had a dangerously vivid imagination. She was also showing a very poorly developed sense of what she considered to be right and wrong behaviour for me, a sort-of-married woman, to indulge in. As she left to go home I decided that I wanted to continue seeing her. But I also decided that under no circumstance was I going to tell her anything else about Kevin and myself, always supposing there was going to be something to tell in the first place.

The house seemed empty when Breda had gone. Ronan was still studying upstairs and after I brought him up some supper and told him where we had walked, I went back downstairs and restlessly couldn't settle to either watch television or read. On impulse I rang the Garda Headquarters and was surprised and pleased that, late and all as it was, Kevin was at his desk. I told him of the pointless hospital visit of yesterday with Ann and then asked him if he could check something for me. I intended to see Cormac soon, and gossip at one time had suggested that he had been arrested in some peculiar situation in Dublin a good few years previously. One of the problems of living in a small village is that nothing will ever escape the notice of everyone in the place. Naturally once one person gets a sniff of any bit of gossip, accurate or not, it will quickly spread. Working in the bank as I do, there is very little that goes on that doesn't get discussed within its confines, whether by the staff or the customers.

I explained to Kevin that, as I was sort of working for him, it occurred to me that he might be able to find out the true facts of that incident as opposed to the gossip eagerly spread by some horrified locals at the time. Perhaps he would let me know if there was anything that was likely to be of benefit in my enquiries with Cormac. I hung up on Kevin's promise to look into it and successfully avoided his efforts to tie me down to the promised dinner that he insisted was owing to me.

I felt more settled after the phone call. Kevin sure wasn't like Franner. He wasn't closed. He wore his feelings comfortably on his sleeve. Or was it in his case on his lips? Why should I care? It was of no interest to me!

As I climbed into my spacious double bed, I smiled at the thought of what Breda's fertile imagination would have made of my phone call to Kevin. As she wasn't going to be told, it was of no consequence and anyway, I rationalised, I did need to know about Cormac's incident, didn't I?

Maybe not at half ten at night, but I surely did need to know about it.

CHAPTER 16

Joan

I was getting no proper rest. I'd have bags under my eyes if I wasn't careful: bigger bags, actually. Sunday morning, I should still be in bed and normally would be. A cup of tea provided by Ronan as a prelude to a late full breakfast fry-up, my job to prepare, was our set routine. On this day we got up, got dressed, had the normal everyday breakfast and went over to his granny's. I had rarely gone to Ray's house since he moved back in with his mother. This was not because I didn't feel welcome to visit my ex-in-laws. I knew Mrs Traynor in particular loved me to call and always made me feel very welcome in her home. My reluctance to call possibly had a lot to do with the process of moving on with my life and leaving past ties behind, which I had to date markedly failed to do.

I always got on very well with Ray's parents, and I know his mother all those years ago was particularly delighted when hearing of our plans for marriage. She, as much as me, thought I would be a steadying or more realistically a sobering influence on her darling son. We both got that one wrong! I liked her very much then and love and respect her even more now. Ray's father I can take or leave. He has a good local profile as the county engineer for Wicklow and is acknowledged as a very capable man. However good he is professionally, it is in a social context that he really excels. He is the linchpin, in his own view anyway, of the local golf club, where he spends a lot of his leisure hours. He plays a lot less than he would give you to believe, and I think it is the social and committee ends of the club he revels in. I had often wondered if Ray got his early drinking habits from his father. But Mr Traynor was always well able to keep up good social appearances and hold down a responsible job, something his son has abjectly failed to do. Maybe if I was more the sort of wife his mother was, I could have coped better with Ray and his drinking. I must say, though, that when I finally threw Ray out, his mother visited me and complimented me on doing so. She said that she hoped it would in no way be a barrier to our continuing friendship or to her contact with her grandchild. Mind you, after he had left our family home I felt she should have let Ray survive in a grotty room somewhere on his own. Instead she took him in and has since, in my view, enabled him to keep on drinking. The curse of soft Irish mothers!

The reason for going early was that Ray's parents always went to Mass at ten o'clock on Sundays and I wanted to catch Ray in the house on his own.

I got there just in time to attach Ronan to the church attenders, much to his granny's delight as she loves showing off her handsome grandson. Ronan went off, his arm linked into his grandmother's, with the half pleasure, half indulgent stoicism of a put-upon teenager. Ray naturally was in bed sleeping off the Saturday night alcohol excesses. I made tea and brought him up a cup. Shades of years and years past! This time, though, I was full of trepidation. My big fear was of a repetition of the blow he struck the last time I tried to prod him.

It started well anyway.

'You're an hour or so early with my tea,' he said with a grin as he sat up in bed.

'Sorry, I'm not too familiar with the licensing laws and the Sunday opening hours.' I said this with a smile, pleased that at least he was in a good humour, and I badly wanted that to continue.

CHAPTER 16 - JOAN

'If of course it's getting in here with me you want, then don't expect too much. I am out of practice,' he added while pointedly moving over slightly in the bed and indicating the space made available to accommodate me.

'Pass,' I rejoined as I opened the bedroom curtains.

'Sorry, I forgot that it's a member of the law you're sharing your bed with at the moment, or so I hear!'

I ignored that barb, as much because I wanted to as because it would be very unproductive to go down that line, knowing Ray's sharp tongue.

'You know that John is in hospital after a suicide attempt, don't you?' I said as I began to dip carefully into dangerous territory.

'Yeah, pity the bastard couldn't even do that right,' was Ray's caustic reply.

Ignoring that jibe, I hastily continued. 'I went in to see him in the hospital. And I talked with Franner. Look, Ray, I am sure now that something did happen and perhaps it would help if I knew what it was.'

I looked intently at Ray when I had put that statement to him. After a slight pause during which he pointedly held my gaze, he said, 'Nothing happened, or at least nothing I know about. Mind you, there isn't anything about that bastard Franklin that would surprise me. Joan, why are you pursuing this? What is it all about for you?'

Getting animated, I said, 'Ray, I told you Ann asked … no, begged me to find out what made it happen. She needs to know what could have led to John killing that poor boy. I was ... we both were his best friend for all those years. There has to be some explanation. One of us must know something …' I finished lamely.

'Well, I know nothing except that he was always a self-opinionated shit and I wouldn't put anything past him.'

Still holding hard and trying to keep the conversation on a positive note, I implored, 'Come on, Ray, I know you fell out with him over taking his business away from you, but all those years growing up he was even more squeamish than you or me and a lot more so than Franner. I remember when we started fishing first, he wouldn't even kill the fish and one of us had to take it off the hook and kill it for him.'

With an impish grin and quick wit so reminiscent of the boy Ray I palled around with, he said, 'Well obviously he isn't squeamish now and that's for sure.'

'That's not funny, Ray. Come on, try and help me on this please.'

Ray's patience was beginning to wear out. 'Joan, just fuck off out of here and leave me alone. I've already told you I don't know anything. There is nothing to know.'

Sometimes, in fact quite often, I just don't recognise when I am beaten. While that may be an essential quality in a competitive game like squash, it is dangerous in this scenario. I pushed it by continuing.

'Ray, we were married a long time. If there is anything … anything at all, you know I would back you, help you with it. I still care about what happens to you. It hurts me to see you just destroying … just wasting yourself.'

Ray's eyes hardened and he almost hissed at me. 'For the last time, I don't know anything. Nothing happened. You just mind your own fucking business and stay out of it ... right? Now get out and leave me alone.'

'But Ray?'

'Joan, fuck off. If you are so desperate to please that fucking copper that's sniffing around, why don't you just let him move in and bugger off and leave me alone?'

With that Ray turned his back and slipped down in the bed pulling the covers up to his chin, clearly signalling the end of the conversation. I knew him too well to think that I would get anywhere further with him. It was time to retreat, so I did.

'Tell Ronan to come home soon. He has studying to do,' I shouted to the prone Ray as I descended the stairs and left. I returned home as defeated as in any confrontation I had ever had with Ray. However, I still had a very strong sense of unease. By now I really did believe that something was lurking in the background. But what? The only consolation I could take from the morning's visit was that at least I parted from Ray without too much acrimony … this time anyway!

CHAPTER 16 - JOAN

That evening I had a visitor, welcome and unwelcome. I answered the door for a change, as Ronan was up in his room, to find the big mass of Kevin shuffling slightly uneasily on the doorstep with a hesitant grin on his face. I'd had a bath and made a sort of an effort, not something I would normally do for a Sunday night in by the television, so his presence couldn't have been a total shock to me. We retreated to the kitchen and tea.

'No match today for the veteran midfielder, then?' I asked.

'We were training this morning preparing for our championship cup match, which is on next Sunday.'

Looking him up and down, I said with a shake of my head, 'At your age you will need to take things easy, save your old limbs for next week, then.'

Smilingly he agreed. 'That's right, eat well, sleep a lot and take extra oxygen before the match is the plan. Have you any more of your lovely tea brack, then? I'm sure it must be good for energy.'

'Where would I get the time to bake, with chasing around and doing your bloody job for you? Have you found out anything about what I asked you?'

Kevin's eyes widened in feigned exasperation. 'Have a heart. It is the weekend and you only asked me last night, for God's sake.'

'Oh yeah, sorry!'

Grinning in triumph, he continued, 'Actually I did run it through our computer. I also contacted a colleague of mine this morning and he clarified information for me. So, smart alec … I do have some news for you.'

Kevin grabbed the first slice of buttered brack, took a large bite and made a noise that I took to be one of satisfaction.

'Your friend Cormac was picked up in a raid two and a half years ago. It was in a large house in the north inner city. Reports had indicated that some young kids were being used for male prostitution in that particular establishment and the Gardaí raided it. Your friend was among the adults present. Six or seven men in total were arrested and taken to the station. They were held overnight, but in the end the Director of Public Prosecutions decided not to charge anyone.'

'And was there child prostitution going on?' I asked with anxiety.

'My friend says yes, but it's so hard to prove. Two or three boys were in the house at the time with the group of men. But as nobody was caught actually doing anything of a criminal nature and no evidence, photographs or the like were found, the case got dropped and they were all just given a big fright. Not that a brush with authority is likely to stop many of them,' he finished ruefully.

'Is Cormac a homosexual, then?' I questioned.

'I don't know for certain, but our concern isn't about the behaviour of consenting adults. They can do what they like. They will anyway! It's the fact that they are involving young boys in child prostitution that we're concerned about. They pick up the homeless, those going through a bad time or kids from messed-up families and lead them into prostitution. The sad thing is that the kids don't want to stop. They see it as an easy way of making money, so it is impossible to get through to them. A lot of the kids are much tougher nuts to get to talk than the adults involved in that carry-on, unfortunately.'

'Depressing, isn't it?' I commented.

'Yeah, a sad business,' Kevin said and added 'I checked fully and Cormac was never picked up at any other time. If he is involved, it is only on the fringes. The guy from the youth prostitution side I met this morning said he hadn't seen him around Dublin in a long time. Actually, the reason my contact remembers Cormac so well is that he too lives here in the county of Wicklow and when he called into the County Council office to get his car tax renewed it was your friend who served him, much to the embarrassment of them both.'

'Right. I'll visit Cormac this week, not that it's likely to do any good,' I said, having made up my mind. 'More tea, Kevin, and just maybe there's a scone or two around somewhere?' Okay, I baked this afternoon as well, so what!

'Thanks Joan,' he said, his eyes lighting up. The baking was worth it.

'Eh, is there any chance I could see *The Sunday Game* on your television?

The team we're playing next week are on and I want to suss them out.'

'Sure,' I agreed readily. 'Go through and I'll get a tray. Do you want a sandwich or something?'

Kevin paused at the door, smiled and said that anything to help build up his strength for the next week's game would be welcome. He has a lovely smile. We sat together in a comfortable silence during which Kevin made short work of the sandwiches and scones while intently watching every nuance of the television's reflections on the day's game. I half watched, enjoying the rare companionship and the silent company. The snack and tea finished, Kevin said 'thank you', keeping his eyes firmly fixed on the television as his hand lightly caressed my thigh in a gesture to match his words. The sensation lingered disturbingly for a long time after the hand had resumed scratching his ear, something I noticed he did absentmindedly while following the moving pictures on the television screen.

He left soon after the match ended. He kissed me, not in his customary following-half-departure fashion, but slowly, lingeringly before leaving the sitting room. I didn't resist. I partook, actually. But I was careful to do so without abandonment. At the door Kevin shouted goodbye to Ronan, who could be heard moving around upstairs, and got a reciprocal response from him. At the gate he smiled and gave me a sketch of a wave before getting into his car. As I closed the door I idly thought that maybe I did miss that peculiarity of his. Things move on, I suppose.

Be careful, Joan: while Kevin and yourself may be pursuing a similar goal in relation to John Franklin, a secondary agenda seems increasingly on the cards, and is that what you want for yourself?

Talking to oneself is a habit born out of loneliness! Perhaps!

CHAPTER 17

Joan

The following morning was a typical Monday at work. Wicklow town always seems to awaken to the reality of a new week at a leisurely pace. Business is usually steady and relaxed, so it is a day I generally reserve for reviewing the business development part of my job. For me, this was a day for thinking, planning and plotting. This morning was no different, or I tried to make it so. Unfortunately, Cormac kept intruding into my thoughts. I was going to have to visit him, and it was not something I was looking forward to. Another step into the unknown, and yet again a step back into my past. Cormac was the most vulnerable and the one I was most likely to damage, and this frightened me. All morning I kept trying to push thoughts of him to the back of my consciousness while I concentrated on official business. However, in spite of my best efforts my subconscious anxiety kept winning the battle.

A further distraction came with the arrival of a caller to the bank. A lady wanted to see me. Mrs Sally Creamer? Strange how her name rang a bell somewhere in my overworked brain, yet a quick check on the computer showed she didn't have an account in our branch. Seeing people who casually drop into the bank has in the past proved to be very good for business. The cashiers know that my policy is to accommodate casual callers if at all possible, just in case we lose a potential new customer to another bank. So, as I was distractible anyway, I asked that she be brought through.

Mrs Creamer seemed, as she entered the office, to be a nice, attractive lady a few years older than myself. However, there was also about her a tension, an inner turmoil, that was palpable. Her brisk handshake, the way she blocked out my welcoming smile, her marked lack of eye contact and the sudden, jerky way she sat on the comfortable office chair all indicated a person who was in an agitated, stressed state. She sat ramrod straight in the chair, her fingers wrapping themselves around the strap of her handbag as she waited, clearly anxious for me to sit and get the interview under way. I am accustomed to and generally at ease with tense customers in my office, so I wasn't disconcerted. I put on my reassuring smile and relaxed manner, but they made no impression. I sat casually in the other comfortable chair, away from my formal desk, but she was still agitated. I offered refreshments but got only a sharp negative shake of her head. Suddenly the tension within my visitor erupted as she obviously decided to take the initiative and move things on. What she had to say took the smile from my face and had me sitting as ramrod stiff as she herself was!

'My name is Sally Creamer,' she blurted out. 'My son Frank, who should be seventeen years old in a few weeks' time, has been missing now for four years and nine and a half months.'

A hundred questions raced through my shocked brain as I tried to comprehend what was happening. However, before I got a chance to catch my breath or say anything, the brief silence was already filled. More disaster for me!

'I understand that you are a friend of John Franklin and that you are helping Detective Sergeant Brady in trying to get him to talk … to tell about my son.' She leaned forward, her face set and desperate just a few inches from mine, as she continued.

CHAPTER 17 - JOAN

'I need to know about my son. John Franklin knows. He knows what has happened to my Frank. Get him to talk. Please, you must get him to tell you what has happened to my lovely boy. Please, Mrs Traynor: I must know.'

'Mrs Creamer, Mrs Creamer,' I hastily said, appalled at the direction this meeting was taking. Desperation flooded me. All I could think was that I was going to kill that bloody detective. What the hell was he thinking, dropping me into this?

'Please, Mrs Creamer.'

'Sally,' she interjected.

'Please, Sally,' I said, my tone softening as I reached out my hand to take her elbow. 'I am really, really sorry about your son Frank. It is … it must be absolutely terrible for you and your family. I … I can't even begin to think how I would cope if my own son went missing. But please, please believe me. I don't know anything about … about … and I don't expect that I will find out anything. How can I? As you see, I work in here in the bank. I am sorry, but I don't know how you can even think … hope that I can help!'

'But you do know John Franklin, don't you? And you have talked with Detective Sergeant Brady? I have got the right person?'

Oh God, I thought, as I desperately strove to get a grip on things.

'Well, yes,' I hesitantly answered, 'but I only agreed to talk to John to see if he might tell me, as an old friend, what happened. I … I wanted him to help me to understand how a man I have known since I was a girl … a kind, gentle man, a friend of mine … how he could possibly have been involved in killing a young boy?'

Mrs Creamer straightened further in her chair, if that were possible. She shook my reassuring hand from her elbow in the process and said, 'So, you are helping the police. John Franklin might talk to you. When he does, you must get him to tell you about Frank. I have to know. I need to know, even if it is only to give my lovely boy a decent Christian burial.'

I could as easily have stopped a runaway train as stop Mrs Creamer from continuing.

'Mrs Traynor, my son is dead. I know that. I am a realist. I have to be. I have believed he is dead for more than four years now. My husband, Richard, held on to hope much longer than I did, but now he too agrees that our son is gone. We love him very much and now all we want is to be able to say goodbye to him properly. We need to grieve, to mourn before we can get on with our lives, before we can make the best of things for our family. We can't do that until we have found our son's body. Please, Mrs Traynor, talk to John Franklin … ask him to tell you what happened to my Frank … where his body is.'

'Joan,' I said softly as I reached over and closed my two hands around hers. The straps of her handbag were held so tightly that they seemed to have cut off the blood supply to her fingers, so I gently loosened her grip. I needed time to frame my next few words.

'I will talk to John and of course I'll ask him for you, but don't … don't hope for too much. I am only trying to see if he would, will talk to me, an old friend, easier than he would to the police. But …'

The 'but' seemed to hang in the air with only our tense sharp breaths and my fingers tightening reassuringly over hers competing with it for dominance in the room. One advantage of doing the job I do is that I am used to allowing silence to hang in a fraught situation. I don't usually feel a need to fill tension with talk. So I waited and waited.

Finally Sally Creamer's body shook as if with a slight tremor. Then she looked at me, making real eye contact for the first time. Her tension lessened some more as she made a sort of self-mocking grimace allowing me, for the first time, to catch a glimpse of the person, the real lady that lay inside the desperation I had seen.

'I'm sorry, Joan … sorry for just barging in on you like this but … you can understand that I have to. I just have to try every avenue.'

I started to say something but she disentangled her hands from mine, let her handbag rest on her lap and took hold of one of my hands.

'The police … particularly Detective Sergeant Brady has thought ever since poor Barry Breen's body was found that this might be the big breakthrough for them in the search for information on my Frank. He believes that this is possibly the best chance to find out about what happened to Frank since the day he went missing nearly five years ago. I … I just wanted … needed to let you know how important it is for Richard and me to leave no stone unturned. I wanted you to see our pain so that you wouldn't let any chance go by that might help us. Oh, and don't forget poor Mr Fitzpatrick … his son Terence. He is in the same state as us.'

Gathering myself, I desperately struggled to find the right words to say. All that came out was: 'Sally, I really am so sorry. I couldn't even begin to cope with what your families are going through. I will see John Franklin. Of course I will. I promise you that I'll keep seeing him. If it is at all possible, I will seek any information that might help you. I need to find things out for myself, for my own peace of mind. I will try my best, I promise. Please don't hope for too much from me but, I promise I won't fail you for lack of trying.'

As she stood up, this attractive lady, just a tense shell of the happy, loving, carefree mother she had been five years before, smiled wanly and took her leave. At the door she paused and delivered a parting shot.

'I'm really sorry for barging in on you like this, but I have to keep on trying. I can't … no, I won't let go until I find my son's body. Thank you, Mrs Traynor – Joan – for your time and for your understanding.'

Sally Creamer left behind her a shattered, shaking bank official. She had also left a card with her name, address and telephone number. The card was sitting on the glass table in front of me and seemed to be glistening in the sunlight. Irritated by it, I picked it up. I twirled it round and round my fingers as my agitation grew and grew. Finally I grabbed up the phone and punched out a number.

It took a few minutes for me to be put through to Kevin. As soon as I heard his bright 'Hello Joan', I exploded as the suppressed anger burst out. How dare he give out my name and place of work to that poor woman? How dare he put me in the embarrassing situation I had just found myself in? I went on without giving him a chance to get a word in.

'You didn't even have the nerve to tell me. You didn't even bloody warn me that she would be paying me a visit,' I spluttered out at him.

Kevin Brady – Detective Sergeant Brady, as Mrs Creamer called him – was still trying to stammer out some questions when I angrily hung up on him.

Five minutes later I was still sitting at my desk trying to recover from the visit when his return call was put through to me. My instinct told me not to accept it, but then I decided to be more mature than that. I wasn't going to give him the satisfaction of saying that I refused to take his call, so I asked my colleague to put it through.

'Joan, before you hang up on me again, listen to me – please let me explain. I didn't tell Mrs Creamer your name, I promise you. I admit that I did tell her that a friend of John Franklin's had agreed to talk to him. Stupidly, I did say that this friend worked in a bank, but that is all I told her. I was just trying to reassure her that we were chasing up every option. I had no idea that she would follow up on that information herself. God, she is a determined and resourceful woman. I have been sitting here trying to rack my brain to figure out how she could have found you. I know that she has a cousin who lives in Wicklow town. She must have got your name from her and then she went on a fishing exercise to find you.'

I tried to get a word in, even if only to rubbish his sporting metaphor, but he wasn't finished.

'I'm sorry, Joan. It just never occurred to me that she would track you down. I … it must have been really terrible for you. I am very, very sorry. I had no idea.'

Silence at both ends of the phone. This one, though, was not a banker's tactic. In this pause I had to quickly appraise my choices. Me, my big mouth and my quick temper! Damn it. Damn him for having me in this bind.

I had no choice but to do a little apologising myself. Kevin accepted it with, I think, some relief. He was gracious enough to acknowledge that he had given Sally Creamer more information than he should have. I even assured Kevin that I understood how he would want to ease her torment in any way he could. Ugh, what was happening to me? I didn't have to be that understanding with him, did I?

We disconnected with a totally different process of communication than the last abrupt hanging up. Deeper and deeper I was plunging, and not just into my four friends' lives.

CHAPTER 18

Joan

Cormac was the most vulnerable of the five of us at that time, and I suppose he always had been. He had never really found himself. He had worked in the motor taxation office in Wicklow town since he left school. He lived in quiet comfort with his mother, a lovely lady. Sadly, however, he also lived with a history of depression, suicide attempts and a number of hospital admissions. Cormac cut a lonely, sad figure around the town. I saw more of him than I did of the others, even including Ray at that time. Sometimes when our paths crossed he was very well: the old bright, alert, intelligent friend of my childhood! Other times he was a shuffling, monosyllabic depressive, a tablet-induced zombie. Cormac was probably the easiest of the old group for me to see, yet strangely he was the one that I had been hesitating most to visit. Possibly it was the uncertainty of the state I would find him in that made me so unwilling to talk to the last of my friends. Certainly if anything was to be unearthed, Cormac was more likely to be forthcoming than any of the others. Yet all my instincts screamed at me to avoid him. Now, however, armed with Kevin's information, I couldn't put it off any longer. So on Monday evening I called to see him at his mother's house.

On the way over I thought of the Cormac I knew before he left school. He was a lovely, gentle lad. That was hardly surprising as he grew up in a very cosseted environment. His father had died when he was young and he was raised by his overprotective mother and his maiden aunt, who lived and still lives next door. They both doted on him and fussed over him to a dangerous degree. Gradually as we got older, Cormac was less and less inclined to get wet or dirty – the exact opposite to the rest of us – and I think now that it was because his two 'mothers' fussed and worried over his getting chills and colds. I wouldn't mind, only I can never remember him being ill at any time in those years.

Funny how odd events jump from your memory bank. I know that Mrs Clifford and of course her sister had great hopes for Cormac and myself. Around the time of our sixteenth birthdays I was invited to tea in Cormac's house on a few occasions. As members of the group never went anywhere singly, I remember bringing John Franklin with me, without thinking, on one of the visits. The reaction of the two ladies was in retrospect a joy to behold. They were obviously horrified at John coming along as well. They jumped on him, asking what he was doing calling uninvited, and before he could struggle to get an acceptable answer out of his confused mouth, they sent him packing, with no doubt the worst invective the ladies could think of to call him. As he left, I remember how much I wanted to go with him, but I didn't have the nerve. I heard Cormac's mother say to her sister, 'Thank God that … that gooseberry is gone, leaving the two young folk to have their tea in peace.' It was the last time that I responded to a not very subtle invite from them. Gradually they accepted that Cormac and I were not destined for each other, though in spite of that obvious disappointment Mrs Clifford and I always exchanged kind words when our paths crossed. What I could never figure, and haven't since had the nerve to ask her, was what she saw in the rough, unkempt, bordering on delinquent tomboy that I was then that could possibly have made her think me a suitable catch for her beloved son.

Mrs Clifford was pleased to see me. She herself was fine, though her hip was giving her a lot of trouble. She told me she was due to go in for a replacement one in the near future. My Ronan was a lovely lad, so like me when I was his age, according to her. The thought occurred to me that I hoped he was not like me at that age, but then wasn't the time to ask her what she meant by that worrying comparison. Sadly, her Cormac was not home. She told me that he had been admitted into Newcastle psychiatric hospital two weeks before after yet another bad turn. The whole thing with John Franklin had really upset Cormac, and he had been doing so well before that, according to his mother. Reluctantly, after seeing him go into his shell, she eventually had to get Dr Wilson out to see her son, and the good doctor had him admitted to Newcastle. Mrs Clifford, winding down, said I was lucky to find her in as she was on the point of putting on her coat to catch the bus to go and visit her son. She didn't feel too much like facing the journey with her hip and all but wouldn't like it if Cormac wasn't visited.

It didn't take much persuasion to convince her to allow me to do the visitation duty that evening, and for her to put the feet up and rest her sore hip. I also promised to get Ronan to call in on her and told her that if she needed anything done while Cormac was away not to hesitate to ask, as my lad would be very willing to oblige. See, my Ronan is a nice lad and not like me when I was that age at all!

Amazingly, I had spent thirty-seven years living in this county and had passed the hospital hundreds of times, particularly when it was on the main road to Dublin before the Newtown bypass was opened, yet I had never been inside it. I entered with a mixture of hope that my quest for information might be nearing an end and trepidation at going into a 'lunatic asylum', surely the threat of many of our youths. I went to the big old building first. This building dominates the skyline but apparently it is primarily now used for administration, so I was directed down to the lower level. The admission ward was a long, low, single-storey building in a lovely setting but looked strangely at variance with the imposing old structure that sat on the plateau above, easily dominating it.

On entering I was confronted by a strange mixture of activity and inactivity. People were gathered in small groups and in the balmy evening weather it was difficult to identify the visitors from the residents. These groups were interspersed with individuals, men and women in dressing gowns shuffling along, many of them smoking, heads and thoughts focused inward, as they made their unseeing way past those conversing together. One or two of the gowned people came close to me, causing a slight tightening of fear in me, but they moved on uninterested in me or my anxieties. My eyes panned around in a desperate search for Cormac. Strangely I knew that by now this was his environment, so it was for succour and support for myself that I was searching him out at this juncture.

'Can I help you?' I heard from behind me, and I turned to see a nurse a few years older than myself standing, an enquiring look on her face. She had an air not only of belonging but of being totally at home.

'Cormac Clifford,' I murmured.

At the mention of his name she looked more intently at me, her interest obviously having been sharpened by my enquiry. I'm sure it was quite obvious that I was visiting for the first time.

'Come into my office, won't you?' she said.

After we sat I introduced myself, explained that his mother wasn't feeling the best and that I had offered to give her a break as I in my own right wanted to see Cormac. The nurse explained that he wasn't very well at the moment and was staying almost all the time in his small ward down at the end of the corridor. She added that though she felt he wouldn't communicate with me, as he was not responding to anyone, it was nice that I came and she would show me down. She had nursed him on many occasions over the years when he was depressed, but he was as ill now as she had ever seen him.

'What does he do all day?' I asked, as much to put off going down to his room as out of any great desire for information.

'Normally,' Kate said – for that was the name by which she introduced herself – 'Cormac would, after his first day or two settling in, go off to the day activity centre. He would put in his day with the variety of jobs and social activities going on over there and in the process mix with the other patients. This time, however, he just refuses to leave his room. He gets up, eats his breakfast or rather picks at it with a lot of coaxing. Then having washed, dressed and shaved, he simply stands at the end of his bed holding on to the bed frame and just gazes out the window at the field and trees behind the unit. He won't go to the activity centre and he won't even let any of the nurses take him out for a walk. I have a few times even offered to put a chair out the back for him so he could sit and at least get some fresh air. At the moment he doesn't even respond, so all we can do is keep a careful watch on him.'

She confessed that all the staff were worried about Cormac, adding, 'The tablets – and he is on quite a heavy dose – don't seem to be having any effect on him at all this time, which is different than on his other admissions. Normally Cormac would have perked up by now.'

'What can you do for him, Kate?' I countered, interested in the sad regaling by now.

'Well, it is up to the doctor really. But at this stage all we can really do is stay with him, try to support him until whatever demon is eating at him relents, and then help him to rebuild himself again.'

Kate paused at that point, obviously appraising me; as if having given me a vote of confidence, she continued. 'The consultant was saying just today that if there was no change in Cormac by the end of this week we would have to seriously consider changing his treatment to a more robust one, which we don't like doing if it can be avoided. It's nearly impossible to know what to do for the best, as we don't really understand what has caused this present breakdown. The sad thing is that he had been keeping very well the last few months. Having said all that, I don't want you to be scared of him. Cormac is in a bad way but it is himself he is eating up, Joan.'

Smiling, if only to acknowledge the act of faith Kate showed in being so frank with me, I commented rather than asked, 'You like him, don't you, Kate?'

'Yes,' she answered after a slight hesitation, 'when Cormac is well, he is a lovely man. He is well read and we have some long conversations, especially late in the evenings when I am on night duty and the place is quiet.'

After a pause while she perhaps was appraising whether she had said too much, Kate asked 'And you?'

'Cormac and I were best friends growing up and I regret that … well … probably because my own life was a terrible mess, I neglected our friendship,' I answered.

Confidences shared, it was with a sense of companionship that I followed as Kate led me down the long corridor, past rooms that seemed to hold four to eight beds in each and down to the last one on the left. As we walked down, the patients shuffling in their self-obsessed way seemed to revive from their reverie to pass a comment or an acknowledgement to Kate, who responded positively to them all. The thought occurred to me that if I were unwell, I would be happy to be left in Kate's competent care. Just let it not be in this hospital, I hastily added in supplication.

Kate knocked and then entered a smaller two-bed room at the end of the wide corridor. Just as she had described, Cormac was standing with his back to us, his two hands resting on the frame at the end of the bed. His eyes were fixed on the green field through the window. His body was rigid and unmoving. Kate walked around in front of him and, in a positive tone, told him that he had a visitor. Joan had come to see him. She had come to give his poor mother a night's break from the bus and the long walk up the hospital drive.

As I came into Cormac's peripheral vision, his eyes moved slowly to take me in then just as slowly returned to their fixed position, his brain focused on the emptiness inside, while his eyes continued to be trained on the field outside. After one or two fruitless efforts from Kate to elicit a response or to get him to acknowledge me, she settled me into a chair between Cormac and the window. Then, after showing me the push-button that would summon her if she could be of any further help, Kate took her leave with a reassuring smile. When I found myself alone with Cormac it occurred to me that perhaps I needed more than just reassurance to handle this situation.

Facing John Franklin in prison or in hospital after his suicide attempt was a doddle compared to this. I'll kill that bloody Kevin Brady for getting me into something I have no idea how to deal with, I thought. Any idle thoughts were better than this reality. Had I actually done a proper psychology course and practised as I'd hoped, maybe, but only maybe, I'd have been better equipped to deal with this situation.

After one or two 'How are you?' questions that got not even a flicker of a response, I moved the chair out of Cormac's direct vision and over to the side. I did this not for him but for me, as the sight of his pale, emaciated face with the fixed expression, looking out over me into an unimaginable horror, was more than I could bear to have to face directly. I talked inanely then to fill the void. I talked of his mother, her hip and my Ronan calling in to help her. It was difficult to know if any of it penetrated. I then talked of us, him and me, of our friendship through the years and how sad it was that in growing up we had moved so much away from each other.

After more silence I started to reminisce about the fun we had as children and the things the five of us did together. That got no response either. Then in desperation I talked of Ray, our marriage and our break-up. It almost felt as if I was on a psychiatrist's couch with an inescapable need to pour my sorrows out. It didn't matter what I said, though, as Cormac seemed to hear nothing. He reacted to absolutely nothing. At least this session wasn't costing me anything, I idly thought.

I stood up, poured a drink from the 7-Up bottle I had brought and offered him some. Not a muscle twitched. There was not a response of any kind from Cormac as he continued to stare out into his abyss. Finally I drank it myself. My mouth and throat were very dry, no doubt because of anxiety, apprehension and the talking of too many inanities into a vacuum. When I had settled back into the chair, I allowed the silence to dominate. I tried to switch off and relax, and succeeded for about three or four minutes. I am not normally a garrulous person, but I have a tendency to let my mouth run away with itself when I find myself in a stressful situation, like when meeting people for the first time on social occasions. Then I fill silences with any inconsequence that comes into my head ... natural shyness, I suppose.

However, I filled the silence finally. Cormac clearly wasn't going to.

Taking a deep breath to get my courage together, I launched into an account of my searching over the past few weeks. I talked of Ann's request to me and of my desire, on the basis of the friendship we all enjoyed as children, to find out if there could be any explanation for John's behaviour. I talked of visiting John in prison and of his suicide attempt. As I recounted that, Cormac's eyes moved around towards me. They locked on to me for a brief moment before returning to their former unblinking rigidity. Nothing else moved. His hands still rested on the bed frame. His body was still rigid and I got no sense of any change from him.

Nonetheless, heartened by the movement of his eyes, I restated my belief that something had happened to John, something that I felt Ray or Franner knew about. I told the shell of Cormac that I needed to discover what it was, if only to help Ann and the children to survive this tragedy.

Something, some indefinable change in Cormac, stopped me at that point. I went silent, hardly daring to move. Something scared me, but I couldn't put my finger on what it was. A tension seemed to course through him as I scarcely even took a shallow breath. A change had taken place and it caused me to tremble.

Suddenly Cormac let out a piercing scream and, still screaming, he ran past me to the window, the object of his focused stare. When he reached it, he banged his head violently against the window frame. Fortunately it must have been specially made, as it didn't break in the onslaught. Cormac then started to bang his head against one of the panes of glass, hitting the other panes with his hands while continuing to screech at the top of his voice. I rushed to touch him, pull him away, do something, anything. But it was like trying to hold back a dam that had already burst. I made no impression on him. The piercing high-pitched noise reverberated around the room and filled me with a fear the like of which I had never before experienced.

In my panic I forgot to press the bell for assistance. It wasn't necessary anyway, as the screaming quickly brought Kate and two male nurses running in to assist. They caught and held Cormac, walking him still distressed to his bed. There they laid him down, holding him in their firm, controlling grasp. Physically restrained, Cormac continued to scream in a piercing, high-pitched tone that echoed and re-echoed his deep pain round and round this fairly small room. I stood transfixed, terrified, out of my depth and feeling somehow responsible for this outburst. Kate rushed out, coming back quickly with a filled syringe which, as they had hastily pulled a screen around to shield me from the reality, I'm sure was expertly and quickly administered. She instructed the two nurses to stay with a now thankfully only whimpering Cormac, and brought me out of there and back to the nurses' office. Needless to say, I didn't need much persuading to get out of that room.

Over settling tea and biscuits I recounted what had happened. I outlined when he looked at me and the point of his explosion. I told Kate more of my history with Cormac and added his mother's comments about this current breakdown coming hard on the heels of John Franklin's arrest. Finally I left. I gave my work and house numbers to Kate before returning home in a state of total collapse. Fuck Kevin Brady, fuck this quest. I would kill that man the next time I saw him.

Lying in bed, my head was still ringing with the torment embodied in the screams coming from Cormac. No sleep again: how the hell would I be able to work in the morning? At midnight or so Kate rang to say that the injection had worked and that Cormac was now sleeping the peaceful sleep induced by sedation. She had stayed late to see him settled and was just about to get home to her own bed. I was very grateful for her kindness in taking the time to ring me and for understanding that, no matter how late the hour, I would appreciate being told how he was. Unfortunately I had no access to sleeping aids, so I tossed and turned all night. I blamed myself for causing such distress to poor Cormac with my stupid, stupid blundering. Mostly, however, I blamed that bloody detective, who of course was not around when he was needed.

intervened and supported my view that as Cormac was in hospital and as I had formed a positive relationship with his mother and with Joan, the initial follow-up should be a meeting in the hospital between Patrick, myself and Joan. Some feathers got ruffled but logic prevailed. It was agreed that Cormac would be maintained in a sedated state for a few days and closely monitored. Patrick did say that he had been so concerned about the acute nature of Cormac's current depressive state that he had even contemplated ECT. However, he hoped a meeting with this new friend Joan might open up better options. As I was delighted with this eventual decision, I agreed to ring her and set up a meeting.

Cormac was still in an induced calm state when I returned to the ward after the team discussion. Patrick and I were both on duty that afternoon and, as I didn't want to waste time or give the outreach team any excuse to take the case back from me, I rang Joan. I got her in the bank and she agreed to come in for a meeting on Friday afternoon after the bank had closed for the weekend. After years of frustration in trying to bring it about, sustainable change in Cormac's long-term psychiatric welfare could, just could, become a reality, and if I had an opportunity to be part of that, no outreach team was going to deprive me of it. Sometimes I've felt that the 'community team' thought that the nurses in the hospital were just glorified carers. We're not!

Cormac's episode should, I hoped, prove to be a catalyst to explore new treatment avenues. I have believed for a long time that while the development of more effective drugs has enabled us to manage patients in distressed states much better, there is a danger that we overuse them to the detriment of dealing with the underlying issues that are the real causation factors of the illness

CHAPTER 20

Joan

I went in to work the next morning but didn't do too much. It was just as well that I had a reputation as a very good worker, as frankly for those past few weeks I had been coasting on it. I rang Kevin hoping that he might help to make me feel even a little bit better about myself and what had happened. He was away down the country somewhere and not contactable. It was early evening before he rang me. He must have been sorry he rang. I gave him an earful about pushing me into this bloody mess and now, when I needed him, where was he? Off gallivanting in some godforsaken hole having an easy time of it, I sarcastically suggested.

Naturally, after I'd shouted my mouth off, it turned out that a very bloody murder had been committed, which of course I would have known about had I listened to the news. Kevin had been diverted to that enquiry late last night. According to himself, all the signs indicated that he was going to be tied up all week on the investigation. In fairness, he was very sympathetic to my plight and very reassuring on the phone. Me, my temper and my big mouth! Kevin promised he would get up to me the second he could, and he did at least manage to sound very concerned for me. Well, he had got me into this and I had a right to demand and expect his professional support, didn't I? That was all I needed … professional support!

I also rang the hospital and again got talking to Kate. Cormac was still primarily in a catatonic state, the one I found him in at the start of my visit, but showing signs of distress on odd occasions. He was well sedated and due to see the psychiatrist, Dr Wilson, once more the following morning. I volunteered to call over to see his mother and suggest that she shouldn't visit until after the doctor had seen him. On my way home from work I did that, and while I was there I also explained to Mrs Clifford what had happened during my visit. I said that I was sorry if I had inadvertently caused her son to get worse. She, nice lady, shrugged it off as just another phase of his ongoing illness. Ronan had called in to see her on his way home from school and had done some shopping to take the pressure off her hips, so I felt a little better for that.

I was knackered, so I went to bed early but again didn't get too much sleep. I had just drifted off when Ronan shook me awake.

'Sorry, Ma,' he said. 'I let Dad in, I had to. He's downstairs and in a bad way: drunk, of course.'

Cursing and swearing, I climbed into my jeans and sweatshirt and went down to face a re-creation of what had been part of my normality for going on ten years.

Ray wasn't just drunk: he was falling-down paralytic. I couldn't for the life of me figure how he even got to my door. Probably one of his stupid and equally drunken mates had dropped him off. At that moment, however, other things were more immediate. Ray was half sitting, half lying on the settee, trying in vain to light a cigarette. All he was succeeding in doing was putting, to varying degrees, his hair and my sitting room at risk. From long practice I manoeuvred him into the kitchen and sat him in my big solid chair. This chair had high armrests and I distinctly remembered buying it for just this purpose quite a few years previously. You know how with babies you buy a high chair? Well, for my particular grown-up baby I had bought a strong chair with arms. When Ray had too much to drink his body always seemed to become flaccid and he would fall off an ordinary kitchen chair. Just as well, I thought, as Ray flopped down into it, that I had never gotten around to discarding it.

Ronan, experienced lad that he was, unfortunately, had already put on the kettle and was busy making coffee. Ray rarely drank it, but the effort of trying to get him to take some and the process of his refusing it often took his attention off having another drink. As a drunk, Ray was usually quite manageable. He was normally subdued and fairly good-humoured. It didn't make any sense to me, but Ray would only ever try to have intense discussions about issues that were bothering him when he was in a seriously drunken state. When he was sober or even just merry I always found it impossible to get him to talk about these topics. Sobriety seemed to induce a state of emotional withdrawal in my ex-husband. I remembered one night less than a year previously when Ray called, after the pub closed, naturally. He was drunk, though not in quite the paralytic state he was in tonight. He was upset as he had somehow come to the conclusion that Ronan was gay. He based this assumption on the fact that Ronan was showing no interest in girls. How he could work this out given how rarely he saw his own son was totally beyond me! Nonetheless, he had called to help me to resolve this very serious problem … and one that I didn't even know I had!

Ray was proposing that we should find some nice girl to initiate our son into the pleasures of intercourse. No doubt this was the combined wisdom of the slightly inebriated group in one of his pub sessions. Being drunk, he didn't take account of the fact that Ronan was standing in the kitchen behind his back when this proposition was being expounded. I was very embarrassed, especially as our son was only fourteen at the time. The following day I made a point of talking to Ronan about it. We had already had the 'birds and bees' talk, so this, I hoped, was just a refresher. Ronan was just amused. He assured me that his Dad and I had nothing to worry about as his orientation was very well fixed. He added that if we gave him the money his Dad proposed to spend on the aforementioned girl, he would be happy to put it to good use in the pursuit of his current amorous objective. That, I think, is when I really started to worry about my son and his strange way of looking at things.

After Ronan and I had distracted Ray by the coffee trick, he settled somewhat. I lit the cigarette for him; ugh, I hate the taste. Then I placed an ashtray beside him to protect the kitchen table from conflagration. Ray, once he had taken a drag or two to get started, slurred out that he wanted a serious word with me. With a grossly exaggerated movement of his head, he signalled for Ronan to go. Ronan shrugged and made a comment on his need for beauty sleep. He gently touched his Dad on the shoulder and then, displaying a maturity that sort of saddened me, kissed his cheek before going off to bed. Me … I was left with my mistake of a husband.

Ray talked, mumbled, rambled and talked. He didn't really make any sense, but then he never did when he was this drunk. However, the gist of his talk seemed to be that I was embarked on a course designed to ruin him and his reputation … what, that of a drunk? And that I would be personally sorry if I didn't desist from whatever stupid thing I was looking for. He added that John Franklin was a murdering queer and that he should be shot for the good of the rest of us. It was two o'clock in the morning before he ran out of steam and dropped off. I was tempted to just leave him to sleep there in the kitchen chair. However, I had gone through too much to get Ray out of the house and in the process to bring some order to my life. So, rather than let any slippage that could be used against me occur, I put shoes and a jacket on and after some very uncoordinated gymnastic juggling I got him into my car; a few moments later I was opening his mother's front door and ushering him in. I ended up undressing him and putting him, my husband of whatever number of years, to bed. It felt strange to be carrying out such an intimate act. But then it was a few years since I had last done it. Actually, as I was settling the covers around Ray, realisation hit me as to how far I had come in rediscovering a positive sense of myself in just a short time. No way would today's Joan make such a mistake. As I was hanging up Ray's suit – habits die hard – his mother, having woken, came into the room. I reassured her, finished the perfunctory job and let myself out quickly.

Kate rang from the hospital and got me in the bank. The consultant had seen Cormac and wanted to meet me. I seemed to be slipping deeper and deeper into the mire, but there was no escape from this responsibility. Timing was difficult, as I still had to continue the pretence of working for the bank, so finally Friday after work was arranged. She told me that there had been no change in Cormac's condition, though he hadn't had any more really agitated outbursts.

Kevin was away and I was feeling so trapped that I needed to talk to someone, so I went for a drink with Breda on Thursday evening. While getting ready I resisted the impulse to wear dark glasses, not because I wanted to avoid being recognised but, more prosaically, to hide the baggy eyes. It was only while sitting in the hotel slowly relaxing that I realised just how uptight I was. When Breda arrived we had a few laughs, mostly about me walking Ray in an irregular pattern from my car to his home in the early hours of the morning. Breda wondered if I could have been arrested for being in charge of a drunken object on the public highway. She was sure it was an offence under some subsection of some code or other. Poor Breda had got a parking ticket in Bray the previous day and was feeling very much at odds with Big Brother at this time. Having got the levity out of the way, we then discussed Cormac. I told her about putting my big feet into that one and how much I was dreading the meeting with the psychiatrist. It was nice to talk it out and to get positive reassurance from a supportive friend, particularly as that so-and-so Kevin had gone off on some silly pretext of having to investigate a murder. Breda reassured me that I wasn't to blame, as whatever happened to cause his sudden outburst, she was sure that Cormac had been ready to explode at any moment. All I did, according to her reasoning, was to precipitate what was going to happen anyway. I didn't believe what she was saying, naturally, but it was reassuring to hear it nonetheless. Mind you,

Breda being Breda, as I was coming to realise, did of course have to put her own slant on things. She said that even if the doctor certified me, which wouldn't surprise her, she promised to visit me in the hospital, at least once anyway. Even if that was only to gloat! After the week I'd had, nonsense was just the tonic I needed. I relaxed and felt almost human. All the same, I didn't let my guard down totally. I was very careful not to tell her about the phone call to Kevin or our 'Sunday evening cosy television by the fire' episode. Had I done that she would have had a very interesting and amusing night for herself, mostly, no doubt, at my expense.

CHAPTER 21

Kate

The follow-up meeting between Dr Wilson, Joan and myself was more relaxed than I expected it to be. Patrick, who was clearly taken by Joan, got her to settle by starting with questions about herself and then focusing on her studies. He seemed very sympathetic about the difficulties she had encountered in getting employment as a psychologist before she settled for working in the bank. He also commented on the lack of psychological support in our own clinical team. I had the fleeting thought that he would have been very happy to have Joan working professionally with us.

The discussion then moved on to the business in hand.

Joan relayed again her history with Cormac and his friends and the task set her by John Franklin's wife. Patrick was very interested in her quest and the conviction she had that some incident or series of incidents had occurred involving the four young lads.

It also, surprisingly to me, emerged that Joan had done a lot of reading up on abuse and its effects on the victims. Rather than becoming just a fact-finding exercise by Patrick, the meeting evolved into a discussion on abuse and its implications for victims. An interesting and refreshing exchange!

When Joan left, Patrick lit his pipe and sat deep in thought for a few moments.

'If you ask me, she would be a great addition to our psychiatric team,' he said finally. 'Ah well, banking's gain is our loss, I suppose. Anyway, to Cormac! What do you make of Joan's story and how it relates to our patient, then?' he asked me.

The suddenness of the question threw me for a minute, but after some hesitation I blurted out, 'I have little doubt that something happened, something that Cormac has kept buried for a long time. Something that may well be at the root of his issues.'

'I agree,' Patrick said, 'and maybe, just maybe, this has been the catalyst for his persistent recurring depressive episodes. I sometimes felt that Cormac was beating himself up by denying his natural homosexual inclination and that if he had only acknowledged it, accepted it as his normality, he would have been more at ease with himself. Now I wonder if he hasn't got stuck at an earlier stage of his sexual development because of whatever the incident or incidents were and he hasn't allowed himself to explore these issues properly.'

'You mean,' I asked, 'that he is not homosexual at all? That he just hasn't allowed himself to move on in his normal sexual development?'

'At least we owe it to Cormac to explore the possibility, and God knows nothing else we have tried has really worked for him. It seems possible that he might have turned his guilt back in on himself, with disastrous consequences.'

'How should we handle it, then?' I asked.

Patrick paused for quite a long time. Then he surprised me.

'I think I might do an abreaction on Cormac, use meds to depress his defence mechanisms and see what emerges. Yes, yes, that's what I am going to try,' said Patrick, getting more animated. 'Cormac is in such a distressed state that we need to try to force a breakthrough, and maybe his expression of real anger the other night is the first step in the process.'

CHAPTER 21 - KATE

Interesting! Sure I'd heard of psychiatrists doing it, but I had never seen it happen and didn't realise that Patrick would be comfortable with using that approach.

'Monday morning, then, Kate: I'll do it Monday morning. It would be good if you sat in on it as well and then we can both report back to the clinical team. Let's just hope something positive can come out of it.'

'Do you want me to get Cormac's consent and maybe his mother's?' I asked.

'Yes,' he said after some thought. 'It might be best to get both of them to sign consent forms. And let's hope that Joan's quest can benefit us in our treatment of Cormac.'

An abreaction, and I was going to get to sit in on it. What I knew of it was that the doctor would use medication to create a relaxed state in the patient, almost like a hypnotic effect, allowing for a freer disclosure of painful repressed issues.

A first for me, and I couldn't wait!

Before I went home I rang Joan at home and thanked her on behalf of Patrick as well as myself. I outlined that Patrick was going to start a special treatment programme with Cormac on Monday and he was hopeful that her new information would be of benefit to Cormac. I promised to keep in touch if confidentiality allowed. A different than normal finish to my week's shifts! Patrick never gave a thought to the fact that I might be off on Monday. I was, actually, but nothing was going to stop me from coming in, and even after all my years working in this hospital I couldn't wait for the following Monday to come around.

That night as my house settled, my thoughts, as they had frequently done since I had arrived home from the hospital, drifted to Monday and the planned abreaction.

One of the many stories my old mentor, boss and trusted colleague Michael was fond of telling came to mind.

In the seventies, when he was just a student nurse, the job he most hated was attending the regular ECT weekly clinic. Patients would either shuffle or be wheeled in for their treatment. Michael frequently stated how uncomfortable he had always felt at having to restrain patients as they were administered this shock treatment. It was incomprehensible to him that this process actually seemed to have a positive impact on some patients. However, his only function was to carry out instructions from senior staff.

One particular case left a big impression on him.

A nice young couple came in to the outpatient clinic, where he was assigned to take their history. Young, married less than two years, they seemed like nice people and he was particularly struck by the kind, loving way the husband acted towards his clearly depressed wife. He completed the information sheet and introduced them to the duty doctor. As a junior student he didn't sit in on the interview and, his job done, he moved on to the next patient.

Michael was horrified some six weeks later to recognise this young woman as she slowly moved to a bed. She was the next one of the group of patients for that morning's treatment. The period in hospital had clearly not improved her.

Michael often reflected on what happened next, as it made a lasting impression on him. As this young woman lay sedated on the table, the doctor paused, then talked quietly to the three nurses gathered around the bed.

'This lady is not getting any better and her three previous sessions of ECT haven't seemed to help, so I am going to just give her a small extra dose of sedative and try and do an abreaction on her.' Michael stood transfixed, as he didn't have any idea what any of this meant.

After a moment the doctor started to talk to her, with her responding in a quiet monotone. As the conversation moved on she began talking of how when she was a young girl her father used to come into her bedroom and have her fondle him. This progressed to more serious abuse as she got older.

All of this was related in a detached monotone. The doctor didn't press and stopped quite quickly after muttering some quiet, reassuring words to her.

CHAPTER 21 - KATE

He then depressed the syringe, putting her fully unconscious.

'I think we now know the underlying issue with this lady and, with a bit of luck, we can now really help her'.

He proceeded to administer ECT, the prescribed treatment, to her.

Probably the reason Michael returned to this story so often was his surprise that the doctor carried on, as to his way of thinking surely the root cause of the severe depression was now clear and aggressive medical treatment should no longer have been indicated.

So, now I had an abreaction to attend on Monday and, thank God, I was working in a changed, though far from perfect, psychiatric system from the one Michael faced in his early years.

CHAPTER 22

Joan

Saturday morning I slept, slept and slept. Ronan wisely left me alone and got his own breakfast. On waking I was conscious that this last while I hadn't been fair on him and had left him far too much to his own devices. Fortunately he is a great self-contained lad who just gets on with his life. As I thought about it I realised how supportive he had been to me in this present upheaval. These thoughts were drifting across my mind as I sat in the kitchen over a basic breakfast, so when Ronan came in I expressed my thanks to him.

At that he smiled and said, 'No sweat,' then with a grin added, 'but I reserve the right to revert to my normal teenage state at any time, unless of course you see your way to increase my allowance.' I knew I was right to worry about Ronan, and it suddenly occurred to me with a pang of regret that he was a very attractive boy who would soon have many females other than his mother in love with him. He would need to do something about his strange sense of humour, though!

Kevin rang me later, but it was not a satisfying call. He was still stuck with his murder investigation down the country. Actually, as far as he was concerned, it was very much an in-house affair and not one he should have been called into. Nonetheless, as it was coming to a critical point, he had to stay with it both day and night, so he had no hope of getting up to Dublin, not to mention Wicklow. He did tell me how sorry he was for not being around when I clearly needed someone to talk to. I, typically and mostly untruthfully, told him that I was managing fine.

Kevin was distracted, though. His greatest anxiety seemed centred on the football championship match he was due to play the next day. Being stuck down the country and working around the clock meant that he hadn't been able to train with his fellow players in the run-up to the match. This wasn't ideal preparation and could, he worried, cause him to let the team down. That I should feel sorry for his football worries after all he had left me stranded with!

Now that I was up, I didn't feel as rested as could have been expected. This was probably because I kept waking during the night with my mind full of the week's turmoil. Expectation of Monday also tended to intrude on my sleep pattern. I was glad of the extra bed time nonetheless. Late in the morning Breda rang enquiring as to the outcome of the previous day's meeting and expressed disappointment at not being given the opportunity to visit me in the 'psychiatric wing'. Actually she confided that she also carried quite a degree of anxiety about the outcome. I suppose that if something had emerged it could also have changed her life. While her life might not have been perfect, she and Franner had found a balance that seemed to suit them both. More immediately, though, she was worried about the effect of facing Franner with something he had been avoiding for so many years. That girl has tremendous insight. I realised later when I thought about her phone call that she, even more than me, now believed that there was something buried deep in her Franner, and from that she surmised that it was also buried within the other three.

I did the weekly shop on autopilot: after all, Ronan and I had to live too. Then I forced myself to visit Ann and the kids. Five minutes in the

CHAPTER 22 - JOAN

house and I was climbing the walls with the continuing depression that hung over the place. It felt like a fortress with the drawbridge up to keep out the invading reality, but that reality was already inside before the defences were raised. Ann told me that John was not really talking to her and her visits consisted mostly of strained silences broken only by her sporadic and usually futile efforts to engage him. He was still in hospital rather than in prison and he expected to be there for some time yet. I didn't tell Ann anything about Cormac as she wasn't in a fit state to be able to hear it and interpret it, nor, I felt, could she handle any hope that it might raise.

After just ten minutes in the house I couldn't stand the depressive feel of the place, so I bullied the three of them to come back with me for tea. Thank you again, Ronan, as the children livened up to some degree. Ann sat in silence through my television choices and in truth there wasn't too much to be said about them. Anyway, I got her out for a short, silent walk along the beach, which couldn't have done either of us any harm. I also tried to get them all to stay the night; while the kids were on for it, Ann wouldn't stay and Brendan particularly wouldn't let his mother go home on her own. Reluctantly, but not before they had supper, I walked home with them in the late evening. When I got back Ronan commented that while Maura seemed to have come around a bit, he felt sorry for Brendan, whose spirits couldn't be lifted much at all. Ronan felt that the poor kid was trying to take on the father role in the house and was totally unable to cope with the pressure of it. Brendan's real need, according to my perceptive son, was to deal with his own grieving process for the loss by imprisonment of his Dad.

Kevin rang on Saturday night. It must have been very late as I was already in bed. Did I remember him, he asked? Sure I did. I always remember so-and-sos who get me into messes and then leave me in them while they gallivant all over the country. Kevin wasn't really in a mood for banter, as he was very concerned about the game the next day. He too was hopeful about the outcome of Cormac's session but didn't see how it could benefit his case. He hoped to have a short break after the match and promised to get down to

Wicklow on Monday if he was able to engineer the time out of his current enquiry.

Sunday passed, as they do. Breda rang. She had a real approach–avoidance thing going on. She wanted to help Franner lose his compulsion to work, to prove himself and to be even more financially secure. Yet she was worried that the result might be even worse for them than what they already had. A really good outcome of all this was our evolving friendship. Living in a small town and with a very fixed social pattern, it is nice to have an outsider to help bring perspective to things. An outsider! Is it only in semi-rural Ireland that someone who has lived in an area for fifteen or so years and is married to a local would be still considered an outsider? A good if solitary stroll around Wicklow Head was a nice antidote to my anxieties, even if a sudden shower caught me unprepared.

'Ronan, love, will you come down and record this programme from the television for me?' I shouted up the stairs.

Terrible at my age, and me using computers all the time in work, that I couldn't even record a programme on a video machine. Obligingly, Ronan came down.

'What programme is it, Ma? You don't usually pay much attention to the box,' he enquired as he came into the sitting room.

'*The Sunday Game* is just about to start and I want to tape it,' I said, much to his amazement.

At his age he probably wouldn't be expecting too much sense from his mother anyway, so he casually checked the label on a tape, shrugged and inserted it before pressing the required buttons. However, as he was leaving the room he turned and asked me the question that had just occurred to him: 'Ma, why are you recording a Gaelic match? You normally don't pay too much attention as a rule unless Wicklow are playing?'

'Kevin Brady was playing in a championship match today and I thought it might be worth recording,' I answered casually.

'God, I forgot all about the fact that he was playing, if that is what it could be called, today,' Ronan said in a tone that reminded me, as if I could forget, that he was a son of mine. With that he came back in and settled beside me on the settee to watch the programme.

'Do you know the result of the game?' he asked as the highlights began.

'No, and I don't want to,' I answered sharply, worried that he might, out of devilment, blurt it out.

'No danger from me. I had forgotten that Kev was playing,' said Ronan while subtly moving me out of the prime viewing spot on the settee.

'He's big, isn't he?' said Ronan after a minute or two as Kevin, in his white and blue hooped jersey, seemed to fill the television screen.

Five minutes later we were both on our feet shouting at the reflective images before us as one of the opposition punched Kevin in the face. He fell to the ground and a skirmish developed, with players from both teams pushing, shoving and occasionally striking each other. Kevin, lying prone, was clearly in danger of receiving further injuries from the trampling boots of the protagonists. When calm was finally restored and Kevin was treated for his injury, the referee admonished all and sundry. He might as well have been swatting flies for all the notice the players took of his wagging finger. As the game was about to resume Kevin was highlighted and his jersey clearly showed spots of blood against the blue hoop across his chest. Suddenly his immediate opponent, the one who had struck him, could be clearly seen to punch Kevin again on the blind side of the official. I felt strangely proud when I saw Kevin's elbow 'accidentally' make contact with his assailant's stomach, causing him in his turn to fall to the ground in discomfort. It was a tough game, lacking in real skill according to the commentator, but then 'Gaelic football is a man's game,' he added, obviously pleased to be on the microphone side of the contest. Kevin's county lost, as expected, but he seemed to discharge himself quite effectively. He played some good football, I was pleased to note.

Ronan, before going back upstairs, commented, 'Kev sure is one big tough copper. He can play a bit too. Mind you, I wouldn't like to get on the wrong side of him, Ma, would you?'

His departing back precluded a reply, fortunately, as various ones drifted into my consciousness. Some were not the kind normally shared between mothers and their teenage sons. After supper was over and the breakfast table set for the morning, a bad habit picked up from my mother of which I can't rid myself, I was on the point of retiring for the night when the doorbell rang.

'Behold the vanquished hero,' I said as I walked back through the hall into the kitchen, leaving Kevin standing at the doorstep before he slowly followed me with a sheepish grin on his face. I'm going to have to reset the table for breakfast, I inconsequentially thought as I got together tea and some light refreshments. He was 'a bit hungry', so some heavier refreshments in the form of thick sandwiches joined the tray before I carried it into the sitting room. The thought that he would cost a fortune to feed came to me as I watched him devouring the repast.

'Always get starving hungry a few hours after a match,' Kevin mumbled through a full mouth.

'I thought the next time I saw you it would be on one of my prison visitations. That is, after you had got yourself arrested for assaulting all and sundry on a football pitch,' I said. This seemed to please as well as amuse Kevin.

'You saw the highlights, then?'

'Highlights?' I snorted. 'You wouldn't see as many punches thrown on one of the Sky Sports pay-as-you-view boxing nights … You're all bloody thugs.'

'It was a bit rough all right,' said Kevin, grinning. 'That's the trouble with playing against one of your best friends. Joe Dunne, the fellow who hit me, we play together on the same club team in Dublin. We also live beside one another in our apartment block. We really are great friends, but any time we come up against each other it's inclined to sort of get out of hand. You know, poor Joe had to get strapping on his ribs after the match. It seems they somehow or another got badly bruised.'

Kevin's grin belied the concern implied in his words.

CHAPTER 22 - JOAN

'You ought to be ashamed of yourselves, the whole lot of you,' I said with false indignation. 'I'm sure you've put guys in prison for using less violence than that ... Were you disappointed to lose?'

'Not really. They're a much stronger team than we are, so it would have been a big surprise to beat them. I thought we did well enough, really.'

Laughingly, I said that in my opinion, if nothing else Kevin's team seemed to win the punch-up hands down or, in this case, hands up. Kevin smiled, then held his hand up to his mouth grimacing at the discomfort the laughter caused to his bruised face.

'The inside of my mouth is cut from a punch,' he said in explanation.

'Let's have a look,' I said as I leaned over to, well, not exactly admire the cut inside what was clearly a very bruised mouth. His left eye was also swollen, so wordlessly I went out and got some ice wrapped in a cloth and placed it on his temple, instructing him to hold it there for a while to keep the swelling down to reasonable proportions.

While sitting there we discussed the developments of the past week. I went into detail on my contact with Cormac and the hospital. It seemed incongruous that here we were discussing our hopes of the enquiry while he sat there with his big hand holding an ice pack to a swollen eye. Kevin told me he had to go back down the country to wrap up the investigation he was tied up with, but he hoped to have time to focus on the Franklin case after that. At one o'clock in the morning, suggesting that I had best get off to bed, I got up and took the ice pack from him. Looking intently to see the results of the treatment, I suddenly found myself gripped by the waist within his encompassing hands as he gently eased me closer to him, bringing my lips once again into contact with his. This time it wasn't with haste, although, given his bruised state, neither was it with much pressure. Rather it was a controlled tender contact. It was a contact that somehow seemed to change the whole tone and structure of our relationship. I found myself sitting beside him, my head on his chest, feeling secure, comforted and safe in his embrace. Ten minutes of not talking was wonderful ... no conflagration, just contentment. Finally and reluctantly rousing myself from my reverie, I looked at Kevin and said I had better be off to bed.

'Alone?' he questioned quietly.

'I have a teenage son asleep upstairs, so yes, alone,' I replied softly.

'Unfortunately?' he queried with a lift of his eyebrows.

Talk about being asked to make some sort of a declaration! After a pause I said, 'Yes, unfortunately.'

'That's okay, then,' said Kevin, lifting his bruised body from the chair. He smilingly took his leave, promising to contact me the next day – no, tonight now – to hear the details of Cormac's treatment revelations, if any. He gave me a last kiss as he removed himself from my door to exit into the quiet night.

Sleep didn't come too easily, but lying there I basked in the warmth of my feelings. Worries about unimportant things like baggy eyes were a long way from my thoughts.

CHAPTER 23

Kate

Me? I was on tenterhooks all weekend. The time couldn't pass quickly enough for me, and I was in early and over to the ward to check on how Cormac's weekend had gone. He had been withdrawn and stayed in his room the whole time. But at least he had eaten some food and taken liquids. There had been no further outbursts and the staff felt that much of the previous week's extreme distress had left him.

Cormac walked quietly into Patrick's office accompanied by one of the student nurses, who promptly left. When he came in he smiled at me and nodded to Patrick.

'Are you sure you're okay about me doing this procedure with you, Cormac?' Patrick asked quietly.

Cormac hesitated for a long minute and then said 'I can't go on like this any more. I have no life and I ... I owe it to myself and to my mother, so yes, yes I'm willing to try this ... anything to change my life.'

'Fine,' said Patrick, then more positively, 'right, you can sit there in the chair or perhaps you might be more comfortable lying on the couch.'

Cormac looked at both of us and then moved over to sit and then lie on the couch. Patrick pulled a chair up beside him and I just sat where I was, riveted. 'I'm just going to give you this injection into a vein in your arm,' said Patrick, taking the prepared syringe off a tray.

'You'll feel just a bit different, almost as if you're here in the room but not fully here,' Patrick said as he inserted the needle. 'It's not a large dose,' he said quietly, depressing the plunger. 'I hope I've gauged it correctly.'

'Are you okay, Cormac?' he said as he withdrew the needle. 'It didn't hurt, did it?'

'No,' Cormac answered in a flat monotone.

'Just relax, Cormac.' Then, showing his own anxiety, Patrick went over and poured himself some water and drank it. He offered me some, but I was too absorbed in what was happening to want any distraction, so I shook my head. Patrick then resumed his seat beside the couch and began.

'You grew up in Wicklow town, didn't you?'

'Yes'

'With your mother?'

'Yes, just me and my mam.'

'Were you happy growing up, Cormac?'

'Yes. It was nice with Mam, and my auntie next door.'

'Were you lonely then?'

'No, it was just nice, quiet but nice.'

'You went to school nearby. Did you like it?'

'It was okay.'

'Did you have a lot of friends at school?'

'No ... not really, I didn't mix well. Then near the end of primary school we started to hang out together.'

'We?'

'Ray, Franner, John and me sort of started to go home from school together.'

'They became your friends?'

CHAPTER 23 - KATE

'Sort of ... but not really until Joan joined us, then we were always together.'

'How did that happen, Cormac?'

'Joan was being bullied one day and we came on it. So we protected her. She then beat up this big bully and from then on the five of us became a gang. Friends for life was our motto.'

'That's a nice motto, Cormac. Did you like being part of that group?'

'Yes, it was great. I had friends and they looked out for me. We looked out for each other.'

'Was your mam happy you had friends?'

'Yes, mostly; up until then I was quiet. I had friends in school but nobody special before we joined up together. Then … sometimes Mam thought they could be a bad influence on me ... not Joan, though. She always liked Joan.'

'It must have been great as a child to have such close friends.'

'Yes, I was really happy in those years.'

'That's good, Cormac. Are you all still friends?'

'No, not really. We don't see each other any more.'

'"Friends for life" was your motto. So did anything happen to come between you and cause the break-up?'

Cormac hesitated for the first time. Patrick sat back and let the silence hang in the room. I hardly dared to breathe.

'Yes. I suppose so.'

'Can you tell me what happened, Cormac?'

The room was still. The only noise I could hear was Cormac's quiet breathing. I was trying not to in case I broke the tension.

'Alastair,' Cormac said suddenly in a monotone.

'Alastair,' Patrick repeated quietly.

'Yes.'

'Who is he?' Patrick blandly asked.

'Someone John met in the library.'

'The library.'

'Yes. Joan used to go to the library to look things up. Things like how to tie a fly for fishing … anything really. It became a running joke between us, but then we all started to go.'

'He broke you all up, did he, this Alastair?'

'Yes.'

'Would you mind telling me how he came to break you all up, Cormac?'

'John wanted to go up to Alastair's big house. He said Alastair printed magazines. He wanted us all to go up together. He told us Alastair said it was okay.'

'And did you all go up?'

'Yes. Not Joan, though. I think she was away on holidays.'

'Can you tell me what happened?'

'Alastair showed us around. He was rich and it was a big house. He had loads of pictures, pictures of models. He showed them to us. Then he showed us his cameras. He had loads.'

More silence, and Patrick just waited.

'Then he started to take pictures of us all. It was fun for a while. We were all joking about and making faces. Then Alastair suggested we pose like the models and John took off his clothes down to his underpants ... and then we all followed him. Alastair took loads of pictures of us all standing funny and making faces.'

'Anything else happen?' prompted Patrick.

'No ... no, we went home, all four of us, and Alastair said to come back up the next evening and he would have the photos developed for us to see them.'

'And you all went back up, did you?'

'No, no ... we met. John was all excited, anxious to get going. Franner and Ray refused to go back up and ... and I didn't want to, but John persuaded me.'

'So the two of you went back up to Alastair's house?'

'Yes ... over the next three or four weeks we went up a good few times and … and then Alastair moved house. He moved away from Wicklow and I never saw him again.'

'That's good, Cormac. Thank you for telling me that. And Joan, did she …'

'No, no, she was away for the first few weeks. On holidays with her mam and brother, I think. We would never have gone up there if she hadn't been on holidays. I've often wished she was around at that time. So much that happened wouldn't have! She wouldn't have let it happen. And now she'll hate me.'

'Nobody will hate you, Cormac. Kate here, Joan, me and, I'm certain, your Mam won't think any the less of you. We all like and care about you.'

'But I did bad things.'

'No, Cormac. You were only a child. Children don't do bad things.'

'I did.'

'When you have rested, would you be okay to talk to me more about all of this, Cormac? Would you mind?'

'No, I … I wouldn't mind. I think I want to, really.'

'Right, just rest now. Have a sleep, and you and I will talk later today. Okay? Just remember – and trust me, Cormac – children never do bad things.'

'Okay.'

'Rest now, Cormac. Kate and I will stay with you for a while. Now get some sleep.'

A short while later Cormac was fast asleep and I arranged for him to be wheeled back to his own room and delegated one of the nurses to stay with him on observation. Only then did I remember that I wasn't actually on duty, so I hastened in to my colleague, apologised and handed the patient's care over to him.

Patrick and I retreated to the canteen for tea, sustenance and unwinding. All those years of hospitalisations! Years of floundering around in the dark, and now we had a real chance at helping Cormac. Work rarely gets this good.

As I sat quietly enjoying what I knew to be a big breakthrough in our care of Cormac, I was reminded that I needed to ring my mentor, Michael. He would be so pleased that our treatment had moved on from medical crudeness to a recognition that therapy was a far healthier way out of damage such as this.

Patrick and I met again that afternoon just prior to our follow-up meeting with Cormac.

'Any questions?' he asked.

'No,' I answered. 'All good.' Then I blurted out, 'This morning when Cormac spoke of his encounter with Alastair, you didn't press him for details.'

'No, you're right, I didn't. To be honest I was tempted, but I wasn't comfortable about probing too deeply and pressing Cormac to talk about what actually happened while he was under hypnosis. He needs to talk about the details of what happened in a setting where we can immediately support him in dealing with his revelations. Therapeutically I didn't feel it was wise to go into any more depth during the session this morning.'

'Do you think the abuse was bad?'

'I'm not sure. But clearly John Franklin was aroused, and for whatever reason in his background, upbringing, or just his own state of sexual development at that time, he was ripe for exploitation. With him it would have, I feel, escalated rapidly. Unfortunately, unlike the other two boys, Cormac didn't have the strength in himself or in his personality to withstand the pressure John Franklin put him under. Both of them were probably sucked in and couldn't retreat from it, even as soon as their second visit. I'm certain this Alastair guy was, and probably still is, a serial abuser.'

These horrible thoughts came with me as we walked from Patrick's office to Cormac's hospital room.

CHAPTER 24

Joan

Imagine three whole days when I was able to devote my energies to the bank that puts the food on my table. Naturally my thoughts flittered frequently to the hospital as I wondered what was happening after my session with Kate and Dr Wilson. I felt it had gone well and hoped that Cormac was doing okay. My six-monthly bank review of the companies in the town that we were funding was due, and that was a useful antidote to my personal distractions.

On Tuesday after business had closed for the day, Jim and I went through my various reports. We also discussed, as always, potential new businesses that we might target. This regular review was always positive, particularly as our relationship, arising as it did from the high regard he had for my mam, was a core constant of my adult life. It occurred to me that Jim, apart from being the bank manager and my boss, was actually one of my closest and best friends. Reliving the friendships of my childhood was forcing my mind down strange avenues.

Just as we were finishing up, Kate rang me from the hospital. She told me that Cormac had seen Dr Wilson and herself. With their consent, she explained what Cormac had told them about what happened to him and John, and assured me that I had been on the right track in my pursuit of the truth. Kate added that while Cormac was definitely better, it would be some time before they could allow anyone outside of his medical team to discuss it with him. She also thanked me from all three of them, as they felt a big breakthrough in Cormac's treatment had been made as a consequence of the information I had provided.

This led to me filling Jim in on the detail of what had evolved since John Franklin's arrest. Now I had two men to depend on if I needed to. Jim was absolutely delighted when I told him about Kevin and our evolving relationship. It was nice to have a father figure to replace my long-lost dad, if only he wouldn't keep nagging me about doing the bank's degree course.

CHAPTER 25

Joan

Ronan came home early, grabbed a quick snack and then went off to play a football match and stay late with one of his friends afterwards. Fortunately he was so rushed that he didn't notice my distraction. The banging of the gate and the screech of his accelerating bicycle signalled his departure as I was left again with my thoughts. An hour or so later Kevin rang. I told him about the phone call from Kate. Why hadn't I rung him, he wanted to know? Why didn't I tell him this immediately? I couldn't properly answer him. I suppose the truth was that I didn't have the energy to ring anyone. I hadn't absorbed the impact of the revelation sufficiently inside myself to move on. I had not yet reached a point where I could easily share my thoughts with anyone. All I could do was apologise and try to explain that I was struggling to take it in for myself before I could talk to anyone, even himself, about it.

Kevin was ringing from down the country and hoped to be soon setting out for home, having finished tying up the investigation he had been working on. The brother was due to be charged with the murder, much to the amazement of the local Gardaí. Kevin was almost purring as he suggested that he would come straight to my place if that was okay, so that I could tell him in detail what Kate had said. He hung up on my assent, and with considerable effort I tidied up and got myself ready for his arrival.

Kevin bounced in an hour and a half or so later, asking twenty questions at once while also telling me that he had been on to the prison. John was still in hospital and we could visit him any time we liked. Kevin was so animated, so excited.

'Tell me everything,' he said, his big body standing so solid, his open, enthusiastic face showing such expectancy. He didn't even complain about me not ringing with the news last night.

All I did was to go over to him and place my arms around his frame. He held me, so strong and safe. Suddenly I was crying, weeping inconsolably for no reason at all. I just stood there, encased in the security of his arms, and cried and cried. I suppose I cried for my youth, my friends, my loss and their loss; or maybe it was just the realisation that all five of us had missed out on so much, arising from Cormac's revelations.

Kevin held me and held me. I felt so stupid, so childish. But he just stood there allowing me to cry it out, to rock and whimper, while he slowly caressed my back and whispered soothing words some six inches over my head. Slowly, I cried myself out.

'Are you okay now?' he said, reaching over and plucking a tissue from a box on the dresser.

I looked into his open face and through it looked into my own stupidity. I saw above all reflected in his caring eyes my own sadness. Then without conscious thought I slowly took his hand in mine and walked ahead of him upstairs to my bedroom, where I lay down, pulling him alongside.

For a man who had been so rough and tough on the football field a few days before, he exhibited a gentleness, a softness, unexpected yet oh so welcome. I didn't give a thought to the fact that this was only the second man I'd had sex with since the day I married. A lot of years had passed since I had last indulged in this activity. It didn't matter. Nothing did. It was so loving, gentle and reassuring. I lost myself and my cares for a long few moments as desire and release engulfed me. Did I want him for himself, for myself or to purge the traumas of the past few days and the guilt they evoked in me? I didn't know or care. I just needed to be held, to be loved and to feel wanted. Kevin seemed to understand. He never spoke. He just gently and lovingly held me, caressed me and made love with me.

The telephone rang some minutes after it would have been very anti-climactic, if that is not too Freudian, though not before my breathing had regained an even rhythm. I answered! I can't not!

Breda was on the phone. She wanted to know how I had got on.

While I struggled to get my thoughts together, she got hers and asked if she had rung at an inconvenient time.

'Not totally,' I answered, struggling for and markedly failing to find a suitable reply. Breda, for whom a ready reply was second nature, hung up laughing, but only after suggesting I should ring her when or if I had nothing better to do. She paused before finally hanging up and just said, 'I'm glad.'

'Remind me to boot that bitch Breda up the rear end,' I said to Kevin, the first words we had exchanged since I'd walked him up my stairs.

When he asked why a sweet girl like me would want to do something like that, struggling for words I replied, 'Because ... that's all ... just because!'

At least the call had the effect of rousing me and stopping the easy drift into contented dozing that my body was suggesting, so I got up.

My 'I suppose you're hungry and want something to eat' got a big smile from the naked policeman, so I retired to refresh myself and rustle up a not inconsiderable mixed grill, all the while feeling more fulfilled than I had felt in a lot of years. While watching my provisions supply being quickly eaten into, I brought Kevin up to date with the little Kate had told me.

He said, 'So, all four of the boys went up to this Alastair's house and had pictures taken. Then two of them refused to go back the next day, but Cormac and John did. And it is likely they went back time and again, though we don't know how long it continued. Is that the essence of it?'

I nodded in agreement while Kevin added 'If you are right, it was John Franklin that met this guy first, brought the other three to visit him and then Ray and Franner wouldn't go back. But John and Cormac continued to go, and things got more and more out of control.'

'That appears to be about the size of it.'

'Who is this guy, and where does or did he live?' asked Kevin, reaching for more bread.

'That's been puzzling me ever since Kate told me,' I said, checking that there was more bread in the bread bin before putting on the kettle for another brew of tea. Domesticity felt nice.

I hadn't a clue who the hell this man could be or even where the house was. Nothing had come to me on that subject in spite of worrying myself around it through another sleepless night. 'Never mind,' said Kevin, wiping the bruised mouth carefully with a napkin as he stood up. 'If we can get John Franklin to talk in the hospital we should now be able to find that out, and with luck I can locate the graves of my two missing boys. Their parents will be so relieved. I can't wait to tell them and put them out of their misery.' Kevin paused at that point and with a half grin added, 'Stupid, isn't it? Most times I hate going to houses and telling people their relatives have died and here I am almost looking forward to telling these nice people that I have found the bodies of their beloved children. Who was it that said it was a crazy, crazy world?'

Late and all as it was, Kevin and I drove to the hospital in a heightened state of anticipation. The drive home was a slow, more purposeful, more depressing journey. Ann had been to visit John before we got there, but he was on his own when we arrived. The guard, who was obviously permanently situated inside the hospital room, informed us that he hadn't said anything all evening and never once spoke to his wife during her entire visit. He added that she had left in an even more tearful and depressed state than usual. However, Kevin and I had the key to his talking, so it was with great confidence that we opened the door and entered.

As we came into the hospital room, John looked from Kevin to me and back to Kevin. Then he retreated back into himself, seeming to shrink into a little ball. He paid not the slightest heed to my social blandishments. I talked and talked into the vacuum he had created. Finally Kevin, tiring of this, decided to take a hand. He sat within a few feet of John on the side his face was turned to.

'We know now what happened in Colestown,' Kevin said. 'We know about Ray, Franner, Cormac and yourself. We know about the photographs and the videos of Cormac and you.'

From my safe distance I could see John's body stiffen under the covers as this information was relayed to him, but he didn't move his head. Kevin said afterwards that he didn't even blink.

'Tell us who this Alastair is! Tell us where we can find him!' Kevin said. Nothing. 'Come on, I can now understand what happened. I know what caused you to kill poor Barry. I can understand and even sympathise with you. I now know that it wasn't all your fault. Tell me the rest and we will help you as much as we can. Help us to nail the bastard who started all this. This Alastair is the one who should be in prison, not you.'

John just lay there with a fixed stare, unmoving, unresponsive.

'John,' I pleaded, 'you know Ann asked me to try and find out what happened? What made this tragedy come into your family? Help me. I know a lot now. Help me to put it all together for … for Ann's sake … for the children. They'll need something to hold on to in the years ahead.'

Silence dominated the small hospital room. It lay on the three of us for a long time. Then slowly John turned his head away from Kevin and towards me. He held me in a fixed stare for a considerable period of time before talking for the first and only time that evening.

'Fuck off, you,' he said and then turned away from both of us and slid down into the sheets till they covered his head as well as his body.

Five minutes and no movement later, Kevin signalled to me and we left, our high expectations in absolute tatters.

Journeys home are often much quicker than the outward ones. It was definitely not so in this case. The twenty or so minutes it took for Kevin to meander through the light inner-city night traffic was in total silence. The silence of shattered hope! Eventually as the speed began to pick up along the dual carriageway, I broke the silence by saying, 'I'm sorry.'

'For what?' Kevin said in a surprised tone, glancing at me for the first time since we left the hospital car park.

'How the hell do I know what I'm sorry for?' I barked somewhat brusquely before adding in a more modulated tone, 'Sorry for building up your hopes, for thinking it was all sorted out, for thinking I could solve this riddle. Or probably it's just that I'm feeling sorry for myself,' I added lamely.

'You have done absolute wonders to get us this far. You should be proud of yourself, not sorry,' Kevin said, stretching the considerable palm of his hand over and caressing my leg.

He drove on in silence but, while the pall of depression still hung over us, the sense of shared comradeship acted as a comforting antidote. Kevin put a tape into the cassette player and gradually its soporific effects made inroads into my sense of futility. I was mildly surprised at his choice of music. It was some light classical piece. I idly wondered if I would have the same amount of trouble with Kevin as I do with Ronan. Ronan takes issue with not just the type of pop music I listen to but also the volume I like to play it at. Whatever, in this moment the muted tones of that gentle piece of classical music were just what we both needed.

At the house I got out of the car and came round to the driver's side. 'I'll give you a ring tomorrow and we'll see where to go from here,' Kevin said, and on my nod of assent he slowly engaged gears and pulled away, leaving me to my own thoughts. I went in and called up to Ronan. His response assured me he was home, as if the bag full of dirty boots and damp football gear lying in the hall wasn't proof enough. Having put the gear into the washing machine I went, as ever, to put on the kettle. No sooner had it been plugged in than the doorbell rang. When I answered it, there stood Kevin, looking sheepish. A man his size standing with a sheepish grin was quite comical to my eyes.

CHAPTER 25 - JOAN

'Now I'm sorry, Joan,' he said. 'I just drove off. What must you be thinking of me after what happened earlier and what you mean to me? How could I have just driven off?'

'Is there some strange ritual unique to the part of the country where you grew up that I am not aware of and need to acquaint myself with?' I asked in a sharp tone, though the glint in my eye must have belied it.

Kevin's not too-innocent face took on a look of puzzlement as he said, 'I don't understand what you mean.'

'Don't you, now? The first time you called to this house you left and then came back and kissed me. The next time out the gate you went, then turned around and tried to do the same. What is it now? Coming back for more sex is it? After all, if I don't understand your rituals, how will I know how to respond to them?'

'I'm sorry. I just left and drove off. Not even a proper goodbye. I was so wrapped up in my own thoughts that I wasn't thinking straight. I turned back when I realised what I had done, or hadn't done.'

At that, noticing the laughter in my eyes he stopped, grasped me in a hold that didn't brook any defiance and kissed me hard, then much more tenderly and softly. Letting go, he half turned away and added.

'You know it's not, as you so smartly try to suggest, a local ritual, but I do intend from now on to kiss you every time I take my leave, and …,' he added from the gate, 'it just may be that I will leave you very, very often.'

Grinning, he sent me a sketchy wave as he got into the car, and the tail lights winked back at me as he turned out of the road.

'Was that Kev driving off?' asked Ronan coming down the stairs. 'Why didn't you invite him in for something to eat, Ma?' he continued as he progressed to the kitchen to help himself to a snack.

I hastily followed, though not because I was so domesticated as to think it was my job as a mother to prepare the food. It was just that I absolutely hate cleaning up the mess that his self-created repasts always leave behind.

CHAPTER 26

Joan

'If you want a loan, a bank is just the right place to come,' I said to Breda as she settled into one of the comfortable chairs in my office. Isn't it grand to be able to have a cuppa and a chat with a friend under the guise of working! Out came her cigarettes and with a shrug of resignation I dredged the ashtray out from the drawer of the desk where it lay for just this contingency.

'To hell with all the bank stuff! I just couldn't wait to hear what was going on and as you were obviously too occupied to have any thoughts of me yesterday, I had to call in. So come on, tell all! What happened?'

'Well, I went into the hospital with Kevin to talk to John,' I started to say but Breda interrupted.

'Yes, yes, of course I want to hear about that. Not yet though! First things first! What was going on when I rang you? I was right, wasn't I?'

'Does the right to privacy not exist in this country? What happens to me is personal and private, I'll have you know.'

'That's okay, then,' Breda interjected. 'But you're going to have a hard job explaining to the manager why one of the few customers whose accounts are in credit decided to move her money to another bank. I could be forced to do this because of the poor cooperation of his staff: one staff member to be precise.'

'You wouldn't,' I said, in mock fear.

'I would, and Franner's business account would go with me as well. So come on, talk.'

'Hold on a minute,' I said, my hand raised, vainly trying to stave off the inevitable. 'Neither you nor your husband bank here, so out you go.'

'We use this bank … eh … just not this branch, so come on, stop prevaricating. Explain yourself!'

I told. I had little choice, though to be honest I was dying to confide. We indulged in a not-so-quiet game of retrospection as I recounted my entanglement with Kevin. I couldn't, of course, answer her questions as to what was going to happen next, as I didn't know myself. I hadn't even begun, either intellectually or emotionally, to dissect the implications of the loss of my virginity again after such a long time in that wilderness. That of course didn't stop Breda from projecting all sorts of developments into the situation. She should be writing Mills and Boon stuff with an imagination like hers. On second thoughts, her imagination ran on too carnal a track for them.

Gradually our lightness eased off as I recounted the information given to me by Kate and its revelations.

'My poor Franner,' she said when I had finished telling her of Cormac's story. 'Men are so bloody daft, if you ask me. Has he been living in a sea of guilt and self-denigration from that bloody childish episode? Does he really think I would love him less if I found out about that? The torment of guilt that he has put himself through! Damn and blast the bastard who got them involved. I am personally going to find the guy who owned that house and when I do I'll strangle him with my bare hands. You, my friend, better keep very well in with that detective of yours, because I'm going to need him to cover up for me when I do commit murder.'

'There is a little problem there,' I said, and outlined to a riveted Breda what had happened when Kevin and I confronted John in the hospital room.

'I haven't a single idea as to who it could be that inveigled them into those activities,' I added.

'Do I get this right?' Breda eventually summed up. 'We have Cormac and John who won't or can't tell us and Ray and Franner as the only options to finding out who he is.'

'That's about it,' I concurred. 'Cormac will probably tell us, but my guess is that Dr Wilson is going to hasten very, very slowly with his treatment. I'm afraid it's going to be a long time yet before he'll be able to talk about his childhood abuse in a way that won't be detrimental to his own mental wellbeing.'

After lighting another cigarette and standing up to pace the room, Breda asked me if there was any chance that Ray could be talked to about all this again, in the hope that he might come up with the name we wanted.

'No way in this earth am I going to broach that subject again,' I said. 'Judging by the response I got so far – and up to this I have only been prodding around – it is quite likely he would decapitate me if I told him that I knew anything about all of this.'

'You never know your luck,' said Breda with a rueful grin. 'He just might divorce you on the grounds of knowing too much.'

'Actually,' I mused, 'I had sort of wondered if he might go to see someone and deal with his drink problem. If I could reassure him that this childhood thing didn't change how people thought about him, then maybe he could take control of his life.'

'With men you never can tell,' said Breda. 'They are strange creatures, no mistake. Still, I don't think it is advisable to talk to Ray at this juncture. From your response just now I can tell that his reaction is just too unpredictable. So it looks like it is up to me to try to prise it somehow out of poor Franner, doesn't it?'

'It does seem to be the best chance,' I agreed, though without pushing it.

'Strange – now that we have come this far I am really scared. The life

Franner and I have together is quite nice, really. It suits us, or him at least. If I open up this can of worms and if this stupidity is part of the cause of his being so driven, so closed up, the outcome of such a revelation can't be totally predictable. It will certainly change things between us. And I have to admit that I am a little worried that the change won't be for the best. After all, if I burst his bubble, breach this protective wall that he has built around his emotions, he might not like it and he just might blame me for taking away his defences and hate me for it. He mightn't let himself believe that I do love him. He may not want to believe that what did or did not happen during his growing-up years doesn't have any bearing on how I feel about him now. I suppose really I'm sort of scared that he could end up pushing me even further away.'

'Don't do it, then!' I said in agitation. 'Leave it to me, Breda. Look, I'll go back to John Franklin as often as it takes until I break him down. I'm sure he will talk about it eventually. Kevin needs him to talk anyway, as he desperately needs to find those missing bodies. Don't you do anything yet. Let's think things out.'

By now I too was on my feet, pacing. 'In the first place, Cormac isn't well enough to tell. Ray certainly won't and Franner is dangerous for you. So, leave it with John Franklin and me. He is totally fucked anyway. He has nothing left to lose so he will talk eventually. He has to!'

With that we both paused and looked intently at one another. Finally Breda placed her two hands on my shoulders, and holding me hard, she said, 'No, Joan – leave it to me. I have to do it, not for my sake but for Franner's. He may hate me for it, but he is entitled to the opportunity of burying a ghost that haunts him. I owe it to him to try and help him do it. If I can support him through this, life is bound to be better for both of us and for the children. I know there is a soft, vulnerable bit locked inside Franner and if he can trust himself to share it with me, it will be much healthier for both of us. I know he loves me. I just have to trust that our love will get us through this.'

With that she turned to leave the room. Her face was full of determination and, not for the first time in the past few weeks, I regretted the wasted years when we could have been such good friends. At the door she paused and, after giving me a bright, open smile, departed with an admonition.

'Don't ring me. I'll ring you. It's just that I get so irritated when people ring me at an inconvenient time, like when my breathing is a giveaway to my actions. I do so hate any sort of interruptions, don't you?'

She departed quickly, but not so rapidly as to miss seeing me stick out my tongue at her. Five more minutes of time paid for by the bank was wasted as I took the space necessary to get myself back on track before returning my concentration to financial matters.

I made a quick visit to Newcastle Hospital on my way home from work. I didn't go to see Cormac, though I half wanted to. Actually my visit was to see Kate on foot of a phone call from her. I was puzzled and intrigued as to her reason for asking to see me for the second time in a week. In truth I kept trying to think of something I had done wrong, something to incur Dr Wilson's wrath. It was bad enough feeling guilty meeting policemen; now I had the same guilt complex when the psychiatric hospital rang me. And I knew I was perfectly normal. The problem was, of course, that I couldn't be certain that everyone else shared that view!

I met Kate in her office and at first she seemed, if anything, to be more nervous than I. Finally she told me that this meeting was at the request of Dr Wilson, though he would deny allowing Kate to talk to me about these confidential matters. He wanted me to know something that Cormac had said. She also made it very clear that Cormac was aware of and in agreement with her telling me. Now I was really worried, but I solemnly assured Kate that I would treat any information I was given with very good care. At that Kate nodded and then told me that Cormac had said that the sexual activity involved not just John and himself but also the man who owned the house. He had also said that the two boys had tied each other up at this man's suggestion. Cormac was scared during those games, as he was hurt a little during the session. Dr Wilson felt I needed to know about this extra information in view of the interest that I was taking in the terrible death of that poor boy.

Having given this information, Kate relaxed and assured me that Cormac was making slow progress, but progress nonetheless. He was so lucky to be in their care. Kate really likes my old friend, I thought, as I walked slowly back to my car. Better to think those thoughts than the ones that I was trying to blot out. I drove home in a frightened and anxious state.

By now I was very worried at the can of worms that I had opened … and how it was going to impact on all our lives.

CHAPTER 27

Joan

It's amazing how much I enjoyed a simple daily routine. By now my normality had become so abnormal that I basked in the familiar. I got up, went to work, then came home to cook dinner for Ronan and myself. After watching a few hours of television, I unfortunately had to do a small bit of ironing. I then went up to my own bed and for a change had a refreshing eight hours of sleep. The bank also got my undivided attention, though there were two customers with over-exuberant overdrafts who were going to regret my concentration on that day. Ronan even commented on the meat and two veg as well as the roast potatoes put before him, unusually so for a Wednesday, before he disappeared upstairs to his studying. He made short shrift of them, mind, so he wasn't exactly complaining.

Kevin rang to see how I was. He wanted to take me out for a meal the following evening, which sounded good to me. No word from Breda, but it was a bit early to expect anything from that quarter. I rang Ann. She was fine. The kids were fine. In fact everything was fine. So, worried as to how they really were, I promised to call in to her on my way home from work the following evening. After a long soak in the bath, sleep came quickly and deeply, though the bags under the eyes hadn't disappeared in the morning. How is it, I wondered as I put on my work face, that it takes such a short time to develop them but a long time, if ever at my age, to lose them?

Ann again said she was fine when she opened the door to me. Her face, her clothes, her demeanour all told a different story. I got her or rather forced her to have a long soak in the bath. It worked for me, so why not for her? While she was in the bath I cooked some dinner for them. This took much longer than expected, as there was nothing much edible in the house and Maura and I had to go to the supermarket to get some provisions in. Ann wouldn't come to the shops with us. She hardly ate anything either. Over dinner, which I didn't eat as Kevin was providing this for me, Ann talked of the frustration of going into the hospital to see John. He wouldn't talk to her. He never asked about how things were or about the children, and she found the visits an absolute trial. Brendan was still refusing to go with her to see his father in spite of his mother's and sister's repeated requests. When Maura went in with her mother, John didn't say anything to her either. This upset Ann because Maura, being the only girl, had always been very close to John. Maura herself didn't seem too upset by her Dad's lack of response to her. She reasoned that he wasn't well at the moment and things would be sure to improve as her Daddy got better. She always hugged and kissed him on leaving, but it was never reciprocated.

What could I do for Ann? I felt so helpless. I didn't tell her of Cormac's revelations or my visit to John the other day, as it seemed pointless until I had some concrete progress to report to her. I got home later than projected, so it was fish and chips collected on the way for Ronan.

'Normality resumes,' he commented as he tucked in, referring to the contrast with the previous day's repast. I just don't know where he got that sarcastic streak.

Quick shower, quicker change and time spent over make-up with emphasis on the eyes. Was I getting neurotic about those bags? Then I was

CHAPTER 27 - JOAN

ready to meet Kevin for what in reality was the first date I'd had in sixteen-plus years. A last look in the mirror didn't reassure me; rather it left me feeling that I would just have to do.

I opened the door to leave, having given Ronan his instructions. You know – bedtime, have his supper, all the usual things that he would totally ignore – and there standing in front of me with an expectant expression on her face stood Breda, her hand suspended in a mock door-knocking position.

'Oh, did you not get the message from Ronan? Or are you dressed like that for me?' she said with a smile. However her smile was tinged with the anxiety of someone set fair for a good chat, who was picking up the message that I mightn't be around to share in it with her.

'Ronan!' I shouted up the stairs.

'Yes, Ma' came floating down, followed by a hesitant 'I meant to tell you that Mrs Crowley rang to say that she would be calling around to see you'. This was followed after a perceptible pause by a 'Hi, Mrs Crowley, how are you?' in a light, bantering semi-apologetic tone.

'Come in, Breda,' I said, withdrawing to the kitchen while I appraised my options. Having gone sixteen-plus years without a date, I didn't suppose another few days would make too much difference to my romantic life.

'Is there anything you have to say that would benefit from the presence of a policeman, a plain-clothes detective at that?' I asked.

With barely a hesitation Breda answered to the effect that if this meant that she got the opportunity to meet this big fellow and maybe do the 'in loco parentis' role of assessing his suitability for me, then maybe she could find something of moment to discuss with him.

'Seriously,' she added, 'there is an end result from my discussion with Franner that he could help with.'

'If I get him here in what … an hour and a half or so, we can have plenty of time to ourselves first,' I suggested, and on her nod of assent I rang Kevin at work and told him of my problem. In fairness to him, he agreed without much demurring to defer the meal and to come and join us later. As I was hanging up a thought suddenly came to me. I rang him back and, after much hither and thither it was agreed that Kevin would bring a Chinese takeaway to the separate requirements of Breda and myself as well as a large order to stuff himself with on his arrival.

Tea made and the ashtray having been produced before it was asked for, I settled in the chair and, with a tremor of expectancy, said, 'Come on, then – your turn.'

Just as Breda was about to start talking, I got up and from the bottom of the stairs shouted up to the listening walls, 'Don't think you've got away with not giving me the message from Breda! I won't forget, don't worry.'

Returning to the kitchen I heard, as if in the echo of my own voice, the comment, 'You never bloody do, Mother.'

Breda smilingly commented, 'Nice kid you have there, very mannerly as well.'

'Sure,' I said with agreement. 'I just like to remind him now and then that he isn't bloody perfect.' Unable to contain myself further, before I was even sitting down, I asked, 'Is everything okay with Franner and you?'

'Yes, don't worry. Everything is very all right,' reassured Breda. 'Very, very all right in fact,' she added.

'Good. So?' I said into the hiatus while she inevitably lit up a cigarette.

'First of all, let me tell you that I have, or at least I think I have, the information that you need,' was Breda's opening remark, and she proceeded to tell me of her strategy and encounter with Franner.

After a lot of thought she had decided not to talk to him on the Tuesday night but organised for Noeleen, her regular babysitter, to come in the following evening. She then rang Franner and arranged to meet him at his favourite restaurant. A nice meal … then home. The kids were safely asleep, and so they retired.

Breda joined Franner not in bed but rather on the bed, facing him. She sat in her nightie, one he particularly liked, with the light softly glowing. She started by outlining what he knew: my quest for information about John Franklin and what might have made him do what he had done. At that stage, she said, Franner looked not so much worried as wary, so she hastened on to my discussions with Ray as well as my visit to their house. She finished by recounting to him, in a flat, impersonal tone, what Cormac had said.

At that point, seeing the beginning of panic in Franner's eyes, she caressed and held him. She reassured him of her love for him and of the fact that whatever might have happened to him when he was a young boy was not going to change in any way how she felt about him now. She cradled him to her bosom (my interpretation – I must be a romantic at heart!) and caressed him for a long while. Eventually she could feel the tension leaving his body as he held her and then responded to her ministrations by slowly rubbing her back.

The next bit surprised me, as Franner then started to talk to his wife not about the lads but about me. He told Breda how he had loved me as a kid. How he bloody well knew once I had called to see him the other week that there was going to be no end of trouble. Knowing me as he did, I was bound to find out what had happened. He then told Breda about the first time he saw me. He described seeing me being shaken off the back of that big bully and how I had beaten Thomas Mooney through pure doggedness and determination. He talked about the fact that all through our growing up together I was the strongest one of the five of us. I was, according to Franner, certainly the most determined and ruthless person he had ever met. He knew from prcvious cxpcricncc that I was going to find out about that bloody Alastair come hell or high water. He knew and hated the fact that I would discover the secret they had hidden from me for all those years. At that point Franner asked Breda if I knew all that he had done and if I despised him now. She reassured him that I only felt sad that such a stupid, stupid bloody thing was let get in the way of the great friendship we had. Now, in retrospect, it had so clearly ruined the five friends as a group as well as doing so much damage to all of the boys as individuals. Breda then told him that what I was really sad about was the fact that my perception of the five of us as the greatest of friends was turning out not to be true at all.

Franner then said that at the time of the visits to this Alastair's house he wanted to tell me about it, and nearly did a few times. But the others, particularly John and Ray, had insisted that nobody, and that included me, was to be told. They believed that if knowledge of what they had done got out they could all have been taken away from their families and put into homes or reform schools. He knew now, of course, that this was a load of rubbish, but to a vulnerable, frightened twelve-year-old it was a very real threat. Franner remembered so well that this fear was planted in them all by Alastair.

Franner then moved on and told Breda how he had loved me, or thought he did, and hated the fact that I married Ray, who in his view was never good enough for me. He himself had wanted to ask me out for years but didn't have the nerve to bring the subject up, as he felt that nobody could love him after what he had done. This, he added, was of course old history, and he wouldn't swap Breda now for, well, at least some of the tea in China. Relieved that he could make a joke Breda then said that neither how he felt about an old friend twenty or so years ago nor whatever stupid thing he did as a kid was going to change the love she felt for him. Franner, reassured, relaxed a little and told his wife all he knew about Alastair and what had happened in that house all those innocent years before.

John met this Alastair guy, who was an old man – or old in twelve-year-old eyes anyway – while he was visiting the library in Wicklow one day. There was some photographic exhibition on and John was looking at the pictures on display when this man came in and started to look at them as well. Franner, as an aside, explained to Breda that all the lads had gotten into the habit of calling into the library because it was something that Joan had always done. He said that I was forever going in and checking things out. Hearing Breda say that, I smiled, remembering how strange my friends had thought this habit of mine was. That is, of course, before they discovered for themselves the usefulness of a local library.

CHAPTER 27 - JOAN

Alastair got talking to John about the photographs and then invited him over to his house to see his own photographic studio, which he said was fully equipped to take professional pictures. John went over on his own first, then came back and told the rest of the lads about it. Needless to say, all four boys went over the following day. They were very impressed not only by the studio, which was used for taking professional photographs, but also by a room that was equipped for making videos.

This Alastair, according to what Franner said, lived in a house with a bit of land around it just about halfway between Colestown and Wicklow. It seemed to be a huge house to the lads at the time. Alastair told them that he ran a mail-order business and needed the studio to take photographs of the models for his catalogue. After getting the four boys interested in the whole process, Alastair then took a few photos of them in humorous poses to demonstrate the lighting and backdrops that he used. He promised to develop the pictures and let the boys take them home to their parents if they called back the next day.

Excited, the four of them were delighted to visit the next day. Sure enough, Alastair had the pictures ready and they all had a good laugh at the poses and funny faces that were shown. What impressed the boys most then, according to Franner, was the obviously professional set-up. Alastair showed them the catalogues he had and some of the pictures taken for them in the studio. He also demonstrated how the whole thing worked. He showed them the process of transferring the pictures to the catalogues. All of this was wonderful and exciting to the boys. But then things started to change.

While they were having something to eat, Alastair showed them some pictures of girls modelling underwear. These pictures were set up for the next edition of his magazine. They all had a good though self-conscious laugh about those and then he suggested that they should copy the poses of the real models whose pictures they had just seen. This started out for the lads as just a lark, but by the end they felt both excited and scared, knowing that what they were doing was wrong. They had by then started to adopt suggestive postures, wearing less and less until finally they were in their underpants. John actually took off all his clothes for some of the pictures and they could see how excited he was by it, though Franner didn't really understand then what was going on for John.

The next morning, feeling a bit embarrassed about the whole episode, Franner met up with the lads. John particularly was on a real high. He was anxious to get back up to Alastair's house to see the developed photos. Franner and Ray, who felt guilty and scared about what they had done, refused to go. John, though, was totally consumed with going back, and he pressured Cormac into going with him. As far as Franner could remember, John and Cormac went to Alastair's house each day for the next week or so and then suddenly Alastair had apparently moved and none of them, to his knowledge, ever saw him again.

In the evening of the first day that John and Cormac went up on their own, John called to Franner's house and, Franner presumed, to Ray's. He told Franner that Alastair had developed the pictures of the four of them posing in their underwear. According to John, if they said anything to anyone about the house, Alastair would send copies of their pictures not only to their parents but also to the police. Ray and Franner discussed it and made a pact never to say anything about that day or what they had done to anyone, ever. They agreed specifically that that included me. It wasn't that for one second they believed that I would ever betray the group, but they absolutely didn't want me to know what they had done.

For at least a year after those few days, Franner went around in a state of fear. He was scared of being arrested every time he saw the local sergeant on his bike and even used to hide from him. One day the sergeant came into their classroom and, Franner said, he nearly wet himself with the fear of his guilty secret being found out; and that was six months after that stupid day in Alastair's house.

Ray and himself never talked to John or to Cormac about what went on up in the house. Nor, in fact, did they ever enquire as to why the lads stopped visiting, or even about your man's sudden disappearance from the area. At no time since then did any of the four mention that episode to each other, unless Cormac and John talked about it, but Franner doubted even that. Franner said that he believed now that things were never really the same after for the lads.

The inseparable friends held a guilty secret and it unglued them. Sure, they still hung around together. They still did everything together as a group, but the easy spark had gone. Franner felt that the only thing that kept them together after that was me and the allegiance they all had individually to a friendship with me.

Franner added that he didn't know what John and Cormac got up to on the days they went up to Alastair's on their own, but in hindsight he could bloody well guess. At that point Breda told me that Franner's revelations dried up and he became a little anxious about what might happen if all of this came out now, and particularly how it might affect their own children. He was also worried about how his parents might react. He didn't fancy the idea of his strait-laced lawyer dad having this to hold against his successful son.

Breda said that she had to spend quite a while reassuring him that it was unlikely that any of this about himself, Ray or Cormac would come out. Anyway, all those who loved him would understand that it was easy for a twelve-year-old to be manipulated by an expert like that bastard Alastair. Nobody would blame him or hold it against him.

'What has been really bothering me,' I said, 'is how all of this could possibly have gone on without me knowing of it.'

'Franner's memory is that all of this happened during a fortnight when you were away on a family holiday. Judging by how close you all were then, I reckon that there was no way this could have possibly happened if you had been around,' Breda said.

Thinking back all those years, I reckoned it must have been one of the times that Mam took us to stay for a week or two in Jim the bank manager's caravan in Courtown. As I said, he always respected Ma and her struggle to bring us up and gave her the use of his caravan every year. To think that all this happened because of two coincidences: John meeting this guy in the library and my being away at that same time. Shrugging off the sense of anger this realisation brought upon me, I came back to Franner and Breda's encounter.

'I hope you were able to convince poor Franner that nobody was going to give a bloody damn what he or the other boys did one afternoon twenty-five years ago,' I said.

Breda agreed with a grin that she had worked hard at doing so.

'I hope the effort didn't tire you out too much,' I said.

Breda's grin just got broader.

'You mustn't have got too much sleep,' I said. 'Your eyes are a bit puffy.'

I should never have given Breda such an opening.

'I suppose you would have to be an expert in that area,' she retorted.

Things could have got very nasty, given how touchy I am on that subject, only for the arrival of one big, very broad detective who took the attention of my friend Breda away from me. Mind you, it didn't stop her from repeating her smart comment, much to his amusement. My insistence on him arresting her for defamation of character or insulting behaviour or any other trumped-up charge he usually used in these situations failed to alter his amusement at my expense.

Isn't it amazing, the silliness that we adults can indulge in when we are trying to ease the tension created by such fluctuating emotions?

While the banter went on, Kevin and I dished out the takeaway he had brought. As we set about demolishing it, I was pleased to note that he had got the order right. He had even included – I was delighted to note, as I hadn't put it in the order – a meal for Ronan, which he gratefully took up to his room.

Hunger satiated, we, or rather Breda, briefly recounted her developments with Franner. Typical policeman, Kevin wasn't at all interested in the emotional tangles involved and was focused on the pursuit of the identified criminal. Who is this Alastair guy? Where did he live at that time? Where is he now? What is the name of the mail order company he runs? The questions came tumbling out one on top of another, giving me room to pause, as I hadn't yet moved away from the protective emotions I was feeling for my four childhood friends. I was also still caught up in the relief of knowing that Franner and Breda seemed to have come out of the revelations okay. Dominating all my emotions, though, was the surging anger that I was feeling towards this Alastair guy.

'Slow down, Kevin,' I said. 'Give us time to catch breath and we will start to think along your lines. And while we do so, you may as well take the dishes out to the kitchen.'

With a smile … I liked his easy smile … he removed himself and the plates into the kitchen. Over the noise of the washing-up, which I hadn't asked him to do, Breda whispered, 'I hope you are going to hold on to that one. I can see how he would make your breathing go all shallow and deep. My God, he is big, isn't he?'

I was only just finished making a face at Breda while secretly agreeing with her when Kevin re-entered, wiping his hands on a tea towel. He threw it at me as he tumbled down into the couch, seeming to totally fill it.

'Right, girls, give!' he said, looking with mock expectancy from one of us to the other.

Breda, who was continually surprising me, said that Franner and herself discussed most of the questions Kevin had harangued us with. The only one they could answer for certain was the whereabouts of the house. Franner knew nothing beyond Alastair's first name and the location of the house.

Half an hour later, Breda had gone home and Kevin and I were sitting in his car looking, albeit in almost full darkness, into a driveway with a security call system and electronic gates. We were satisfied that we could at least see from a distance the outline of the house where this Alastair had once lived. Kevin got out of the car and paced around examining the defences protecting the distant house, then he shrugged, obviously deciding not to bother the present occupants at this late hour. He sat back beside me with a determined look on his face.

'I'll find him, don't doubt it,' said Kevin in a grim voice as he started the car to take me home. I had no doubt that he would. Neither of us could predict whether it would help John, make Ann and the kids feel better or aid in the solution of Kevin's other big agenda. What I could predict from Kevin's tone was that he wouldn't rest until he had run this Alastair to ground.

'Tomorrow morning I'll call into the Garda station in Wicklow and see if they have any information on Alastair whoever. If they haven't I can always go through the old census registers. Time consuming but usually productive,' said Kevin in a grim, ruminative sort of tone as he pulled up outside my house.

CHAPTER 28

Joan

It's late, eleven o'clock at night, certainly very late for me, a separated lady, to be bringing a man into my respectable home. You couldn't exactly sneak this one in unnoticed with his size, but brazenly I walked with him up the drive and entered the house. Ronan was in the kitchen getting himself a drink before going to bed. He didn't appear to be having any of the reservations I was imagining were going on behind some of the curtains in the houses on the road.

Hi, Kev, how's it going?' he said. 'Thumped any footballers recently?' he added in a typical Ronan-type remark. Honestly, I just don't know where he gets his sense of humour from!

'No, not recently,' answered Kevin, 'but I could be tempted to sort out a certain smart alec teenager if he isn't more careful with his comments.'

They shared mutual grins as Ronan in mock retreat took his toast and coffee with him out of the kitchen. 'Goodnight, Kev. Night, Ma. Oh, and thanks for the Chinese,' he said as he was leaving.

'Night, love,' I answered, adding, 'I haven't forgotten yet about the Breda message I didn't get.'

'No pocket money for a month again I suppose … not that I get enough anyway,' rang out from the stairs, much to Kevin's amusement.

'Don't encourage him,' I said, hitting Kevin lightly on the shoulder as I put on the kettle. Turning, I came straight into Kevin's body and his arms went around me. He held me in a strong, tender hold. I let myself just be there, enjoying the release of some of my pent-up tensions. Slowly he kissed me, a gentle soft touch, and without a conscious decision I felt my mouth open and somehow found myself drifting into a pool of calm comfort. We seemed to pause there in a rigid tableau where the only movement was internal lip against lip as our tongues gently touched. I stood there thinking, well not thinking really, but the thought at some point did come into my head that all that nonsense about drowning in someone else's embrace was not total nonsense after all.

Repressing a sudden impulse to push Kevin away, I gently eased myself out of his embrace. The kettle was just switching itself off anyway, so more than me was in danger of boiling over. In some confusion I turned and busied myself making the tea. Usually I don't clank the crockery together like this, I thought to myself.

'Do you want anything to eat?' came out sounding more normal and controlled than I felt inside.

'I suppose I could manage a sandwich. I do feel a bit peckish,' Kevin said, moving over to the bread bin to help himself.

'Peckish, and you only finished the takeaway an hour and a half ago. Thank God you don't call here too often. You would eat anyone out of house and home,' I stated as I struggled for normality.

Kevin paused in the buttering of the bread, looked at me seriously and asked 'Do you really not want me, that is me personally, to be calling to see you regularly, Joan?' Crunch time, and I brought it on myself. I carried the tea tray into the living room and sat down. Kevin joined me as his solution for peckishness sat dominating a plate that rested on his knee.

Oh well, here goes, I thought. 'Look Kevin,' I said, my serious face turned towards him, 'I'm thirty-seven years old. I have a failed disaster of a marriage long behind me. I hadn't even thought of another relationship before all this and then you and I ... well it ... it just happened. I was upset, vulnerable really ... not that it wasn't lovely: it was, you know that. But it doesn't mean anything. You don't owe me. I don't expect anything of you. And I certainly don't want it to happen again.'

His face, strong and impassive, showed a sense of pain in the flicker of his eyes but he remained quiet. Into the silence I continued. Why can't I just leave silences hang? In work I do it all the time and it works very well for me there.

'I don't know anything about you, Kevin, really, whether you are married, single or even living with someone. You have to understand that apart from this whole John Franklin thing I feel personally very vulnerable. I am not into nor could I handle a casual fling just because we are thrown together in this case.'

'Do you think that what I want is just a casual fling, as you put it?' Kevin asked quietly, taking my hand.

'In truth I just don't know,' I answered softly, adding, 'I don't have the experience to tell in this kind of situation. I can't decide whether our making love came from a developing relationship or just a physical need.'

As I struggled to find a word – any word that wouldn't dig me in deeper – Kevin quieted me with a slight movement and said, 'Look, let me put my cards on the table.' With that he held my hands, engulfing my two in his. 'I'm not married, never have been. I did get engaged once some six or seven years ago, but working for the murder squad, as I have done for ten years now, is a very disruptive way of life. I am permanently on call and often so caught up in the horrors of the cases we have to deal with that I certainly was no use to any woman, let alone myself. My then fiancée, who really was and is a lovely girl, couldn't handle my lifestyle. It ended when she, after a few horrible rows, called the engagement off. She now lives in Portlaoise. She is married to a man who has a nice regular nine-to-five job and she seems very happy with her kids and her life.'

'Do you see this girl often, then?' I enquired with just a tinge of bitchiness in my tone.

'No, I have hardly seen her at all in the past few years, but my mother does and she likes to keep me well informed. You know the sort of thing? "See what you have missed out on! When are you ever going to get around to having a few grandchildren for me to spoil!" Anyway, for the past five or so years it has just been the occasional, very occasional, one-, two- or three-night stand, and that with girls who wanted no different for themselves. I have stayed away from any emotional relationships since then. Of course the fact that I was playing both club and inter-county football and trying to keep up with the training demands of that further complicated things. Between work and sport I was left with very little spare time in my life.'

At that Kevin paused.

'Well?' I said eventually.

'Well what?' he answered with a slightly confused look.

In some exasperation I said, 'Are you telling me that what happened between us was just a one-night stand or one that you wouldn't exactly object to turning into a two-night one, then? Is that what you mean?'

'Absolutely not,' he insisted, his face lightening and a broad smile coming into it. 'I would much prefer to have, let's say, a two-hundred-night stand and then we can discuss where we go from there. Seriously,' he added looking intently at me, 'I like you very much, Joan, and I certainly don't want this to be a stand of any sort. I was hoping we could get to know each other much better and see how we go from there. I absolutely don't want not to see you again after this case is finished. Surely you've picked that much up from me. I have never met any woman that I liked as instantly as I did you. Why the hell do you think I kissed you the first night?' I had a smart comment on the tip of my tongue, but Kevin stopped it coming out by placing a finger lightly over my mouth before continuing. 'Why do you think I made such a fool of myself going in to apologise?'

CHAPTER 28 - JOAN

As Kevin's finger was still in range I attempted to bite it, and as he hastily pulled it out of the way I got my retaliation in. 'That mother of yours should spend less time keeping you up to date with the goings on of your ex-fiancées and much more on giving you lessons in the art of saying the right sort of things to sweep a girl off her feet.'

Smiling, he enquired with an innocent expression on his face, 'Your child-bearing days … they aren't over, are they? I mean Mother will ask.'

A girl, or in my case a sort of a girl, can only take so much. So I threw him out at that point. Not before there was time for some more embracing, but certainly before any conflagration that might give hope or anxiety to his mother took place. As Kevin went out the gate he turned back to me.

'Not again,' I said smiling.

'No, smarty, not that! I just wanted to say that as I am supposed to be off tomorrow, or is it today, I'll call to the station in Wicklow and maybe drop into you at the bank and let you know how I get on. I want to see if I can get a handle on this Alastair guy.'

Notwithstanding this peculiarity of his, I had to kiss him again. I just hoped the neighbours had gone to bed and were perhaps doing what I wanted to do but wouldn't allow myself. After all, my son Ronan was in the house.

CHAPTER 29

Joan

Breakfast time, and Ronan struggled down.

'Where's Kev?' he enquired casually. 'Didn't he stay the night?'

'He most definitely did not,' I answered, as if the thought had never occurred to me.

'Don't lose this one, Ma. After all, you're not exactly young any more,' he said over his shoulder, taking his cornflakes with him into the sitting room to watch MTV, something he knows I hate him doing in the mornings. I was so taken aback at what he said that he watched TV with impunity, that morning anyway. Strange … here I was racked with guilty thoughts and anxieties about how my son would react, and he just took it all in his stride. Which of us was right? Oh Lord, the child was becoming the adult!

One of the great things about working in a bank is that it often mixes the role of social centre with that of a financial institution. That morning I did a lot of socialising. Mrs Clifford, Cormac's mother, called in early. She had visited her darling son the previous night. He seemed a little better and had talked to her. She was very pleased, as it was the first time during his present hospitalisation that he had been able to converse with ease. They talked about the important things in their lives, like how much the cat missed him and how she was managing in the house without him. Cormac was very pleased to hear that Ronan had been calling, and he sent his thanks. I suggested that on her next visit she might ask Cormac if he would like an old friend to call and see him, as I would be delighted to, if it wouldn't upset him.

A short time later Kevin called. He was not happy with his morning's futilities. This Alastair was not registered in the voting lists or on the census around the relevant period, and no records showed up on the computer against anyone at the address he lived in then.

'Never mind,' I said as I brought him into my office through the security entrance. Well, he was security, wasn't he? We had only just sat down when I was called out again. Breda, wouldn't you know! So in she came as well.

'Borrow a razor and buy a new shirt, did you?' she said to Kevin with a deal more meaning implied than I would have had the nerve to say to anyone.

'Terrible the way girls' de-fuzzing razors don't work properly on a real beard,' responded Kevin, rubbing his clean-shaven face.

I wasn't sure if I liked the easy familiarity they were enjoying with each other as much as I should. Strange, that!

'When you two have finished, this is my office and I dictate the agenda, right?' was my contribution.

Kevin filled Breda in on his fruitless morning and all three of us took to silent contemplation while we pondered on the next move.

'Got it!' I said, as inspiration struck.

They looked much as friends must have looked at Archimedes after he shouted 'eureka!'. Mind you, I was not jumping out of a bath and I was dressed in regulation bank issue. While studiously ignoring their quizzical expressions, I looked up the local telephone directory and dialled out. It was no harm, I reckoned, to keep smart-alec Breda out of the limelight for once.

'Could I speak to Vincent Coffey, please?' I asked of the female voice that answered.

CHAPTER 29 - JOAN

'Hello Vincent, it's Joan Traynor here from the bank! Good, thank you, and yourself? Is there any chance that I could call and talk over a situation that happened some twenty or so years ago that you might be able to help me out with? Urgent? I would say so!'

After a silence at my end I answered, 'Well yes, I can take my lunch break now and I can be out with you in ten minutes if that's okay. Thanks very much and ... oh is it all right if I bring some person or persons with me? Great, thanks Vincent. See you soon.'

Hanging up, I grinned at the two open mouths looking at me.

'That was Vincent Coffey I was talking to. He retired as a Garda sergeant here two years ago. He was our local policeman as I was growing up and he is sure to know about anything that went on in the town or the surrounding area, whether legal or illegal. I'm on my way to see him if anyone cares to join me.'

Neither of them hesitated in following me to the car park. Breda's car, being the biggest, was the one we piled into. As she drove I asked her how Franner was the previous night.

'Just fine,' she said.

I swear that girl can make a simple comment like that sound suggestive. Smiling, she added, 'Oh, by the way, Franner wants me to invite both of you over for dinner on Sunday next. Is that on?'

'Sure,' said Kevin looking towards me.

'As long as you do a lot of cooking, because one of us takes a lot of feeding,' I added.

'Yes, well, I didn't want to be the one to bring up the fact that you have put on a bit of weight!'

Kevin giggled, which didn't amuse me. Breda was driving, so I couldn't hit her, and if I had made any response it could have led us down a track I wouldn't like, so I kept silent.

I knew well where Vincent Coffey's house was: in a small rural area or a small town everyone knows where a certain number of local notaries live. We could all unerringly find the priest, the doctor and even the useful electrician and plumber as well as the nurse and policeman either at their office or at home. Over the past few years, with everyone having cars and many working great distances from where they live, such connections are being taken over by phones and contract services … regrettably. As I was neither a criminal nor one whose path was so pure as to be comfortable in the friendship of the local policeman, I had never previously been in the Coffey home.

They had a lovely house on a few acres some miles the other side of Wicklow town in a quiet country setting only barely out of sight of Brittas Bay, a stretch of sandy beach and dunes that is, for me, the jewel in the crown of our beautiful area. And that is saying something! Vincent's garden was a delight: clearly he and his wife enjoyed tending it. The contrast between the roses section, the apple tree cluster, the flower beds and the sunny veranda area made it the sort of beautiful, restful garden that is the fruit of tender loving care and an awful lot of consistent hard work.

After I had introduced Kevin and Breda, Mrs Coffey – another Joan – invited us to sit outside as it was a nice afternoon. I commented that it must be lovely to live so close to the beach. Vincent agreed, adding that as he was originally from the Midlands of Ireland, as far inland as was possible in this country, the sea was a constant source of delight. Kevin interjected to ask if Vincent and his wife hadn't considered going back to his roots, as many people do when they retire. After sharing a quiet smile, it was Joan who answered, saying that this was now their home and that many thousands of roots had been planted in these acres of land by them both. A minor calamity then occurred as Kevin and Vincent discovered that their families were relatively close neighbours in County Laois. Then, when the football got mentioned, Breda, the other Joan and I shrugged and got talking of children and the vicissitudes of menfolk. Finally realising that I was the only one with a time problem as I was on my lunch hour, I called conviviality and men talk to order and we got down to business.

I outlined in brief where we were at, how we had reached it and our desire to trace this Alastair. Vincent was always a nice, pleasant man, though never one to suffer fools or criminals gladly, so he listened with great concentration. Joan, whom I knew of but hadn't known to talk to previously, brought out tea and cake. Then Kevin outlined his issue of the missing children and our failure to get John to talk. While Joan was pouring the tea, Vincent suddenly stood up and excused himself. He strolled off, head bowed in deep thought, down to the bottom of the well-tended garden.

His wife reassuringly explained to us that he was in the habit of going down beside the stream that ran across the end of the garden when he wanted to do some thinking. She suggested that we carry on having tea and trying out the cake she had baked only that morning. So we settled, ate, drank and waited. It took Vincent ten minutes to return, wearing a satisfied look. As he resumed his seat he said, 'Sorry about that, but the old brain isn't as quick as it once was.'

As nothing ever had got or would now get past him, I took that with a pinch of salt.

'I have him; well, sort of,' Vincent said. 'I'm sure it is the right case, though it was a long time ago. One day I got an enquiry from a policeman in England about a man. I can't quite place his surname, but I'm sure that Alastair was his first name. This policeman was following up complaints of child molestation in his patch. He had received two complaints from parents about possible abuse of their young teenagers by a businessman who had suddenly left the area. This policeman got some information to the effect that this Alastair had moved to Wicklow and asked me if I would interview him. The police in England at that time didn't have a warrant out for his arrest or anything. They just wanted me to ask him about these allegations. Anyway, I went out to interview him on foot of the information I had received. I remember he was very polite, very smooth, and though he agreed that he had lived in the area … Bedford, that's it … he totally denied the allegations that had been made. I rang back the officer in England and relayed my information to him and he promised to get back to me. I remember being very impressed by that constable's commitment to his job, so I told him that I would be happy to be of assistance if he wanted me to do any further follow-up.

'In fact, a lot of the reason I remember the case so well is that my own superintendent, a real old-timer he was, was horrified at the cost of my phone call to England, particularly as there was no warrant out for the arrest of the man. He actually, as I recall, instructed me to drop the case. A few weeks later I got another call from my friend in England, and he told me that the boys and their parents had withdrawn their statements, so he was not in a position to follow up on it any more. Mind you, he did advise me, as if I needed it, to keep a close watch on this Alastair whatever his surname is, which I promised to do. Anyway, within a day or two of that call I noticed that the house this Alastair had lived in was up for sale. Later I discovered that your man had only rented it on a short-term lease and had moved on. I never found out where he went, though to be honest I didn't exactly try too hard.'

Kevin said, 'You did a lot more than most Gardaí I know would have done,' which with barely a trace of a shrug Vincent acknowledged.

After a pause Vincent looked at me and said, 'Really, Joan, what you are telling me is that this guy, while living in my jurisdiction, abused four of the lads in the area and I didn't spot it or stop it.'

All three of us in unison jumped in with 'How could you …?' and 'Don't blame yourself!', but Vincent hardly heard them. He continued talking, though in reality it was more in the nature of thinking out loud.

'In those days we knew nothing about sexual abuse. Mostly we didn't think it even went on except for the occasional "dirty mac guy", of which most towns would have one or two. Now it seems to have been going on all over the place: even, if the papers are to be believed, in some of the most respectable of homes. Still, I really should have followed up more thoroughly, no matter what the superintendent had said. Whatever you nice people might say to reassure me, I really should have.'

CHAPTER 29 - JOAN

He had nothing to blame himself for. Even the kids in the town like me knew that he was always a very conscientious policeman.

Vincent then stood up and shook himself as if converting his self-anger into decisive action. He told us not to worry, to leave it to him to find out who that guy was and, if possible, where he was now.

Alastair, I thought to myself, you haven't got much chance of staying hidden with Vincent on the warpath. More practically, Kevin asked him how he would find Alastair, and Vincent assured us that he was certain he could find the old notes on that enquiry as nothing was ever thrown out of the filing room in the Garda station. If it became absolutely necessary he would ring the English police to find out what he could. England was not anything like as far away now as it had been twenty-five years before, he added with a rueful smile.

'Besides which,' Kevin commented with a soft, disarming grin, 'I bet the old super is well retired by now.'

As I looked at my watch I realised with a start that my lunch break was well up, so we left in a hurry after expressing our gratitude to both Vincent and his wife. As we pulled out of his drive we could see Vincent getting into his own car, hastily putting on his jacket and his glasses. He wasn't going to waste any time in starting his pursuit.

Fortunately, my credit in work is still good, so they weren't too upset by my late arrival back from lunch. I made up for it by diligence, as much to stop the thoughts running around my head as commitment to the job. Then just at closing time, in strolled a very pleased-looking retired Garda sergeant.

We adjourned to my office and to business.

'Got him,' said Vincent with satisfaction before he even sat down. 'Nobody is going to commit offences like that on my patch and lie to my face and get away with it if I can help it. It took me a long while rummaging through the old files to find my notes, but I finally got them. I told you that nothing ever gets thrown out down there.

'His name is Alastair McKinnon and he now lives in a small village on the

Dublin–Meath border. The real problem I had was getting that final piece of information.'

'Well done!' I interjected with feeling.

With that Vincent sat back and relaxed with a satisfied grin on his face. 'I only hope that the duty sergeant won't charge me for the phone calls I made this afternoon.' This was said in such a way as to make it clear that in the first place it wouldn't happen and in the second he didn't really give a monkey's whether or not it did. Leaning forward, he expansively filled me in on the afternoon's success.

After getting hold of the old files buried deep in the storeroom, Vincent had commandeered the superintendent's office. The present super, an old colleague and friend, was away on holidays. Four or five phone calls to England finally tracked down the constable Vincent had originally dealt with. He was now a divisional commissioner in his area and a man blessed with a very good memory. This Mr McKinnon had started a mail order company on his patch originally and seemed on the surface an astute, respected and reputable businessman with a lot of good contacts and an interest in local charities. He was heavily involved in the local boy scout troop as well as the Variety Club.

It was in following up some concerns from parents of children in the scouts that the now divisional commissioner visited Mr McKinnon. By the time the boys' statements had been formally taken and a police colleague had got around to serving a summons on McKinnon, the quarry had flown. It was when they were trying to trace him that the trail led to Wicklow, and to Colestown in particular. By then the parents of children who had made statements, realising that Alastair was now out of the country, asked that they be withdrawn and the case dropped in order to, as they said, let the children get on with their lives. Because of that, Vincent's English colleague had no choice but to let the enquiry lapse. However, the commissioner was able to give Vincent the name of the mail order catalogue company, no less. Though based in Ireland, it dealt with Britain and the European continent. It had a monthly magazine circulation and a special quarterly mailing catalogue. The catalogue that the commissioner had got hold of gave the company name and a registered address. It was called the FOR Company and had two main monthly magazines, *FOR MAN* and *FOR WOMAN*. According to Vincent's informant it was never sold in Ireland due to our censorship laws, but it was very popular in Germany and the Far East.

Vincent, armed with that information, made a few calls and talked to the sergeant in the Meath area where Alastair McKinnon's company was now registered. According to him, McKinnon had been living there for many years and was well respected in the area. He lived alone in a very big house and was known to have many visitors from abroad, including models coming and going to do with his business. All of the company personnel stayed over at the house when they came to work, so they didn't mix with the local community. No concerns had ever been raised in that locality about his behaviour, and certainly no sexual improprieties had been even hinted at, according to the local sergeant.

Copies of the original statements dug out by the commissioner in England were being couriered over to the superintendent in Wicklow. Vincent suggested that if Kevin would liaise with the local Gardaí he could perhaps be allowed access to them as part of his ongoing investigation into the John Franklin case. Having been withdrawn by the parents, they could be used only as information, but he felt that 'my' Kevin might like them as references. Abusers, Vincent suggested, like most criminals, probably tended to follow a regular pattern of behaviour, and he wondered whether McKinnon's English modus operandi might be mirrored in Ireland.

When Vincent finally wound down I could only be impressed at the speed and thoroughness of his afternoon's work. No wonder Colestown was such a lovely place in which to grow up: a town where in those times cars were left unlocked and front as well as back doors left open as a matter of course. Vincent Coffey had left a very positive legacy for the community he served. Mind you, I was glad never to have fallen foul of him.

I promised to get hold of 'my Kevin' straight away and suggest that he might link with his colleagues in Wicklow.

'Nice young man that, good detective,' Vincent commented as he showed signs of leaving. 'I'd hold on to him if I were you,' he added. 'Nice girl like you needs a fellow like that as a companion and support.'

With feigned shock I retorted that I was horrified at him, a retired police sergeant, making such a suggestion to me, a good Catholic married woman.

'Don't hold with all these new separations and second relationships as a rule,' continued Vincent, 'but in your case with that fool of a husband of yours I would make a very clear exception.'

'Are you importuning me? Wait till I tell your wife,' I said.

Laughing, he added, 'If I didn't say something like that to a lovely girl like you, it's getting worried about me my dear wife would be. She is certainly not going to give out to me for it, that's for sure.'

We rose together and as he moved to go I gave him a big hug and chaste kiss on the cheek. Another big man holding me tight and comfortingly: wasn't my personal life coming on? Just as Vincent left he turned, the smile fading from his eyes, and looking intently at me he said, 'I forgot to tell you: our Alastair McKinnon ... guess what? He's very involved in the boy scouts movement, according to the sergeant I was talking to, and has personally run a troop in the Meath border area for years now. They have even won national awards, and it seems people in that area all think our friend is the best thing since sliced bread.

'The real worry for me, though, was the reaction I got to my call. I don't think the sergeant in Brownstown is too bright. If someone had rung me with the query I made this afternoon, I would already be pressing the panic button. He just seemed to dismiss my query as of no consequence.'

'He's a scout leader. Oh fuck,' I said, not even noticing that I who don't curse was doing so.

'"Oh fuck" is right,' Vincent said, touching me lightly on the shoulder as he left and adding, 'You make bloody sure that your Kevin lad nails that bastard for me as well as for all those poor kids.'

CHAPTER 29 - JOAN

Turning away from my office, Vincent bumped into Jim, the bank manager. Naturally, as two long-term professional people in the town they knew each other very well, much better in fact than I had been aware of. When they had exchanged social comments, Vincent told Jim that he should be proud of me and all the good detective work I was doing in the Franklin case. As I was feeling guilty about the time it was taking from my real work, I hastily changed the subject. All I needed was for these two lovely men to talk about me as if I wasn't there! So to distract them I suggested to Jim that it was time I got back to my desk.

A short time later the bank was closed; the public's money was safely locked away. And I remained alone in the building, looking at the walls and thinking unthinkable thoughts. Finally rousing myself, I raised Kevin at his apartment and told him in brief of the follow-up from our lunchtime meeting. Now three of us in three separate places were aware that our hornet's nest had become an awful lot bigger!

'Oh fuck' is right.

Just before I left the bank to its normal weekend restfulness, I quietly placed an envelope on Jim's desk to await his arrival for work on Monday.

I know just how much pleasure he will get from my actually applying to do the bank's management course. His years of pressing me are finally working.

CHAPTER 30

Joan

Saturday dawned and the sun made its gradual climb to its noontime height while I dozed on. The lassitude brought on by the turmoil of the week's developments had left me with little desire to face the day. A call to the door, however, answered by Ronan, had me leaping with the vigour of sudden panic, as Kevin was to be heard entering the house. Such inconsideration, and on a Saturday!

I faced him with tousled hair and a modest dressing gown hiding much, but unfortunately not the unwashed, unadorned face.

'So that's what you really look like,' he said grinning as he tucked into a bowl of cornflakes.

Ronan was feeding his own face from a sister bowl to Kevin's. Not fast enough, though, to stop him from adding, 'This isn't by any means the worst she can look. At least the hair is pulled back. When it isn't Ma can look like a fright with her hair curling all over the place.'

'Can you two not find a different topic to practise your duo act on? I suppose neither of you thought to put on the kettle.'

Kevin did insert a 'Yes, I did', but it was too late, of course, to stop me nearly burning my hands as I placed them around the kettle to check its temperature. At least the result of my over-reaction was that their cabaret act was at least temporarily abandoned.

'What the hell are you doing here of a Saturday morning?' I asked to divert further from their target audience. Mistake, of course.

'Called to see you,' Kevin said, to which Ronan quickly added, 'And you're sorry you did.'

When the laughter had diminished – isn't it easy to amuse children, particularly grown-up male ones? – Ronan started reading the paper while moving on to attack the toast. Kevin told me of his visit to Wicklow station. He had obviously been on the go early that morning. The documents as promised had arrived. Included in the package were statements of complaint by two young scouts about abuse of them by Mr McKinnon. These were now twenty-five years old but significant nonetheless. That commissioner sure was thorough. He had not only couriered over the information on foot of the withdrawn statements but also included copies of the mail order catalogues *FOR MAN* and *FOR WOMAN*. We opened and perused them. Kevin and I focused on the *FOR MAN* one. In reality, though a lot of the clothes advertised in it were underwear and swimwear, the magazine was not much different from the catalogues now readily available in Ireland. It seemed to me that the difference lay more in the suggestive poses of the male models we were looking at than in the kinkiness of the clothes. Mind you, I was not an expert on this subject, as I rarely read even the regular women's magazines in the hairdressers. Ronan, meanwhile, was taking advantage, as that brat was prone to do. While Kevin and I were looking through one magazine he was salivating over the other. A slap on the hand, more to do with his earlier jokes at my expense than with his reactions to the catalogue, accompanied my taking it from him.

'Ouch, arrest that woman, Mr Detective, for assault on a poor, helpless child,' he cried, doing a very bad piece of overacting.

Ronan retreated up to his bedroom in disgust with what was left of his toast when he finally gave up trying to get his hands on either magazine. After a long while of silent contemplation we finally put the magazines aside. Kevin and I then talked of our, or rather his, options. He had sufficient cause to perhaps pay a visit to Mr McKinnon given that he was in the process of investigating possibly three serious crimes. However, he felt he would need a statement from one or more of the lads incriminating Alastair to have enough grounds to apply for a search warrant and to raid his house. We agreed that while Cormac appeared to be the best option for getting the necessary information, he also seemed to be the one, outside of John, with the most complications.

At least now, thanks to the magazines, we also had another confirmation of McKinnon's address.

CHAPTER 31

Kevin

I needed to get a statement from Cormac to make certain that I would get a search warrant on McKinnon's house. And as I had just left Joan's, I was already in Wicklow. 'Sod it,' I said as I made what could have turned out to be a futile decision and turned the car in the direction of Newcastle Hospital.

Personally I have always found that I get better results by just turning up in places rather than using the conventional phone system to make an appointment, so that is what I did. In my line of work I've had to visit many a psychiatric hospital, and this wasn't by any means the worst I've been in, I thought, drawing attention to myself as I stood inside the entrance waving my badge around.

I got lucky!

Dr Wilson, the consultant, was on the premises, so, as they didn't know what else to do with me and I was showing little sign of leaving, I got in to see him. Fortunately, through Joan he knew a lot of detail about the case, though understandably he was also protective of his patient. He was certainly more open to talking with me than many a psychiatrist I had had dealings with previously. I think it was when I expressed my belief that McKinnon continued to be a huge risk to young boys and, in my opinion, was almost certainly involved in the murder of Barry Breen that he re-evaluated his primary responsibility for Cormac.

Finally, after excusing himself for a moment while he spoke with a colleague, he returned and agreed that I could have a brief interview on two conditions: (1) that a staff member was present and (2) that it would be terminated if they judged that it was in any way distressing Cormac. I readily agreed and assured him that I would be very respectful of his patient's welfare throughout the interview. So, as the senior nurse would be on duty the next day, we agreed to do it then.

Sunday morning dawned, and fortunately I remembered that I was supposed to be having dinner out with Joan and her friends. As this was much more important, I rang her and made my excuses. Two o'clock on the dot and I was in Senior Nurse Kate's office being briefed by her.

Cormac was a little tense, but after she assured him that he could stop at any time he wanted to, we began.

In a quiet, almost detached way he told me how John and himself had continued to go up to McKinnon's house after the other two lads refused to, and this lasted a couple of weeks. John, he said, seemed to be very excited the whole time and readily agreed to all suggestions McKinnon made, and when he, Cormac, was reluctant to follow, they both put him under pressure. Photographs and, he thought, two videos of them in varying states of undress were taken in those weeks. I felt that Cormac was more relieved than distressed to be talking about this time in his life, but I was also very conscious of how long he had kept it locked inside himself. So, rather than push my luck, I said that I had got as much information as I needed and that I was happy to stop at that point. I added my personal thanks to him for the courage he showed in giving me this information and that I was sure he was in the best of hands in the care of Dr Wilson and Kate. I quickly wrote this up in the form of a statement, and after Cormac slowly read and then signed and Kate witnessed it, I left. Kate escorted me to the door and said she was very happy with how it went, and that in her opinion telling this to me could well be a step forward in Cormac's long-term care.

Mind you, just as we parted she did add, 'And you mind Joan: she is a lovely woman.' I wasn't sure if I should take that as a warning or a compliment!

Now all I had in front of me was a lot of paperwork in order to guarantee a judge granting me a search warrant … a warrant that I so desperately wanted just had to be granted!

CHAPTER 32

Kevin

Bloody hell! I had a search warrant, the culmination of a lot of hard-graft police work, and of course staff were short on the ground. Gillian and Tom, two young, inexperienced Gardaí on placement, were ready, willing and waiting when I got to the office. Ron, an often less than inspiring colleague, was also press-ganged into coming, but where the hell was Con? He had been out on a job right through the night and was in no state to join me. Anyway, why would he be needed, he had argued before he made his tired way home and to bed. Reluctantly, he had agreed to rouse himself if I became absolutely desperate.

The four of us made our way through the early morning traffic to Brownstown Garda station. Gillian in particular was quite excited as it was her first 'raid'. God, she made me feel so old. I was greeted in the station by Sergeant Crane. It was clear that I was going to get the minimum of help from him. He had no enthusiasm for acting on the search warrant and he couldn't spare any officers to assist us. He actually read it through a few times, hoping, it seemed to me, to find a reason to nullify it. 'Five is overkill if you ask me,' he complained. It appeared to me that he was reluctant to compromise the very good relationship he enjoyed with Mr McKinnon, who, according to the sergeant, was a man of impeccable manners and, as he stated more than once, a pillar of the local community. Finally, and with patent reluctance on Sergeant Crane's part, we set off. The four of us followed in my car as Crane drove on alone, as if this in itself might distance him from us and our intent.

Alastair McKinnon himself answered the front door. He certainly was a man of impeccable manners, and I hated him on sight.

Sergeant Crane introduced us and we were politely ushered into the opulent front room. I formally outlined that certain allegations had been made in respect of videos and photographs taken of children under the age of consent and produced the search warrant. He read it carefully and said in a controlled manner that we were welcome to search the house, though of course, as he pointedly assured Sergeant Crane, this had to be a case of gross error.

Gathering himself, McKinnon assured us he understood that we, like him, had a job of work to do, however erroneous it would turn out to be. If he thought that his smooth charm was going to make any impression on me, he was sadly mistaken. Crane, on the other hand, seemed anxious to play that game with him, so I left them to it as I walked outside to get a proper perspective on the whole place.

What a set-up! The main building was big and sprawling, set in about three acres of land with an impressive driveway. Stables and a fenced-off area indicated the presence of a small riding facility. The original house was a large old two-storey-over-basement one with four bedrooms on the top floor. The main dining room was magnificent: my own apartment would have fitted into it with room to spare. The kitchen and main living room and downstairs bathroom were connected by a wide corridor. A single-storey extension comprising a series of big rooms off a central corridor came out at right angles to the main structure. Although new, the extension seemed to stretch up to the full height of the house as if to embrace it. Mind you, Con is the failed architect turned detective and he could have better understood its complexities.

Alastair showed us the extension, outlining that this was the 'hub of my business empire'. His modest smile as he said this grated on me. He added that he had time constraints as he was on a deadline to get the latest magazine issue out. In view of this, he hoped that our intrusion would not be prolonged, as he really was under pressure. The sergeant nodded vigorously and seemed to increase his walking pace as if this would hasten the conclusion of our search. I directed the young officers to search the house while I followed McKinnon into the studios.

There were two rooms: one was a video room and the other looked like a photographic studio, with backdrops hanging on rollers and banks of lights reminiscent of a theatre. All I could think was that this was a perfect honeytrap to lure unsuspecting adolescents. It was with great difficulty that I masked my rising temper within a professional exterior.

Through a haze of anger, I heard McKinnon drone on about the professional studio work having been completed in the previous two weeks and that he needed to do the final editorial work on their two main magazines, *FOR MAN* and *FOR WOMAN*, today. The layouts of them were on the worktops all around two sides of the room. He showed them to me, gaining in confidence, it seemed to me, as he went on. I nodded as if interested and asked to see the office section.

If the studio set-up was impressive, his storage and filing systems were immaculate. Every single edition of the magazine was catalogued and filed in order. Every video and photograph was marked and references for each one were not only available, but accurate and easily accessible. Obviously Alastair McKinnon was a man of meticulous habits. I quickly learned the structure of his system, and it was patently obvious that whatever he might have to hide wasn't located in this area of the house.

He had a secretary, name and address supplied, who came in two days a week. It seemed to me she was unlikely to be of much use. An hour later all I had was that everything was above board in this, the professional end of the operation. Sergeant Crane and the three officers came in to report a fruitless search. Crane was visibly relieved and all for abandoning ship there and then. However, I assigned the two young officers the task of checking out each and every photograph and video catalogue against the files.

McKinnon showed real exasperation at this point as he could see, as I wanted him to, that this task would take hours. It was then that his veneer of civility cracked and he threatened to ring his solicitor. Crane tried to pacify the situation by promising that we would be out of the house in a very short time. I interjected, stating that we still had a long way to go before the search was complete. McKinnon then declared that he was going into his house to ring his solicitor. As he set off I instructed Ron to follow and remain with him at all times.

'Does that include my having to go to the toilet?' McKinnon asked.

Good, the veneer is definitely cracking, I thought, ignoring his question.

I too wanted a bit of space for myself, so I went out to my car and asked dispatch to connect me with Con. When he had surfaced out of his sleepy stupor sufficiently, I begged him to get down there quickly before we lost everything. I urgently needed his expertise. In fairness, Con is as driven a cop as I am and, once he picked up on my desperation, he promised to be with me within an hour.

I left the two young Gardaí to their fruitless task and wandered around the house.

How the other half live! It was opulent, indulgent and beautiful. It just made me sick.

McKinnon had definitely been frightened when we had all descended on him, but that had gradually turned to cockiness. I was certain there had to be something to find. I didn't know what it was, but it was here. And the most annoying thing of all was that this bastard thought we were too stupid to find it. God, I would have hated for him to be right. I needed Con and his talent: he was a genius at a search, having trained to be an architect but left it to become a detective. He has a feel that I simply don't have.

A car coming up the drive shook me out of my reverie. The solicitor already! McKinnon must be a good client to get him here so quickly.

CHAPTER 32 - KEVIN

'Thomas Sullivan,' he said, proffering an outstretched hand. 'I am Mr McKinnon's lawyer.'

I left them to consult and went walk-about around the paddocks. I shoved my head into the stables, noting two horses in residence. Though it might have seemed I was primarily giving the solicitor time and space to consult with his client, I was actually just putting in time awaiting Con's arrival.

Mr Sullivan finally ran me to ground in the large barn and asked if I would come back to the house. Sergeant Crane sat at the dining room table across from McKinnon. Mr Sullivan rather pompously pointed out that I should leave, having completed the terms of the search warrant. McKinnon went on and on about his deadline. I didn't interrupt him, and when he finally wound down Crane stood up, relieved, I thought, that his day's ordeal seemed to be coming to an end. He agreed that the house had been searched and nothing untoward found. However, I insisted that all the photographs and videos still needed to be checked and verified given the serious nature of the complaints.

Mr Sullivan spluttered insisting that he had an urgent court appointment in the afternoon. McKinnon's veneer slipped further and Crane put his eyes up to heaven. Me? I was just pleased at the reaction I had achieved, but of course didn't show it.

We could take them all away, McKinnon suggested, files and contents, verify them and return them to him. He would trust us to treat them with care and respect.

My God, I thought, he really is desperate to get rid of us ... definitely there was something to find. I too could play that game. Half an hour went by while I got on to my office and arranged for them to organise a van to do the necessary removal. McKinnon kept bleating about how urgent it was that he got on with his editorial work. The office rang back. The van would be with us in a few hours. The tension in the room eased a bit, and it seemed to me that McKinnon even began to relax a little.

'Of course I still have to search the outbuildings, stables and barn,' I dropped casually into the conversation. Mr Sullivan went red with frustration. Crane's mouth opened, no words coming out. McKinnon just smiled and shrugged at my foolishness. Time wasting, in my experience, isn't always wasted. And I had my own agenda.

Into this tableau my friend and colleague Con finally entered in his usual jaunty way.

I excused myself and briefed Con. We had found nothing but I knew, just knew, that there was something. The detective in Con took over and he went off to explore. I took Tom and Gillian to visit the barn and stables with me and left Ron with the other three. In truth I knew there was nothing to find in the outbuildings, so I just wandered around in a desultory way,

Time passed. Finally Con found me in with the horses. 'Getting back into your country roots, I see,' he said in a typical Con-like greeting.

'How is Mr McKinnon?' I asked.

'The natives are getting restless. The solicitor is ready to revolt.'

'I suppose he has to earn his fee somehow. Anyway, what do you reckon?'

'That's one fancy gaff he lives in. Strange one, actually! It's a big house and one with an even bigger extension.'

'Anywhere in it we haven't looked?' I asked.

'Funny you should ask that. I had that same thought myself! Did you notice the way the extension is joined onto the original house?'

'I saw it, but ...' I couldn't put my finger on what Con was hinting at. 'Go on,' I said.

'Looking at it logically, that should be a flat-roofed extension, as that is all the space it gives from the inside. It's also what it feels like from inside. So come over here and have a look at it, Kev. See, it's joined just below the top of the original building. With the gentle slope of the new roof, it should really have an extra floor, but there are no stairs and no doors. This got me thinking. If I was planning that extension I would have put a window upstairs to allow for an extra room. There is no window, but if you look up there are two roof windows, so some light is going in there. But where, is the question!

'You think there is a room, then, but I didn't see any door on the top landing of the original house,' I said.

'Neither did I,' replied Con. 'But interestingly, when I went up to the top floor, McKinnon followed me. When I went into the bedrooms, he stayed on the landing and I got a feeling of tension from him. Because of that I didn't look too closely at the end wall. I didn't want him to think I was interested in it.'

'What do you think we should do?' I asked.

'Let's go prod a snake, Kev.'

'But gently,' I added.

'As if I'd be anything else.'

We went back into the extension to be met by Thomas Sullivan, bristling with indignation.

'Detective Sergeant Brady, this is ridiculous. My client has had his day wasted by this pointless search.'

Con, like myself, ignored this and walked around looking up at the ceiling. Finally he pointed to a large section in the corner.

'Does that give you access to the attic?' he asked.

'Yes,' said McKinnon. 'We have a large storage area. Very useful. I put a lot of paintings from the old house into it and some other odds and ends.'

Con and I both picked up the slight change in his tone.

'Has it got a built-in ladder?' Con asked casually.

'No: we … I … meant to install one but never got around to it.'

'So, how can we see into it?' I asked.

'Eh ... eh, we have a step ladder. We keep it in the tool shed, but the gardener always locks it before he leaves work.'

'No, he didn't: I told him to leave it unlocked,' I said, to McKinnon's obvious annoyance.

I fetched it, and Con was soon on top, peering into the attic, shining a torch around. I watched McKinnon while this was happening, and he was giving off some tense vibes.

Con quickly dismounted, pointedly confirming that it seemed fine and that he didn't think we needed to concern ourselves with the attic any more.

Tension seemed to release from McKinnon.

Con accompanied me as I carried the ladder back out to the shed.

'Well?' I said when we were alone.

'I just said that in there to calm McKinnon and give us a bit more time. There is a huge space up there not explained, and I couldn't see any sign of the sky lights. I'm certain that he has a secret room up there and the entrance has to be from the top landing of the original building.'

'Look,' Con continued. 'McKinnon was on edge when I went up to the top landing of the house. That's where I'm sure the entrance to this room is, and it's a big one. It must be nearly 15 foot deep by 20 foot wide. There is an entrance and we're sure to find it, Kev. And also, I think, it is one of the new ones that opens electronically.'

'Electronically?' I queried.

'Yes, in America they are already using cards instead of keys in hotel rooms. As you know, I love gadget magazines, and I was reading up on them. Trust me, everyone in this country will be using them soon and keys will become redundant.'

'I never heard of them. Hey,' I said as excitement grew in me, 'John Franklin is an electrician and it says in his brochure that he specialises in security locks. Why don't we make sure McKinnon and Sullivan are out of the way so we can take a look at the upper landing without being watched?'

Returning with Con, I spoke quietly to Ron and asked him to gather everyone and make sure they couldn't see us. 'Tell you what, Ron, tell them all that I'm satisfied that we have nearly completed the search and that I'll join them in a few minutes. That should reassure them!'

With them safely out of the way, Con and I made our way up to the landing undisturbed.

I looked at the gable wall, bemused. Con was different. He was bouncing with energy.

'See that picture hanging over on the left side?' he said.

'Yes. So?' I asked.

CHAPTER 32 - KEVIN

'It's wrong,' Con said. 'You wouldn't put it there. It should be bigger and hanging in the centre of the wall, not on one side.'

With that Con went straight over and shone his light around it, then lifted up the bottom and showed me a clear narrow aperture that had been covered by the bottom of the picture frame. Then, with that as a guide, we saw the outline of the cleverly disguised door.

Untypically, Con turned and hugged me. I hugged him back.

'Where is the key or whatever, do you reckon?', I finally asked.

'On him: bound to be,' Con answered with a grin. 'Did you by any chance see what he has in his wallet, Kev?'

'No, but I sure am going to now.'

With that we walked together down the stairs and joined them all. McKinnon met us at the door. He addressed his solicitor.

'Well, are they finished? Can I get back to running my business, finally?' Before he could answer, I said, 'I'm just waiting for the van to come to take the files away.'

'You can all wait in the sitting room and let me get on with my work.'

'I have a small question to ask if you don't mind,' I said to McKinnon.

'And what is that?' he replied briskly.

'My colleague,' I said, indicating Con, 'noticed that the attic only seems to take up half of the roof space. The ceiling here is joined to the top floor of the original house, yet there is no entrance from upstairs or from this room.'

'I never noticed that,' McKinnon answered quickly – too quickly – and I, and I was certain Con too, detected a major shift in him.

'Is it for storage ... like the attic?' I asked innocently.

'No, no, not that I know of.'

The shift in the timbre of his voice was now very clear. 'Maybe,' I enquired casually, 'it is for running heating, electric wires, those sort of things?'

'It must be that,' he agreed readily … too readily.

'Can you show me your wallet?' I asked quietly.

'My, my wallet ... what for?' he stuttered. 'This is just ridiculous,' he said to his solicitor.

Con and I exchanged a quick glance. So, he had noticed the now marked tremor in McKinnon's tone.

'The wallet,' I said more briskly. 'It's within the governance of the search warrant.'

Thomas O'Sullivan nodded, and McKinnon slowly took his wallet out of his pocket.

'Empty it on the table, please,' I said and suddenly the tension in the room was palpable.

A lot of gold credit cards, more cash than I had in my bloody bank account, three photographs of himself and two plastic cards with nothing on them were put down on the table.

'What are they?' Con enquired, pointing to the cards.

McKinnon looked at his solicitor, who was of no help.

'They're just blank pieces of plastic ... of no relevance,' he said.

There were definite vibrations in the voice box, much more than before.

I looked at Con. He too was on megawatt alert now. I stepped back and left it to him, at the same time signalling to my colleagues to stay alert. Not necessary, actually, as even the two young, inexperienced Gardaí were clearly tuned in to the change in atmosphere. Con picked up one of the 'no relevance' cards, tapped it on his fingers a few times and slowly moved out the door and started up the stairs. Everyone followed as if pulled by a magnet. He went over towards the picture hanging on the wall in the corner.

'This is ridiculous. Get him to stop,' McKinnon said to his solicitor. The rising panic in his voice couldn't be missed now. Con lifted the picture off the hanger, looking intently at the wall. He felt around with his fingers, made a noise of satisfaction and then inserted the card into a well-camouflaged slit. There was a click, and a hidden door sprang open. A sensor light came on, showing a large room. An opulent area with four comfortable chairs surrounding a large, quality rug.

Thank God the van was on its way. I was certain we were really going to need it now!

CHAPTER 33

Kevin

The door opened to reveal a cornucopia of treasure and, judging by the strained paleness of McKinnon's face, he did not want the trove to be made available to us. The room had two skylights and very modern lighting and, I noticed, an air-conditioning system. There were wall-to-wall luxury carpets and some storage cupboards behind a large desk with a computer on it. A quick perusal showed that the filing and storage were a direct match to the system used downstairs for the company's business, though miniature by comparison. It was soon apparent that while the filing and cataloguing were just as meticulous as downstairs, the contents were very, very different.

Downstairs, the photographs and videos related to the company's magazines. These, if the photographs quickly viewed were anything to go by, were all lewd images of pubescent and prepubescent boys. Ten seconds was all it took for me to have to strive desperately to contain the rushes of anger and elation that battled for supremacy within me. A burst of anger threatened to engulf me as realisation hit that this was probably the very room in which poor Barry Breen had taken his last breath.

It was at this point that I realised that my quest to find the missing boys and find out what had happened to them was hopefully entering its last long stretch. That thought allowed me to get some semblance of control back.

I invited Sergeant Crane to formally arrest McKinnon, which he did with alacrity. We informed McKinnon that all the material in this room would be impounded and taken to Garda headquarters for forensic examination.

The solicitor, who seemed to have completely forgotten his urgent court appointment, was informed that he was welcome to witness the collection and safe storage of all the material in order to protect his client's rights. Thomas Sullivan just nodded, clearly shaken, as the implications were clearly impacting on his usual bombastic manner.

I didn't feel the least bit sorry for him.

McKinnon, trying to regain some composure, began to bluster, but I couldn't take any more of him and asked Crane and Ron if they would just get him the hell out of my sight. They could take him anywhere, to any cell they liked: just get him away from me.

Tom and Gillian stayed behind to await and supervise the van and the removal. Con disappeared back towards his bed with my thanks. Unusually, and for the second time, we hugged as he left. I drove off on my own. I went for a long walk and then tried but failed miserably to eat some much-needed food.

When I finally got back to the Garda station, my energy levels were very low. Fortunately I wasn't really needed. Sergeant Crane was in full flow. McKinnon had been arraigned and would remain in his cells for the night. He was due to appear before a judge at ten o'clock the next morning. Two community Gardaí from Brownstown would quickly peruse the evidence, identify just a few of the victims and prepare an initial set of charges against McKinnon to ensure he was detained.

As I left, Crane shook my hand, apologised and said that, with all his years of experience, he couldn't believe he had been taken in so badly.

'It happens to all of us at one time or another,' I said by way of a sort of forgiveness.

CHAPTER 33 - KEVIN

I needed to go home and try and rest, but I knew I first had to make my way to Wicklow, as Joan would be climbing the walls by now.

• • • • •

The meeting with Joan didn't take too long. By then I was drained, and she recognised it. She fed me while I briefly filled her in on the day and its result. I needed to get ready for McKinnon's court appearance in the morning. As Joan was very anxious to get a glimpse of the hated one, she needed directions to the court and nothing, not even work, was going to stop her being in the public gallery. So, promising to talk to her after McKinnon had been committed, I kissed her, thanked her and made my weary way home. As I started to drive I got an awful feeling that I was missing something – something really significant – but I couldn't figure what it was.

Sleep came, but it was fitful and discordant.

CHAPTER 34

Joan

So, McKinnon was in a cell and due up in court the next morning. Maybe, just maybe, this could be good news: if not for John, at least for his family. Kevin had repeatedly told me not to hope, but it just kept springing. Poor Kevin, he was washed out. Triumph at McKinnon's arrest, sure, but there was so much more to do. He ate, sparingly for him, and went home for a much-needed rest. I rang Jim and, as he was still ecstatic at my decision to undertake the banking course, time off was no problem. No point in talking to Ann until things got more clarified … so I went to bed. A restless night!

I had been in court on a few occasions, fortunately on bank business only. As I took my seat in the gallery of the large courtroom, I was anxious yet full of anticipation.

McKinnon was loathsome, but then I was programmed to think that! Kevin outlined the facts of the search and arrest to the judge. He asked for committal to prison pending trial and clearly expected it to be a formality. Not so. Thomas Sullivan made a strong case for his client to be released on bail.

He based this first on McKinnon's own recognisance and then, at his client's urging, on his leaving a very considerable deposit and his passport as security. I began to feel that the judge might agree.

Kevin, however, strongly argued that this was a very serious matter and, as much of the enquiry would now be related to the lives of young boys in the immediate area, it would be unwise to allow Mr McKinnon out on bail. As the judge was still hesitant, Kevin continued by arguing that he should be detained at least until the Health Board and all the children's families had been contacted. A clever move, I thought! The judge would surely be wary of having any decision he made later being questioned by another government department.

A close thing, but finally the judge remanded McKinnon in custody to appear before him again in two weeks, when he would reconsider the issue of bail. Relieved, Kevin began to gather all his notes together and talk to his legal consultant. My eyes, however, were totally focused on McKinnon. He was obviously angry and exchanged harsh words with his solicitor. Then, jabbing his finger into Thomas Sullivan's chest, he passed him something with his other hand. The solicitor looked shocked. His eyes swivelled and locked on a well-dressed, grey-haired man standing at the back of the court. As I was on the balcony, I had to shuffle a bit to pick this man out.

McKinnon was led away in handcuffs, but my eyes followed his solicitor. As he got close to the courtroom exit, briefcase in one hand, he very inexpertly handed something to this grey-haired man with the other one. Alarmed, I hurried down the stairs and over to Kevin.

'Do you know that man just leaving?' I asked, cutting across the conversation he was having.

'Sorry, what?' Kevin said, having difficulty in tuning in to my interruption.

'That man … him,' I said, indicating the grey-haired man who was just moving out of the court.

Kevin looked. 'Whitely! Bloody hell, what's he doing here?' he asked of nobody in particular. 'I wouldn't have expected him to be here.'

Kevin took me aside while I quickly related what I had seen. When I had finished he stood still, quiet and thinking for a few moments.

'I interviewed him twice about Frank Creamer's case, but I never connected him with McKinnon. I'll have Sullivan's guts for garters … but maybe not just yet, in case what I'm thinking turns out to be right. If so, maybe that's not the best course of action. I knew I was missing something vital. I just knew it. Joan, you're a gem,' Kevin, his brain obviously moving in many directions at once, said before briefly hugging me and apologising as he moved off quickly to talk to a group of Gardaí.

After some consultation, two of them hastily left the court. The other, a young policewoman, came over with Kevin. He introduced Gillian to me.

'You'll take over from Tom at the house tomorrow morning and call me on my bleeper if anyone comes near it, right?'

Gillian nodded.

'Now go and get some rest. You're going to have a long day tomorrow, and thanks, Gillian,' said Kevin as she left quickly.

'Let's get a sandwich and we can talk,' he said, turning back to me and linking his arm around mine.

So we adjourned to a reasonably quiet café nearby.

'Thank God you spotted that, Joan,' Kevin said when we sat, food in front of us. 'I've had an uneasy feeling that I've been missing something, something big, and I needed to figure out what it was.'

'What?' I asked.

'I don't know. I woke about five this morning and I started to think that maybe with all that we found in the house, actually none of it relates directly to the death of Barry or the missing boys. You saw how desperate McKinnon was to get bail, so maybe there is something we've missed. To get so close … damn it, we just can't mess up now. If only I could put my finger on what I'm not seeing! Anyway, I've sent Ron to follow that fellow Whitely, and Tom has gone back to McKinnon's house to stand guard, unobtrusively I hope. I'm doing that just as a precaution. If nothing else it will buy me some time … time to think.'

'What, exactly?' I asked, fascinated.

'I don't know. I only know that Whitely is connected to this in some way. It has to be linked to the missing boys. I just need to figure out in what way … and soon. Look, I'll have to get back to my office. I have so much to do.'

'What about me? If I don't get back to the bank I could lose my job.'

'What? What? Oh yes, of course,' Kevin said, but his mind was a long way away already.

CHAPTER 35

Joan

Amazingly, I slept well that night. Actually I went straight to bed after checking that Ronan was all right over in his granny's. He was, but he missed me and was looking forward to seeing me the next day, or at least he was kind enough to say so.

The next morning I spent the first hour in work with Jim. In that time all I seemed to do was listen while he gloated over my decision to do the management course. Fine for him – it was me that was going to have to do some hard studying. Actually it was really lovely to see how pleased he was. Clearly he took all the credit for my decision, and maybe, after ten years of trying to persuade me to do it, he deserved that much. Suffice it to say that he already had both our working lives mapped out. According to him I would be formally appointed as the assistant manager at the completion of the first year of the course, and then I would take over as manager when he retired in about six years.

When Jim wound down a little, I filled him in briefly on what I had been up to and the emerging outcome. It was nice to be able to spend some time talking it out with such a long-time friend, and particularly with someone who was more or less detached from all the people involved in the case.

A while later Kevin rang briefly, really just to say hello. He told me that he was in trouble over continuing the tail on Brian Whitely, which so far had been a total waste of time. The superintendent absolutely refused to assign extra unit personnel to the task. However, after telephone contact, and no doubt unsubtle pressure, Tom and Gillian had been forced to take turns guarding the house, while Ron was still keeping a watchful eye on Whitely's movements. Kevin said that all three of them hoped and believed that these assignments would pay dividends, and they were as committed to keeping it up as he was. The superintendent was bleating about the cost, but due to the success of the McKinnon arrest he had reluctantly agreed to let it go on for a day or two more.

As McKinnon's detention was not picked up by the press, Kevin suggested that we should postpone going in to see John until the following evening. He was up to his ears trying to get all the relevant parties – nurses, doctors, social workers, child guidance as well as the police – together for a major case conference. This was proving to be a huge headache, as he wasn't prepared to tell them what the conference was about until they could all meet. It now looked as if first thing Thursday morning would be the earliest possible time he could get all the agencies together. With the adjourned court hearing due in a fortnight, there was little time left to plan for the major investigation that would be needed.

I was glad to get home after work. Only six o'clock of a Tuesday afternoon and I was already totally washed out. I felt as if a week at least had passed since I set out the previous morning. I brewed a cup of tea and sat, almost wishing that I smoked, as the events of the past few days tumbled in constant distortion through my memory bank.

Whatever about the murder of Barry Breen, I now knew for a certainty that McKinnon had abused to a greater or lesser extent, whatever that could possibly mean, the four friends and companions of my youth. How differently the passage into adulthood would have evolved between the five of us without this tsunami was difficult to imagine. Suffice it to say that the fragmentation of our unique bond would have been far less absolute without the fateful few weeks when I was away on holidays.

God, I so hated that man McKinnon!

Suddenly tears just cascaded down my cheeks. I had no real idea why they were engulfing me.

My lost youth!

The traumas of the past few weeks!

Maybe it was a response to the euphoria of victory over that so-and-so McKinnon. Somehow that victory was a hollow one and much more a matter of sorrow than of celebration. I now knew what I had set out to discover.

The brutal rape and murder that John Franklin had committed could be explained and understood, if most certainly not justified.

Knowledge, however, carries its own sadness.

Ultimately, the tears bursting forth left me sitting in my kitchen feeling, in my own eyes, pitiful and pathetic. Yet I suppose I knew that the weeping was mostly a release of grief for my lost love. The seeds of incompatibility in my marriage to Ray lay in my hands. He had looked to me to reassure him of his virility, to reflect to him his masculinity and allow him to heal the guilt and recrimination that lay within. But I failed him miserably. Maybe nobody could have succeeded, but I didn't know that. At that moment I certainly didn't believe it.

All the knowledge available to me was of my failure: to Ray, my husband; to Ronan for depriving him of a real father; and to all my own dreams of happy families. Anger welled up in me. Anger at my own failures, sure, but also the violent anger I felt towards McKinnon, who had ruined my life and the lives of my friends.

'Hi, Ma' echoed around the house as Ronan arrived in from football training. In desperation and haste I tried to cover it up, but the ravages of crying were all too apparent to him as he came into the kitchen. Ronan, my lovely son, had never ever seen his mother crying, and somehow that just made more tears come. He held me and comforted me. Was this the beginning of the change from mother–child to an adult son–mother scenario?

Slowly and with growing composure I told all. Well, not all, really: Franner and Ronan's dad were left out, but the essence of the rest of it. He understood. My lovely son took it all on board and just chided me for not sharing it with him sooner, for not allowing him the option of helping more. This led us to talking in a way we hadn't really done before. Now it wasn't mother minding son or son comforting mother. Rather, it was a meeting of two equals.

I talked of his childhood, of my struggle to hold a relationship with his dad and to maintain some sort of family normality within the parameters allowed to me by Ray's drinking. Ronan reassured me that he understood his dad and, as he didn't have unreal expectations, he didn't get hurt. Ronan knew that his dad loved him but just couldn't often show it as his bigger battle against the bottle got in the way. Somehow, realising that my son, my baby, had grown up and would never need me in the same way again filled me with pride and hope rather than the sadness I would have presumed it would have caused. In a desperate bid to get my baby back again, if only for a last short moment, I pulled my Ronan to me and hugged and hugged him.

Finally pulling away, Ronan said, 'Ma, you gave me such a fright when I came in. I thought Kev had ditched you and that was what was upsetting you.'

'I'll have you know,' I said, working at regaining our normal balance, 'if anyone is going to do the ditching it will be me giving that big lug the heave-ho.'

'But you won't, Ma, will you?' said Ronan in some alarm. 'Kev is a nice man. He's good for you. I've never seen you look so good and so together as you have since he's been around. Now, what about my tea?'

With that he pushed me in the direction of the fridge and began to leave the room. 'You really like him and have no objection to him and me … maybe even seeing each other?'

CHAPTER 35 - JOAN

Ronan kept walking without turning back. I held my breath for his response but all I got was the sight of his retreating back. The door closed behind him and then reopened. Now where did he get that from? Grinning, Ronan left a parting message. 'If Kev stays around, that would let me off the hook from having to care for you in your old age, wouldn't it?'

The tea towel hit a closed door as laughter could be heard ringing through it from both sides. Ah well, it was time for dinner anyway, so I set about preparing it. The potatoes weren't yet boiled when the doorbell rang and in came Breda, her face full of anxiety.

'Are you okay, Joan?' she enquired, entering the kitchen.

'I'll kill you!' I roared up at my son.

Over dinner, which Ronan wisely had in his room (Breda, as she had already eaten, just had a cup of tea and a cigarette), I recounted all that had happened.

'Are you going to the court hearing?' she enquired.

'No, I'm not,' I said.

'Well, I bloody well am. I want to see bloody McKinnon and perhaps spit on him if I get the chance,' Breda said animatedly. 'Franner might come with me,' she added.

'For God's sake,' I said with intensity, 'whatever about *you* going to the court, don't let Franner come within a mile of it. Kevin reckons it is going to turn into a blooming media circus, to quote him. He says we should stay miles away from it.'

'I suppose so,' Breda said with hesitation, 'but I still think I might go, if only to see that bastard in person.'

I have to admit that I certainly felt the better for having seen him squirm and finally being led away to jail. I also reassured her that as the volume of material discovered was quite horrendous, Kevin's view was that any material relating to Ray, Franner or Cormac was extremely unlikely to have much relevance in any upcoming court proceedings. John Franklin's probably would, but only in so much as it related to his childhood abuse and damage.

Breda hugged me as she left. She also thanked me profusely for all that I had done for Franner and, by extension, for herself and the children. As I closed the door I sincerely hoped the friendship that had grown between us wouldn't just slip away. Of course it wouldn't. I wouldn't let it.

Apart from meeting Kevin, her friendship had been the most significant thing to come out of this whole sorry mess for me.

CHAPTER 36

Joan

Half an hour later, washed and powdered, I was off to see Vincent Coffey and his lovely wife. Over tea and cake – that woman really is a pearl – I told him the whole story in great detail. I also passed on, as Kevin had asked me to, the fact that some of the photographs predated McKinnon's time in Ireland.

'Brilliant stuff,' was his final summing up. 'Tell that chap of yours well done. I am proud to have met him. Mind you, I wouldn't expect anything less from a County Laois man … my own county.'

Ignoring the county reference I said with some uncertainty, 'I hope this development will help us to prise open John Franklin.'

'Sure to,' Vincent said. Then, obviously anxious to pass on his good news, he turned to his own Joan and said, 'I better go down to the station, love, and ring that district commissioner chap in England as soon as possible. He is going to be delighted. He might even want to send someone over for the next court hearing, so no time to lose. I know it's late, but I have his home number.'

'You do remember that you're retired, don't you?' she said to him as he put on his jacket, but it was said in an indulgent tone.

As I took my leave I said to Mrs Coffey, 'The other day I realised again how lucky we were growing up here to have such a nice, caring, committed policeman.'

'Yes, dear,' she said, 'but it didn't necessarily make him easy to live with.'

Laughing in shared success, the three of us walked down the garden to the gate.

'Keep in touch, dear,' Mrs Coffey said.

'Sorry about that stupid sergeant yesterday. Every profession has them. Say well done to Kevin and, as my Joan has just said, don't forget to keep in touch yourself,' were Vincent's parting comments as he formally shook my hand. Bugger that. I was a new woman now, so I kissed him and then his lovely wife and left promising to see them very soon.

How to ruin a wonderful day that had been full of highs, tensions and success? Simple … visit your husband!

I called into Ray's parents' house and, surprisingly for nine o'clock at night, he hadn't yet left to go to the pub. Mind you, a few drops, though not too many, had passed his lips that day. After we all shared a quick cup of tea, Ray, at my request, came with me into the sitting room away from his parents. Briefly I outlined what I knew and told him of Alastair McKinnon's arrest, and that it would be hitting the papers within a few days.

'Nothing to do with me,' was Ray's response.

'It's okay, Ray,' I said. 'Kevin says that with all the material that was taken from McKinnon's house, the early ones should be of no interest to anyone and will most certainly be destroyed once the case is over. So nothing can come out of all this to upset or embarrass you.'

I don't know what response I expected from this revelation. Knowing Ray, it certainly wasn't a 'thank you'. What I got surprised me and led to my foolishly fighting back.

'I had no pictures taken. I don't know what the fuck you are talking about,' he hissed, getting quite angry.

I never was comfortable dealing with Ray's anger. Instead of just letting his lie stand, as he obviously wanted me to, I needed to have everything clear and open between us … idiot!

'They will be destroyed, Ray,' I repeated. 'They can't hurt you any more,' I said softly, reassuringly.

With that he got really angry. In a quick movement that took me by surprise, he stepped over towards me and slapped me hard across the face for the second time in all the years I had known him. With words falling out in uncontrolled rage, he hissed, 'You … you know nothing, you stupid, stupid cow. Do you really think I fucking care what the cops or the newspapers or any snotty neighbours might think or say? I don't give a damn. It's you … you not finding out was what I always cared about. I never wanted *you* to find out about it. I didn't care about anyone else knowing. Don't you understand? I only ever cared that you wouldn't know, wouldn't despise me. But no, you had to find out, didn't you? You just couldn't leave it alone. Then you come in here and shove it into my face. I … I hate you. Get out! Get the fuck out of here and leave me alone!'

'Ray, I don't despise you. I never did and I wouldn't. I couldn't despise you. Sure, I wish you would stop drinking, stop killing yourself and spend more time with our son, but I never ever despised you.'

'Get out, go on, fuck off!' he roared.

As his anxious parents came into the room I left in haste and, for the second time in a few hours, ended up in tears. 'You stupid, stupid woman, Joan,' I muttered to myself as I struggled to get the key into the car door and beat a hasty retreat.

Fortunately Ronan was in his room and didn't catch me in the same state twice in the one evening. It took a long time, but gradually my trembling eased. The folly of presumption! How could I have so misread my husband? How could I have been so presumptuous as to think that knowing the photographs were going to be destroyed would heal him?

Sure, it would work for Franner because he was already mostly healed. But Ray: if anything, he was still on the way down to the depths of alcoholism. A state from where he might – well, he could – climb back up. He was right, of course. I was so stupid. I should have realised that my just being aware of the pictures would hurt him more than anything. As indeed the reverse would most certainly have hurt me too.

Intelligence is its own stupidity betimes! The damage I could have done if I had pursued a career as a psychologist!

I drank a cup of tea, had a bath and settled, calmed if still shaken. I rang and got Kevin and told him what a fool I had been. Talking it out with someone who cared was nice. He reassured me that to just survive a day like today was an achievement in itself, particularly as it was so far out of my normal stream of activities. Kevin felt that I had taken too much on without allowing myself the time needed to let the impact of the recent developments properly settle within my own consciousness. Had I let a little time pass I probably wouldn't have rushed into the meeting with Ray, as his reaction, if I had given myself time to pause, was fairly predictable. How I wished Kevin was with me, at least until I commented that he, of course, would have handled it much better. He laughed, saying that naturally women understand men much more than the reverse, so of course females blunder about making bad scenes much worse because of this very understanding.

'Kevin, shut it,' I said in my best tactful manner, 'and tell me what else has been happening at your end.'

The arrangements about the joint initiative between the Gardaí, probation and the Health Board to start picking up the pieces in Crane's territory were so complex and confused as to be almost funny. All the different agencies were arguing as usual about the need for extra resources before they could even talk about intervention. It almost seemed to Kevin that the problem was secondary to the agency processes. He had also met with the scout chiefs and, bloody hell, was it hitting the fan in that domain. Apparently McKinnon's troop had won national awards two years running for being the best trained and disciplined unit in Ireland. The scouting organisation was going to have to totally review its procedures in the light of all this.

CHAPTER 36 - JOAN

At the close of the conversation, I was reassuring him about the outcome of the John Franklin interview coming up the next night. I convinced him, I hoped more than myself, that John would tell all. I also reminded him of the nice things Vincent Coffey had said, and then signed off by telling him of Ronan's cheeky comments. Kevin said he would talk to me in the morning and, as we said goodbye, I was feeling that our relationship was evolving nicely. Perhaps I had been alone too long.

Some days never end. As I was about to get into bed there was a knock at the door. Franner just called to say thanks for everything I had done for him. With that, he gave me a lovely bunch of flowers and a warm hug.

'Make sure we see a lot of you,' he said as he left.

From this I went to bed and slept much more soundly than I would have anticipated. My dreams and thoughts were not of Franner, however, but of an even bigger man.

CHAPTER 37

Joan

Wednesday dawned, and with it a sense of things coming to a head.

Ronan went off to school and I went to work to start the day as mundanely as any other. Jim was still very pleased about my, and by implication his, future prospects. Once again he had me wondering why I had finally taken the plunge and decided to go for the bank's training qualifications. He asked again and I still didn't know how I could answer him. While being so involved in the fallout of John Franklin's crime I wondered how I could suddenly add the commitment of studying and self-development to the issues pressing on me. Perhaps in somc strange way I had carried the blame for the failure of my marriage inside myself, and this had affected my self-confidence.

Sure, I knew I was good at my job, depended on by colleagues and even by my friend the manager. However, I always felt that those strengths were built on the safety net of Jim's experience and expertise, a net that protected me and the bank's interests from any mistakes I might make. Perhaps now, freed of the shackles of guilt, I could grow, and find and rejoice in my true potential. But then again, perhaps it was just a strange evocation of being sort of in love. Who knew or cared? Suffice it to say that I am still glad that I made the decision to put myself through the bank's training.

Speaking of Kevin, if I was, he rang later. He was looking forward to this evening's meeting with John Franklin. He had so much information that, once John was confronted with it all, it would leave him no choice but to talk. His bosses were also ecstatic. The Garda Commissioner himself had apparently paid them a surprise visit. He wanted to bring himself up to date on the developments. This arose following contact that had been made with him courtesy of Vincent Coffey's phone call. The English commissioner had apparently been very complimentary indeed and had asked if he might send over his representative to attend the upcoming court hearing. Resulting from that phone call and the personal interest of the top man, the surveillance on McKinnon's house and the tail on Brian Whitely were both given further extensions without demur. Kevin hoped it wasn't going to be a waste of time, but a few more days on the strength of his recent successes were cleared, so what the hell. At least now Tom, Gillian and Ron, who had really risen to the challenge, would be paid for their overtime and travel expenses without hassle.

'Things are moving. Now all we need is to open John Franklin,' I said as we finished our conversation. Strange how I had always called him John when we were children growing up together and I thought of him as that prior to his arrest. Now in my mind he has duality to his name permanently! Kevin had a last comment to make before hanging up: one I didn't particularly want to hear. Sally Creamer had been on to his office constantly and he wondered if I could have a discreet word with her, as he was tied up and anyway officially he couldn't say anything to her.

I'll kill him. He had hung up before I could frame a spluttering reply. Was this another variation on my role as a consultant?

It did not surprise me to have a visitor before lunchtime. Sally still had that haunted, driven look. She again sat erect on the edge of my comfortable office chair. The handle of her handbag was again entwined around her nervous fingers as she pointedly refused to drink the tea I had placed before her. How could anyone be made to suffer as she had? I didn't want this interview, yet strangely I was quite comfortable with it, years of training coming to the fore.

'Sally, I think Kevin is much closer to a breakthrough than before,' I started. As her face brightened a little, I hastened on. 'Don't build up any hopes, though. Kevin is still certain that your son is dead. But things have happened that give a little more hope that the bodies of the missing children may be found.'

'Thank God, thank God,' she whispered fervently.

I leaned forward and, placing one of my hands over hers, I went on.

'Obviously what I have to say is off the record. I really have nothing to do with the police, but I can tell you that a second man has been directly linked to the investigation and is being held in custody. Kevin hasn't yet connected him to Frank or Terence or even to young Barry Breen, but all the signs are that it is a significant breakthrough. Kevin is hopeful that this new arrest might help him to get John Franklin to talk and that he will now tell the Gardaí more about Frank and Terence. Please, though, I beg you, don't let your hopes build up too much. It has been a significant development, but … but we aren't there yet. What I can promise, though, is that Kevin will tell you as soon as he has concrete information. He feels so much for your family and the Fitzpatricks. He will let you know as soon as he has anything new. I promise you that.'

Strange, but this time, while the anxiety was still there and the intensity hadn't diminished, there was no fight in Sally. She just nodded and stood up. There were no arguments, no pleas for further information, just an acceptance and a resignation of hope.

'I owe you,' she said quietly.

I cried suddenly and then so did she. We just naturally seemed to drift together, where I held and held her. Comfort was given and taken, but who gave and who took? She left and I was shattered. Work was beyond me, so I left early. Jim understood.

In for a penny … I might as well keep earning it. On the way home from work I called in to see Cormac in the hospital. Conscious of the revelations due to hit the newspapers soon, I was anxious to see him and prepare him for them.

Things had certainly changed with Cormac. He was now staying in a single, very comfortable room in the hospital. It had a small television and was decorated in bright, pleasant colours. He was also dressed in his own clothes.

Cormac was welcoming and very much in control when I came in. We talked about my work, his mother and his progress in therapy. To my intense delight it was clear that he was enjoying the fact that he felt so much better. The sight of a healthier friend than I expected filled me with some trepidation given the message I was bringing. Before I had blurted it out, my saviour Kate stuck her head into Cormac's room to say hello.

Two minutes later, after we adjourned to her office, I was bringing her up to speed on developments, and shortly after I was repeating it to the good Dr Wilson. Fortunately he had been delayed with a new admission, so we were able to consult with him. This led to a four-way meeting with Cormac also in attendance where I outlined Alastair McKinnon's arrest and the upcoming court appearance. Though I worked hard at reassuring Cormac that it was extremely unlikely that his name would be mentioned at any stage during the proceedings, I had to tell him it couldn't be totally ruled out. In spite of my anxieties, he wasn't at all bothered about the implications for himself. He seemed much more concerned about the distress all the children and their families were going to experience when the extent of the abuse became public knowledge. He was quite confident in his own ability to handle anything that came his way. I was relieved about this and happy too in the knowledge that Cormac would have great support from the professionals in the hospital. I parted from them in a very positive frame of mind, which was not what I had expected when I arrived.

CHAPTER 37 - JOAN

On the drive home I realised how quickly I had come to feel at ease in a hospital that had previously been a place of trepidation. How things were changing for me! What next, the bank exams? What about finishing my psychology studies? Maybe Dr Wilson was right and I should have gone back to them. These idle silly thoughts helped to shorten the drive.

On my arrival home, reality raised its head in the form of normal domesticity. I rushed in to feed Ronan before preparing myself for the evening's other hospital visit. As I entered the sitting room I could hear Ronan on the telephone falsely describing my state of attire at the time of my late-night caller the previous evening. All I needed was for Breda to form an alliance with my not very subtle son, so I hastily took the phone from him. She, of course, started to make suggestions of improper conduct on my part, but I was up to her. I had to explain to Breda that if she didn't have 'it', whatever that was any more, I could for a consideration give her the benefit of my vast experience, if only to save her the embarrassment of having her husband call on me or any other lady late at night. She in her turn offered me a red light should it be required and then, when the nonsense had run its course, told me that her Franner was unbending so much that he might even touch his own toes soon.

CHAPTER 38

Joan

The drive to Dublin was made almost on autopilot. On the way I tried to settle my mind and focus on the meeting Kevin and I were going to have with John Franklin. However, my thoughts kept being interrupted by my concerns for my godchild. While Ann and Maura were very slowly beginning to show signs of some recovery, my poor Brendan seemed to be caught in a spiral of depression that was, if anything, getting worse. As I thought things over, it occurred to me that surely it would be worth asking Kate if she could get Dr Wilson to see him. A kind, gentle father figure could only help my godson. If not him, then maybe they could suggest someone. The family as a whole could certainly benefit from specialist help.

Kevin was waiting by the parking bay at his apartment for me. After a brief hug and holding my hand he led me up to the apartment, where he filled me in on his day's developments. Everything was set for the following day's major meeting of all the relevant agencies. It seemed to me that it was turning into a real circus. According to Kevin, he hadn't known that so many departments and agencies even existed. They were all wondering what the meeting was about, especially one set at such short notice and for so early in the morning. He had refused to tell anyone except the most senior officer in each discipline for fear of rumours spreading. The good news from his point of view was that the chief superintendent had appointed a senior ranking officer to take over from Sergeant Crane in the handling of the Garda side of the local area investigation. Four Gardaí, two of them female, had been seconded to it. Tom and Gillian were delighted that they had been allocated to join the team after they were finished with their current assignment. As young probationary police officers it was a great opportunity to gain experience, and Kevin was pleased for them as they continued to be so helpful to him. Looking forward to that investigation made the boredom of their present stakeouts, which were beginning to seem like a waste of time, more tolerable. So far Brian Whitely had followed a regular, predictable routine. More urgently, and hopefully more productively, we had a rendezvous with John Franklin.

A quick cup of tea and off with us, so it was eight thirty or so when we arrived at the hospital. At least parking was no problem at that time of night.

As we walked through the now quieter hospital whose silence was broken only by the tread of occasional hurrying feet and the coughing and calling of the discomfited, Kevin told me that John had lost some of his lassitude. He was now tending to dress himself and was even watching television rather than lying in bed uncommunicative, according to the latest reports from the Gardaí on duty at the hospital.

The Garda sitting on a chair inside the door ushered us in with just a raising of his eyebrows. John, dressed in slacks, tee-shirt and slippers, was half lying, half sitting on the bed, propped up watching a programme on the box. As we came in he gazed from one to the other of us and then sat up straighter on the bed, though he neither greeted us nor showed an indication of recognition to either of us. He returned his attention to the television; we moved to find a place for ourselves in the room. Kevin masterfully took charge. He used the remote control to turn off the television while I settled myself in the easy chair. Kevin then sat on a straight chair facing the calm and only slightly interested John Franklin. A briefcase containing two or three photos, duly and officially signed out from the evidence room earlier by Kevin, lay at my feet.

'Alastair McKinnon was arrested and charged by me yesterday,' Kevin said in his most authoritative tone. 'We have obtained videos and photographs that incriminate him in child pornographic activities over a long period of time.'

John did not react in any way. He just continued gazing stone-faced and unblinkingly at the now dark TV screen.

'Do you have any comment to make on that?' Kevin asked.

John looked at me for a second before transferring his gaze to Kevin. Then he just shrugged as if dismissing the information as of no consequence to him.

'We now know what happened between Alastair and yourself and have photographs and videos of it,' Kevin said, standing up and beginning to pace around the room.

'I never said it didn't happen, did I?' John said in a quiet voice.

It was the first sound to come from him since we entered. Actually it was the first full sentence I had heard him utter since his admission to hospital. And it gave me goose pimples!

'No, if memory serves me right you said absolutely nothing at all,' Kevin said. Then in a softer, more conciliatory tone he went on, 'But now you know we can demonstrate what happened. We can argue that what you did wasn't your fault. We can show in court that it was as a result of abuse inflicted on you as a child by that … that man.'

'Get me off, will it?' John asked in a flat tone with a slight tinge of sarcasm.

'No, of course not,' answered Kevin, 'but we can demonstrate an element of cause and effect and at least make the death of that poor boy somewhat explainable.'

John sat up straighter in the bed and in a deeper, bitter tone he said, 'Just what I need … and naturally this will make sure the judge has to insist they open the doors and escort me out into the wonderful world you all live in, won't it?'

Kevin paced around some more and then changed to a conspiratorial tone. 'Look, John, you know how things are for you. Nothing you or I can do will change the fact that most of the rest of your life will be spent in prison. But we can help. We can at least try to explain why it happened. I'm sure we can make people understand how you came to be involved in this.'

His obsession showing, Kevin added, 'We also might as well clear everything up in one go and sort out the other two missing children at the same time.'

'That's the reason for this late-night tête-à-tête is it, then?' John said with biting sarcasm, adding, 'No dice.'

'Come on,' said Kevin. 'I know you killed them as well and I will prove it. But if you can help us now, help to put those poor families out of their misery, then we can use that fact and this McKinnon stuff to help you, at least a little bit.'

'My solicitor told me to say nothing to anyone without him being present. If you think this "I can help you" crap will get me to say anything, particularly on the subject of two boys I know nothing about, then you can piss off.'

However, this repetition held less anger and more resignation in it than the first one.

'I have photos of you naked, in suggestive poses. I have brought one or two with me. Do you want to see them?' said Kevin, reaching down by my feet for them.

Watching John carefully, I put my foot over the briefcase, preventing Kevin from picking it up. John didn't react to Kevin's threat. He just repeated quietly 'Piss off.' Kevin, in the act of reaching for the case, stopped as his gaze locked onto mine. Seeing something in my eyes, he shrugged and moved around behind me, leaving the next move in my inexpert hands.

CHAPTER 38 - JOAN

Only Kevin's heavy, frustrated breathing and the softened sounds of the hospital settling for the night broke the silence. John lay motionless with his head turned away from us. It seemed almost as if he had stopped breathing. I could feel Kevin looking at me in anticipation, his frustration and next move on hold, temporarily at least.

Slowly and without any real thought, I reached down and took up the briefcase. Quickly glancing in it, I removed one of the pictures of John. He was posing in his prepubescent innocence with a very sad, worldly-wise expression on his face. I deliberately picked a picture of him with clothes on, even if the clothes consisted only of a small pair of bright yellow briefs illuminated against his white skin and showing the outline of his developing manhood. I motioned to Kevin to sit, and he perched quietly against the radiator sited along the frame of the window. Then without haste I moved over and sat or rather rested myself gingerly on the edge of the bed, on the opposite side to the way John was facing. He didn't move a muscle. He really had nowhere to go on this narrow bed.

As I sat holding the photo in front of me, I started to speak in a soft, modulated tone. I talked as if to myself and in many ways I lost some perception of Kevin's and even John's presence in the room as I did so.

I talked of my childhood, its loneliness and difficulties with a wheelchair-bound Dad before I teamed up with four mates who became the fulcrum of my existence. I spoke of how my mother worried a lot about me becoming a tomboy. I also reminisced on the sense I had of being at one with my friends, protected and supported by them. I talked of the great sadness that had overcome me in the past weeks as it emerged more and more that my view of this idyllic childhood was false. As I talked I gradually moved further onto the bed, finally resting against the pillow, my shoes kicked off onto the floor. John, his back still to me, didn't seem to move, yet almost imperceptibly made space to accommodate my presence on his single bed.

I spoke of my marriage, its disaster and my sadness at that and the gradual loss of contact with my other three friends. Then I referred to Cormac, the damaged individual with whom I had recently managed to renew contact in the psychiatric hospital, and my hopes for him now. Above all I talked of the seething anger I felt at Alastair McKinnon. I was angry not for how he had blighted the individual lives of my friends or the lives of so many others, but for what he had done to ruin my life. Me, someone he had never even met. Someone who until a few weeks ago hadn't even known of his existence!

Yet in the last while it had become clear that he had impacted so much on my life. I hated him for what he had done to me and to the friends I loved.

Silence again permeated the room as I sat having finished my rambling discourse. I was looking over John's body at the wall in front of him. Kevin sat still on the window ledge, his big frame unmoving. John was still rigidly turned on his side away from me. However, his breathing was now audible in the quiet room. His back was touching me in a few places and, interestingly, not pulling away from contact as I continued sitting on the narrow bed.

After a considerable pause I held the photo in front of me again and talked to it. I spoke of the child I saw in it: one in whom the ravages of pseudo-maturity and a poor imitation of the leer seen in adult magazines were distorting a normally grinning, innocent face. I talked to the picture of how I longed for that lovely child to return to innocence, an innocence he had surely had up to a few days before this image was taken. I talked of how much that innocence meant to me, a young, hopeful girl, one of the best friends of that nice boy. Slowly John turned his head and looked at the picture I held out. I froze for a second, half expecting and fearing an explosion. Then, when it didn't come, I took a deep breath and carried on.

I told the picture how much I needed his friendship. I said how much my future hopes had lain with his and then, gaining confidence from his movement, I slowly put my other hand around John's shoulders, drawing him into my circle. As he lay unresisting if unresponsive, cocooned in my arm, I allowed the tableau to hold as if in suspended animation for a time. Then, placing the picture in the hand that encircled him, deliberately and decisively I tore it up in front of his unblinking gaze. I tore it first in halves, then quarters. When they were all torn once again, I let the pieces gently fall from my grasp on to the bedcover as I slowly gathered John in. I turned him gently into my body, where his head settled against my bosom. Gradually his arm came over and around me. He held me tight then tighter and finally he began to sob, his body shaking and racking, crying deep inside though not a tear came out.

'I'm sorry, so sorry,' he said finally, his unsynchronised breathing making the words almost unintelligible.

'I know you are, love,' I said, gently caressing his head and holding him even tighter to me.

'I'm done, nobody can help me. Nobody would believe me.'

'John, love, come on. I care about you and no matter what you have done, that won't change. I'm sad for you, of course I am. But I'm not angry with you. Tell me about it and I promise I'll believe you. No matter what, I'll not stop caring for you.'

I spoke this quietly, softly cradling him into my bosom, rubbing my hand gently over his hair as his arm tightened perceptibly around my body.

'It's okay, John: tell me and I will help you, I promise.'

'I didn't kill him. I didn't kill any of the boys, honest. But nobody will believe me – why should they?'

I heard this clearly, but Kevin, some feet away, wasn't sure what John had said and made to get up from his perch at the window to come closer. I signalled to him with my eyes to stay as he was and not interrupt John, so he settled back on the windowsill.

'You didn't kill young Barry. Tell me, then, who did?' I asked, my lips just an inch from his ear as I continued to caress the back of his neck.

'I have been so stupid, Joan. I was there, but I didn't kill him, honest. I had no idea he was going to die.'

Silence reigned for what seemed to be a long time as I lay there with John cradled against me. My mind raced with all sorts of hopes and possibilities but, like Kevin across the room, I just stayed silent and unmoving: except for the gentle caresses of my arm against John's neck and shoulders, waiting … hoping … for more to come. Finally John looked up into my face and, with a dead look in his eyes and no expression in his voice, he started to talk. Words just bubbled out.

'A while ago I met Alastair again for the first time since he left Colestown. After the winter storms I was called by a friend of mine in the business to do a big job with him. It was a complicated one and he wanted my electronic expertise on some special parts of the contract. As money was no object if the job was done quickly, I went with him to do it over a weekend. Whose house was it only Alastair's? He didn't recognise me, but I knew who he was immediately. The following week, after I had thought about it, I called over to see him and told him who I was. We, well … we started to see a little of each other and I went with him to one or two parties. Then he rang one day and told me that he had "clean meat" available for our supper that night, if I cared to come over and be part of a small group of his friends who were joining him. I went, but I didn't really know what was going to happen. I thought we were just going to have a session with a young boy. It turned out so different.' John looked into my eyes for the first time and desperately blurted out. 'Honest, Joan, I had no idea what they were like, what they were going to do.'

Then, as if he had expended all the emotional energy he had left, John settled back, his head seeking succour against my breast as he continued in a monotone.

'I didn't know – how could I? – that … that Alastair's friends liked to have sex and hurt the boy in the process. So that is what they did. Then suddenly young Barry died and I felt sick. I went to the bathroom and threw up. It was like a nightmare. I hoped that when I went back into the room it would be like waking up and finding out that none of it was real. But no! When I got back the three of them including Alastair were calmly sitting there drinking and eating sandwiches. I felt too sick to do anything except sit there. Finally Alastair told me that as I had a van it was easy … easy, he said

CHAPTER 38 - JOAN

... for me to get rid of the body. He told me where to take it and bury it. I protested but they wouldn't listen. Alastair told me it was perfectly safe and he gave me explicit directions to the wood and the part of the wood to take the body. I refused at first, then begged one of them to come with me. They wouldn't listen. Now that their fun was over they were almost as dismissive of me as they were of the dead boy. They hardly helped me to put his body into a black bag. They left me to carry Barry's body out of the house and put it in my van. Alastair and his friend Brian just told me again exactly where to bury the body and gave me a new spade with which to do it. Then they slammed the back door of the van shut and turned back into the house, leaving me in a state of panic. Here I was sitting in the front seat of my van with a dead body in a plastic bag in the back. It really was a nightmare. I kept thinking, hoping, that I would wake up and find it was all a bad dream.

'Eventually, not knowing what else to do, I started to drive to the place they described. While I was travelling it occurred to me that maybe Alastair and his friends had really invited me over so that I could do the job of disposing of the body for them. They knew ... they must have known that they were going to kill him. But I didn't ... honestly, I didn't. I wouldn't, I couldn't ... I wouldn't have gone that night if I had known.'

At that John stopped talking and cuddled into me for comfort, for reassurance, for mothering. I just held him and rocked him a little. Kevin sat rigid, his mind obviously struggling to take it all in.

Finally, with a sort of whisper, John said, 'That's the truth – honest, Joan – but I know nobody will believe me. Alastair laughed at me when I rang him the next day. Then he became really nasty. He was so angry at my botching the disposal, as if it was my fault. Then he threatened me. He told me to keep my mouth shut. He said nobody would believe that I wasn't as willing a party to it as the rest of them. He told me that it was just a game that had gone wrong, to keep my head down and forget all about it. At the end he even laughed and said that maybe we would do it again sometime, just not yet, though.

'I … I didn't kill that boy and I wasn't even there when they killed the other two boys. I don't know anything about them except for what I read in the papers … not until I was accused of killing them by the Gardaí.'

John, having run out of steam, went quiet. He just lay sobbing, holding me tight.

'It's okay, John: I believe you. I know you didn't do it and it will be all right,' I said, still rocking him in my arms.

Gradually he calmed and relaxed. By then my arms and body were stiff from being held rigid in an awkward position. Needing relief, I moved a little and John settled down, resting his head against the pillow.

Kevin finally moved off the windowsill and came around to stand over John at the side of the bed.

'Tell me about the body, John. Where were you told to dispose of it?'

John looked at Kevin's big, dominating frame, then looked with anxiety at me and said, 'See he doesn't believe me. I told you nobody would believe my story. It's the truth, I swear.'

As I started to say something reassuring, Kevin gave me a look to indicate that my role should now become more passive. Then he said, 'I do believe you, John. What you said makes a lot of sense to me. But you have to help me to piece things together, if only so that I can nail McKinnon and his friends for the whole lot. Explain to me exactly where he told you to bury Barry's body.'

John looked imploringly at me for a moment but, taking my cue from Kevin, I showed no response in my face. Finally, and it seemed to me with resignation, John answered the question.

'Alastair told me to take it to Grange Wood off the N7, where you found it. He told me that as it was after one o'clock in the morning nobody would be there. I was to carry the body in the black bag along the main path and then take the second fork to the right. I was to go along there for about thirty yards until I came to a clearing to the left beside a holly tree. I was to bury the body in there where the ground would be soft.'

CHAPTER 38 - JOAN

'You never got there. You never saw the clearing, did you?'

'No, I didn't. I parked the van and it was dark and quiet as Alastair had said. So I took the body out of the back and started to walk down the track Alastair had told me about. As I was going along, when I had just passed the first turn, suddenly some people came around a bend in the track above me and I panicked.'

'So you dumped the body over a blackberry bush and got out of there quickly,' Kevin suggested quietly.

'That's right,' John said almost eagerly. 'I didn't think that anyone could have recognised me or the van. How could you have connected all this to me?'

Obviously this point had been bothering John. Kevin paused for a considerable time and then, wanting to build a relationship I think, he replied.

'Well, I reckon you were very unlucky. You drove away without putting on your lights, but as you came to the exit from the woods you had to stop as another car came along the main road. That car's lights picked up your van. The young couple who were out for a very late walk, the ones who spooked you, noticed two things. They felt that anyone who ran off the way you did was up to no good, so they hurried after you and saw you driving off. The man noticed that it was a van and that the lettering was either WX, WD or WW, so we had three counties to search for it. Wexford, Waterford and Wicklow are, as you know, the counties that carry those letter codes, which because of our registration system made checking through all the vans in those counties a big job but not an impossible one. The young girl, whose eyesight was excellent, said that she thought she picked up an impression of a lightning symbol on the van which, she thought, was coloured red against a white or cream background. The rest was hard work and a lot of luck. One of the girls in the office who typed up their statements mentioned an electrician, so I followed that line and it led to you.'

'You believe I didn't kill him, then,' pleaded John, and Kevin, after a slight pause, said, 'Yes, I do believe you. Now my problem is how to prove it.'

'I'm tired now; I think I would like to sleep,' John said in a resigned, very childlike voice. Kevin, after a few seconds' thought, nodded quietly and began to gather up the torn pieces of the picture.

I got off the bed and went round to the other side, and said in as positive a voice as I could muster, 'Don't worry, John: if anyone can prove you didn't kill that boy, Kevin can. Trust him.'

He gave me a wan smile and, after a final hug for John and my promise to visit him again soon, Kevin and I took our leave. At the door as I gave John a last supportive look, Kevin, in a deadpan, non-threatening tone said, 'Oh, by the way, the other men who were in the house with Alastair McKinnon, do you remember their names? You mentioned a Brian?'

Without hesitation John said, 'As if I will ever forget … Robert McMurrough and Brian … Brian Whitely. He was a really nasty individual.'

'Thank you,' said Kevin. 'I suppose if I get a number of photos together you would pick them out for me.'

'Of course,' said John, and with that and just an accepting nod from Kevin, we left.

Kevin then had a short conversation with the officer on duty in John's hospital room before we quietly walked through the now familiar darkened, silent corridors. Eventually we emerged into the night; Kevin gently took my hand in his as we walked, and we continued to be wrapped in our own thoughts. Our journey was made in silence broken only by the steady tap of our feet as they covered the ground. I at least was comforted by the connecting clasp of hands. Probably the greatest comfort to me, however, was the realisation that my task, however unwillingly undertaken, had led to a possible reprieve for my old friend John, and that made everything worthwhile.

CHAPTER 39

Joan

Kevin and I sat in his car outside the hospital still not talking, not moving, just looking into the blackness. I noticed that the car clock indicated 10.00 pm and with a start I thought of Ronan, but then relaxed as I remembered he was again staying with his grandparents.

Suddenly Kevin struck the steering wheel and said 'Yes!' very positively. We looked at each other and grinned in shared triumph, and then he talked.

'You know I owe you so much, Joan. John Franklin would never have opened up to me the way he did to you. While it's a bigger mess than I thought, at least I know or have a very good approximation of what has been going on. I'll definitely get them all now. The two names he mentioned, both were on top of my suspect list. Over the last two years McMurrough and Whitely were interviewed a few times, particularly in relation to the disappearance of young Frank Creamer. I just never connected McKinnon to them. That's why, even after we linked McKinnon to your friend John, the other two didn't come into the picture as possibilities. In Whitely's case not until he showed up at the court.'

After another silence he said, 'I need to get the forensic team to revisit all the material we have from the wood that night as well as Barry's remains and see if we can connect anything at all to either of those two or McKinnon. I'd love to arrest them immediately, but with the tail on Whitely and as we are still watching the house I'll hold off on that for a while yet. I need to think things through carefully before I make my next move. Early tomorrow I'll have to go back and get a properly signed statement from Franklin. And I have a bloody meeting with all those other professionals … so, an easy day, then. But at least I can arrange to recover the other boys' bodies and allow Mr and Mrs Creamer and Mr Fitzpatrick to give their children decent burials.'

'You know where they are buried now, do you?' I asked.

'Oh yes. You see, I know every inch of that bloody wood and I could find the spot John described in my sleep. I just knew the first morning when I was called to that place that the missing bodies were buried there. Actually, I have walked around it a good few times since to see if there were any telltale signs. Now I know exactly where they are buried. Your friend John Franklin was lucky. Imagine the shock he would have got if he went to bury young Barry and unearthed other bodies.'

'A bloody great night's work!'

I then blurted out what had been foremost on my mind since I left John's room. 'You know, Kevin, from the start of this horror I was always certain that John Franklin had killed poor Barry, and it seemed logical that he must have also killed the other two boys. I can't believe that after all this time it is now possible to prove that he isn't a murderer after all. His family will be so relieved. It has made all of this so worthwhile.'

Kevin turned in his seat and looked intently at me, causing a shiver to go up my spine. Holding one of my hands in his, he said in his most positive tone, 'Come on, Joan: don't for God's sake believe all that crap that John fed us up there in the hospital room. Sure, he may not have killed poor Barry himself, but he is as much to blame as the other three.'

'But …,' I said.

CHAPTER 39 - JOAN

'But nothing,' he cut across me. 'Think about it realistically. John Franklin knew when he decided to go to McKinnon's that night that they were going to abuse and gang rape a poor innocent boy. He knew it was, to use his own term, "clean meat" ... an innocent boy. All four were there because they were sexually interested in boys and you can bet that John Franklin participated as enthusiastically as the others did. The death of poor Barry might have sickened him, but he was there. He participated and then agreed to bury the poor boy's body. The only thing to emerge in John Franklin's favour is that he may not have been involved with the death of the other two boys, and even that is not absolutely certain. Don't fool yourself, love. John is a murderer and, take it from one who has been here many times before, you can't believe most of what he tells you ... sorry.'

In the silence that followed Kevin leaned over, put his arms around me and held me tight.

Such a roller coaster of emotion, and all in one short night! First the hope of escape for John and now this swift, frightening plunge back into despair.

As Kevin eventually moved back and opened his mouth to say something, his bleeper went off and, after a quick hello, he turned on the police radio in the car. He quickly got through to Gillian, who was covering for Ron. She reported that Brian Whitely had gone down to his car at 10.25 pm and was now driving north out of Dublin. She was following at a careful distance.

'Stay well back,' he commanded, 'and if, as seems likely, he turns towards McKinnon's house, park and walk up the drive. Just make sure he doesn't spot you whatever you do.'

'Okay,' she replied and Kevin quickly asked the control centre to pass him through to Tom, who was still at the house. I heard only one side of the conversation. 'If Whitely arrives, let him enter the house and when or if he goes into one of the rooms, leave him, but for no more than thirty seconds. Then go in, arrest him and make bloody sure he doesn't get away. Gillian is right behind him and I'm on my way.'

Kevin grinned, and with hope vying with triumph in his voice, he said,

'Bloody hell, we may really have him now. The surveillance has paid off!'

With that Kevin started the car while also pushing a button on his interconnecting bleeper. He said into it while driving out of the car park, 'Con, you're not bloody asleep again, are you? Look, this case has broken wide open. We have hit the jackpot with Franklin and we're fairly sure that Whitely is on his way to McKinnon's house. Tom is still at the house, I'm on my way so get going as soon as you can. I'll see you there.'

Disconnecting, Kevin put his siren on and, what seemed like only a minute – if a noisy one – later, I was standing outside his apartment block, the key to his flat in my hand and the noise of the siren rapidly fading.

And so I went into Kevin's apartment for the second time that night. Only now all I had to do was pick up my coat, drive home, and hope and think.

CHAPTER 40

Kevin

I dropped Joan quickly – no doubt she will say I just dumped her – and set off for McKinnon's. A roller-coaster journey out of north Dublin onto the main Belfast road, and then I turned the siren to silence and slowed just a little as the last leg of the journey flew by. Gillian radioed through when I was on the motorway to say that her quarry had turned into the house and that she would park near the entrance. I told her to stay put and I would pick her up in a few minutes.

Just as she was getting into my car, Tom said 'Got him!' through the control. So I accelerated up the drive and was out of the car and running almost before it had stopped. Gillian was hard on my heels. Brian Whitely was standing being held by Tom, not in the workroom as I might have expected, but upstairs in McKinnon's bedroom. He was demanding to know what was going on and why was he being assaulted. I ignored his protestations.

'What are you doing here?' I asked forcefully.

Whitely looked hard at me for a second, probably remembering the previous times we had met, then answered in a bland tone, 'Nothing. I was only checking to see that a friend's house was secure. He is … eh … away at the moment.'

'And you started by checking out his bedroom, did you?' I asked, looking at Tom, who nodded confirmation that he had come straight up to this room.

'My friend will agree that I am here on legitimate business and at his specific request, so why are you holding me?' He stared defiantly at me as he said it.

'This is your friend who is currently in prison awaiting trial for the gross abuse of children, isn't it?' I answered, then formally added 'Brian Whitely, I am arresting you for the murder of Barry Breen. You do not have to say anything, but anything you do say will be taken down and may be used against you.'

I noticed a very definite flicker of fear cross his eyes before he blanked his expression and said, 'I am saying nothing until I speak with my solicitor.'

'Fine,' I replied. I then looked at Tom with a slight raise of my eyebrows, and he informed me that Mr Whitely had come into the house and gone straight up the stairs to this room.

'Why did you come up here?' I asked, but Whitely ignored me.

'Did he do anything?' I asked Tom.

'Not that I saw, but maybe he dropped that,' he answered, bending to pick something up off the floor.

'Don't touch it!' I said urgently and Tom stopped in mid-movement, his hand suspended in the act of reaching out, then straightened and moved back. With that, Whitely stepped over and made to retrieve it. I quickly bumped him before he could reach it. He was put off balance and fell over a chair, then stood up blustering that I had assaulted him and he would be reporting me for it.

'Put him in handcuffs,' I said to Tom, ignoring the protest.

While Tom was placing the cuffs on, in walked Con.

'Am I late for the fun?' he typically asked.

'No,' I said. 'But I think Mr Whitely here just tried to put his prints on that card down there'.

CHAPTER 40 - KEVIN

'Now why would he want to do that?' asked Con.

'What I think he was at was trying to confuse the fact that his prints are already on it. Maybe, Con, you could figure out the "why" for us.'

'Another hidden room, Kev?'

'You're the expert – go figure.'

It took Con just three minutes to find a slot in the wall behind one of the bedside tables.

It wasn't a room this time, but a small safe cleverly hidden, recessed into the wall. Even Con might have taken a while longer to find it had he not had the experience of the other night as an aid. Holding the card carefully so as not to damage any prints already on it he inserted it into an almost invisible slot and hey presto! A safe that didn't contain cash, jewels or apparently anything of value. Con just pulled out four videos. He lay them on the table, looked back into the safe and shrugged. It was otherwise empty. A poor haul, perhaps! But I was ecstatic.

'Got you all, haven't we?' I said to Brian Whitely, my triumph clearly showing. He didn't move a muscle in response.

'I don't even need to look at them, do I?' I said to his unresponsive face. 'You're all so arrogant. You think that we, the Gardaí, are just idiots and that you are superior beings, don't you?'

'What … what's in them?' Gillian asked quietly, speaking for the first time since we arrived.

I looked at her then over at Con, who quietly said, 'Bloody snuff tapes: tapes of the murders.'

Shock was evident on Gillian's face. Con and I just looked at one another. We didn't have to speak. Years of working together, and so rarely did we get to share moments of triumph like this one.

These are what make the job worthwhile. Reminiscences later; there were still urgent tasks awaiting.

'Con, will you get Ron and reinforcements if you need them and arrest Robert McMurrough. You remember where he lives?'

'Sure do,' he said, smiling.

'We'll bring his friend here into headquarters for questioning. Well done and thanks, you two,' I added.

Their eager young faces were clearly still trying to comprehend the dynamite we had just unearthed.

The handcuffed Whitely was locked into the car Tom had used to get to his surveillance, and I gathered up the evidence and closed up the house.

As we returned to the car, Tom asked me what exactly was in those videos. 'Did you not hear Con? I'll know for certain when I have seen them, but I have no doubt that they are videos taken by those … those persons during the rape and murder of the poor boys. It will be interesting to see just how much John Franklin was actually involved in the whole episode. If I'm right he, and only he, didn't know that it was being filmed for their subsequent gratification. My guess is it is clearly going to show us how much or how little involvement he really had in the murder of Barry Breen.'

'Jesus!' exclaimed Gillian. 'Did you know they were hidden somewhere? Is that why you had us follow Whitely and watch the house?'

'Honestly, I wasn't sure. I … I felt that we were missing something. All the stuff we had removed was so bad, but nothing gave us evidence to charge them with murder and I, to be honest, just felt – that we were missing something. I never figured that those bastards could be so arrogant or … thank God, so stupid.

'Come on, let's get Whitely locked up.'

I followed Tom and Gillian in my own car. They could get Gillian's another time.

CHAPTER 41

Joan

When Kevin finally rang, it was after two in the morning. I was in bed but not asleep. Knowing he was going to ring, I lay waiting in a semi-dozing state. As soon as the phone rang I became alert and excited. He was buzzing. Whitely was in custody, McMurrough was being picked up for questioning, and watching the videos they had taken from the safe was his next task. Kevin was busily eating the sandwiches I had prepared knowing it would be late before he got back and, of course, he would be hungry. He thanked me for that then filled me in on the night's success, the culmination of a lot of hard, persistent, professional work, and I was so pleased for him. As he began to wind down I realised that he still had so much to do and needed to go, but I had to ask.

'You weren't surprised to find those video tapes, were you?'

Kevin paused before answering. I think he was just coming back to earth, back to reality. His answer, however, certainly was for real.

'Not really, no. I suppose I knew from Alastair McKinnon's anger at not getting bail and then seeing Brian Whitely turn up in court that there was another angle that we hadn't figured on. I felt that they were desperate to cover something up, something we didn't know about. It had to be vital, otherwise Whitely would never have exposed himself by turning up at McKinnon's court arraignment. Also, I couldn't quite figure why McKinnon was so angry at the solicitor for not getting him bail. I mean logically I would have thought that they shouldn't even have asked for it. He was absolutely desperate, but I couldn't figure out why. I felt it was a major factor in the case. That's why I left the tail on Whitely and watched the house. In fact, earlier today Con and I talked it out and if nothing had broken we were going to go to McKinnon's house and search it again with a fine-tooth comb. We both agreed that there had to be something new to be found. When John Franklin told his story in the hospital last night, it just fell into place for me. Then I knew, or thought I knew, what they were hiding.

'The arrogance of McKinnon is staggering. He has got away with abusing children for so many years that he felt untouchable. It was his feeling of invincibility that led him to keep very dangerous evidence in the house, albeit well hidden. I reckon now that it was John Franklin who developed the security system, including the safes, for him. I'm sure it's that very job that dragged him back into contact with McKinnon again. Did you know that your friend John is a recognised expert in that area of electronics? I had asked a lot of questions about him when he was first arrested and I was surprised at the regard he was held in by his fellow electricians.

'Thank God for arrogance, otherwise we would possibly have had great difficulty in proving anything against either Whitely or McMurrough. Actually we might even have struggled to get McKinnon indicted for the murder of Barry Breen on John Franklin's evidence alone.'

'You're certain about what's in the videos, then?' I asked again.

'Absolutely,' Kevin replied. 'Nothing else makes any sense. Mind you, I am not looking forward to viewing them, but I have to.'

'Do you think that it was meeting McKinnon again after all those years that resurrected the early abuse in John and led him back into child abuse and this horror?'

'It's hard for me to say, as I'm not an expert in that area, but it seems most likely, doesn't it?'

'I suppose so,' I answered thoughtfully. 'It's funny, but I remember so clearly Ann telling me that when you arrested him first John said "Thank God it's over … I'm sorry, I'm sorry." That's what convinced me that he had killed poor Barry, otherwise I wouldn't have dug so deep into my friends and their lives to find a cause for him doing it. Now it seems he didn't do it … or, well, not really anyway.'

'Joan, as I said, don't hope for too much in that regard. He almost certainly lied a lot in what he said to us. I'll know soon enough anyway. Look, I'd better get going,' Kevin said, reality taking over from the personal cocoon into which we had briefly retreated.

My life would, I thought, be starting afresh once all this was over. I could look forward with hope and anticipation to a shared, contented future with Kevin.

Or at least the opportunity of exploring it as a possibility!

CHAPTER 42

Joan

I had a brief phone call from Kevin as he was anxious about his morning meeting. He had had little sleep but was delighted at how the case was moving. He confirmed for me that the videos, briefly viewed, were very much as he had expected.

After everything that had been happening, work was a welcome antidote.

In the evening, dinner over, Ronan had retreated to his room to study while I tried to find a reason, any reason, not to do what I knew had to be done. A shower, change of clothes and a deep breath, then I shouted up to Ronan that I was going over to Ann's for a short while. I knew that no matter how much I didn't want to go and talk with her, it was essential that I did, given the rapid changes that had taken place in the last few days.

Maura's smile of welcome on opening to my ring on the doorbell made the visit worthwhile. Clearly she was pleased to have me relieve the by now normal abnormality of family life in the Franklin household. As I went into the sitting room my beloved Brendan glanced at me with lifeless eyes before returning his gaze and notional concentration to some meaningless drivel on the television. Ann, who badly needed her hair cut and some attention to her clothes, made an effort to be social, which was fine except that the effort showed too much. As Brendan continued to be absorbed in not watching the TV, I moved with Ann to the kitchen for a chat.

Tea things were not cleared up – something unthinkable in that house just a few short weeks previously – so I started on them. Frozen pizza for dinner and the breakfast, if my antennae were working properly, had consisted only of tea and toast. Despair almost settled on me. But I was there to bring her up to date, so reluctantly I did. It gave no joy to Ann. While McKinnon's abuse of her husband might help to explain John's crime, it didn't change or take away the disaster of it. When I made tentative moves to leave, Ann caught my arm and, holding tight, begged me to have a talk with the children and bring them into the picture before I left. Patently she was in no state to do so.

Reluctantly I agreed, as I felt that they needed to hear the facts in a constructive way, and preferably from someone who cared about them.

We gathered in the sitting room and, after a brief hiatus while I gathered my thoughts into some semblance of logic, I started. I told them briefly that their dad had been abused when he was a young boy, no more than Brendan's age, and that the man who had done it was now in prison. I explained to them that it seemed as if this might have been the precipitating factor that started the chain of events leading to the terrible situation that he was now in. I explained that knowing these facts at least gave us some understanding of their dad's problems and that this could mean that the specialists would be better able to help him. Maura cried when I had finished, but Brendan just continued to sit emotionless, expressionless, almost as if he didn't hear or take in what I had said. I hugged Maura and allowed her to cry it out a little, though my efforts to bring Brendan into the comfort circle were to no avail. It was terrible, but all I could feel was sorry for myself, caught in the web of this poor family's torment. I tried to give comfort, and perhaps it was of help to Ann and Maura. Brendan clearly needed a lot more help to deal with this new reality. As I sat there I decided that I needed to talk to

Ann very soon about how we might access professional help for him. When Maura's tears had dried up somewhat I explained that this man was going to appear in court soon and that they should expect more stuff to be written in the papers. However, I chickened out on mentioning the photos or the videos that implicated their dad. Instead I emphasised that the man would most likely be charged with offences against young children in the area in which he now lived. I wanted to leave – I needed to get as far away as I could from this toxic environment – but Ann was my friend and Brendan my godson, so I stayed. In desperation I involved them all in cleaning the kitchen and trying to restore the rest of the house to a semblance of the pristine state I had so envied in former times. Ann and Maura seemed to brighten a little during this process, but Brendan's contribution was minimal as he kept drifting back into himself.

A long night that seemed an awful lot longer than it actually was! As I made my way home I could only hope that I had helped a little.

Kevin rang just as I was getting into bed. The first ten minutes was a hoot as he described the chaos of his morning meeting. Every agency, it seemed to him, was arguing about a lack of resources while trying to shift responsibility on to the others. He thought some decisions were made but couldn't for the life of him explain what they were. Most importantly, from his point of view, the Garda liaison section was taking over the coordination function from him.

Laughter over, I anxiously hoped for some good news about John's involvement, even though rationally I knew there was none. There was silence and then Kevin quietly said 'I'm sorry, love, but the video doesn't really give John Franklin a ready out. It doesn't show him actively involved in the actual murder, but he was present and obviously wanted to be. Sorry.'

Another silence! This one down to me as I struggled to come to terms with accepting that reality. Then Kevin filled me in on the rest of his day. Con and himself had gone to the wood that afternoon and identified and marked out the area that he was certain contained the dead bodies. A specialist team had been brought in and they were due to start their grim task in the morning. He expected results from it very quickly. I was pleased to hear that he had also been in touch with Sally Creamer and the Fitzpatricks. He had made arrangements for a liaison officer to meet them in the morning at the site and support them through the ordeal.

The next bit came as a huge shock! Three videos were as he expected but the other was of a boy that hadn't, as far as he knew, even been reported missing. So Con and himself felt that a third body could be found and, as they had no idea who that might be, another strand of the case would need following up on.

The only small bit of good news was that John Franklin was visibly present only in the Barry Breen video and didn't seem to have been involved in the other murders.

I settled a bit in my bed as we moved on to talk of something, anything, else. Kevin then showed the driven part of his nature as he said that Con and himself had gone over the case as they were driving down to the wood. They had come to the conclusion that both of them had been very stupid and could have screwed up the case. When they saw the two cards in McKinnon's wallet, they used the first one to open the hidden room but never gave the other one any thought. A mistake that could have been disastrous, and one they wouldn't make again. I reassured him that he had done an exceptional job, but I don't think I convinced him.

I was lying on my bed and Kevin was, of course, at his desk working late, so we continued to talk of nothing much, yet everything really, before we said a lingering goodnight.

CHAPTER 43

Joan

'Mam, Mam, wake up, wake up!' Ronan's anxious face peering over me brought me quickly out of a deep sleep. 'Nana is downstairs – something bad has happened.'

'Is your dad okay? Has something happened to him?' I blurted out, feeding into his obvious shock.

'Dad? No … it's not Dad … it's Brendan. He's been taken to hospital. Nana was woken by the noise of the ambulance and when she realised that it had stopped outside Ann's house, she got dressed and went over. Nana is downstairs. She came around to tell us.'

I was dressed and down in the kitchen in seconds. Ronan had the kettle on and was comforting his Nana. While he made tea, she filled me in. Brendan had tried to kill himself. Ann heard it and called the ambulance. All she knew for definite was that Brendan was still alive when he was taken off to hospital.

'Is there no end to this?' I asked inside my head. Outwardly I noticed that it was close to seven o clock, the day just starting and already we were confronted with yet another disaster. I thanked Mrs Traynor for coming to tell us and quickly dropped her home, as I didn't feel she would be up to a long wait in casualty. Ronan wouldn't stay with her and insisted on going with me as I rushed to the hospital. Truth be told, I was glad to have him there. Driving to the hospital, all I could do was question myself about how much of a part I had played in pushing Brendan over the edge.

As we came into the emergency waiting room Ann spotted us and she and Maura rushed over to hug us. Ann assured us that Brendan was alive and the doctors were hopeful that he would be all right. She added that it might be a few hours before they could be certain.

Brendan had been even quieter than usual after I left last evening, and that was saying something. He had gone up to his bedroom very early without a word to either Maura or herself. She looked in on him before retiring and was reassured, as he seemed to be asleep. Ann had then gone to bed and sometime later must have dropped off. A crashing noise awoke her and she rushed out to find Brendan hanging from a rope tied to the banister on the landing. A chair was turned over on the hall floor beneath her son. She took Brendan's weight with Maura's help and then sent her to get a knife to cut the rope and free him. Ann lay Brendan down on the carpet in the hall before phoning for an ambulance.

Brendan was alive when they took him to theatre and the nurse had said that it could be a while before they would have any news. Just one disaster after another! The hope engendered by the breakthroughs was dissipated by yet more disaster. We sat drinking tea, holding hands, just hoping for time to travel and praying for positive news. A nurse briefly rushed in and told Ann that Brendan was alive and that they were more hopeful.

Finally Ann dozed off. Maura was resting her head on Ronan. I sat just thinking until Breda calmly strode into the waiting room. We hugged, then I raised my eyebrows towards her. She smiled and quietly whispered, 'We live in a small town and everybody gets to hear things whether they want to or not. I rang your doorbell and your neighbour told me you were here … so I came.'

CHAPTER 43 - JOAN

I muttered my heartfelt thanks as Ronan hugged her before introducing Maura. Fortunately Ann slept on.

We had more tea and sat waiting. Talking is never easy in that environment, so I just allowed random thoughts to drift around my brain. Could Kevin possibly be wrong: maybe John wasn't as guilty as I thought? Could I cope with one more negative? Could Ann? Then suddenly it hit me with blinding clarity. My brain seemed to freeze. How stupid was I? How could I possibly have missed it? Quickly I excused myself and went searching for a telephone.

I rang Kevin and got him at home. He said he would be leaving soon to go down to the search.

'I have to see John Franklin now, immediately.'

'But …' he started to say.

'Now! It's urgent,' I said as he began to argue.

'But I … I,' he stammered.

'Ring, ring and let the prison officer know we're coming. Come on,' I said. 'It's urgent – really urgent.'

Kevin realised that discussion was pointless, so he said that he supposed he could go on down to Grange Wood afterwards as it was unlikely they would have results before the afternoon.

'Thanks. See you in the hospital car park in half an hour,' I said before hastily hanging up in case he changed his mind.

Quietly, keeping my inner turmoil as dampened down as possible so as not to alarm the children, I spoke to Breda. I told her that something urgent relating to John Franklin had come up and I needed to see him as soon as possible. Breda assured me that she was fine about staying on, so, after a word with Ronan, I hastened on yet another drive – this time from one hospital to another.

'What's going on, Joan? Tell me,' Kevin said as we rapidly made our way in.

'Brendan tried to commit suicide – he tried to hang himself this morning,' I answered without breaking stride.

'Shit,' Kevin said, 'is there no end to it all?'

'No end is bloody right,' I answered as we turned down the last corridor to John's room. 'And I think we have all missed a central part of this whole bloody mess,' I said as I strode on.

With that Kevin held me by the arm and asked, 'What is it? What's going on now?'

I'm not certain, but … give me my head for just a few seconds, please, Kevin.' He shrugged and let go of my arm.

The prison officer was sitting as usual inside John's door. 'Got your message,' he said to Kevin. 'I told him to expect you.'

I just nodded briefly as I pushed into the room. Kevin followed right on my heels. John was sitting up in bed awaiting our arrival. Stone-faced, I looked at John, who gazed in puzzlement back. No doubt he was noting a very different Joan to the one who had held and comforted him just a few days before.

'Brendan has just tried to hang himself,' I flung at him.

John's face drained of colour and his eyes went bleak and cold. He didn't ask if Brendan was alive or dead. He just disintegrated inside, and I knew for definite then.

'You bastard,' I said. 'That's what you meant, isn't it, when you said "Thank God it's over" at the time of your arrest? I thought, and so did Ann, that you were so relieved that you were caught, glad that you wouldn't kill again. It wasn't only that, though, was it?' Surging anger caused my voice to rise. 'You weren't worried or caring about those poor dead children, were you? It was Brendan you were relieved about, wasn't it? My godson, your own son and you couldn't even leave him alone. What have you been doing to him? You bastard!'

And with that I snapped and attacked him. John Franklin crumbled and tried to pull the bedcover over his head. I made a grab for it, but before I could wrench it from his grasp Kevin intervened, held my hands in his and pulled me away from John and to his own body.

CHAPTER 43 - JOAN

'Joan, love, don't! It won't help,' he said, urgently trying to pierce my blinding anger.

'It will bloody help. It will bloody well help me … me … my poor godson,' I hissed. With that the strength drained away from me quickly as the anger dissipated and turned to disgust.

'I didn't want to. I didn't mean to. I couldn't help myself,' wailed John Franklin, but I wasn't listening. 'I'm sorry, Brendan, so sorry,' he said as he curled up into a fetal position at the edge of the bed. His arms were raised to protect his body from an attack. But if another attack was coming, it was from inside himself.

'Bastard,' I hissed as I abruptly turned and left the room. Kevin followed and on the way past urgently asked his confused colleague to summon a doctor quickly to tend to his charge. Then he caught up with me and grabbed at my hand to slow me down.

I stopped and clung to my new friend, my new lover, and rocked against his comforting bulk as tears rolled down my face. We stood there for a long time. Kevin just held me, letting me cry. A doctor rushing past before entering John Franklin's room broke the spell.

Getting hold of myself, I smiled a wan expression of gratitude to Kevin. Then at the ward station I dialled Breda at the other hospital. While waiting for the connection I said, 'I am such an idiot. It was my fault. I pushed Brendan over the edge last night when I told him of McKinnon's arrest and of his father's early abuse. I should have known. I should have guessed earlier.'

Tears again, this time of anxiety, guilt and helpless frustration came over me and it was Kevin, holding me tight and comforting me, who spoke to Breda. He reassured her that I was okay. He also promised before hanging up that I would rejoin her and tell her everything in an hour or so. Quietly he led me, clinging tightly to his solid frame, out to a courtyard that fortunately was quiet. After we settled side by side at a small table he told me that Breda had said that I wasn't to worry. Brendan was alive and expected to make a full recovery.

'Sure,' I said bitterly as reality overcame me. 'A full recovery … but to what? To his father, his own abuse, a horrific future and an enemy within him that can destroy at any time in his life. What the hell is a full recovery? God help him. God help us all.'

'Joan, Joan love,' Kevin murmured quietly, holding me more gently. Then more intensely, more urgently he said, 'Joan, come on, it's grim, but surely it isn't as hopeless as you think! He has his mother. He has you. And you know people who can get him the help he is definitely going to need.

'You and I together will do all we can to support him through recovery. It will be a long road, but if we stick together we can make it better for him. Society now understands abuse in a way it never did before. We have therapists skilled in working with victims using methods they never did before. With your love and support Ann can help him … help him to manage these, as you called them … enemies within.'

'And you're going to be with me through all this, are you?' I said looking up into his eyes.

'Of course I am, as long as you want me to be.'

Kevin pulled me closer and I felt comforted and even a little more hopeful.

Brendan is going to need long-term therapy… We can get that.

Brendan is going to need his extended family to stay with him through the hard days ahead … We can do that.

Brendan can do it … He can deal with and conquer the enemies within if we can hang tough through the rough times and support him.

Kevin is right … we can do it!

And maybe through it find a way to survive as a couple as well!

Horrors, even unimaginable ones, can be faced if we love and support each other through them … can't they?

EPILOGUE

Kevin

What a roller coaster of a week.

Two and a half days it took to finish the careful dig in the woods.

Three bodies were exhumed. Two we knew about and one, also that of a young boy, we didn't. Having already watched the videos many times, this didn't come as a surprise to Con or me.

I grieved with Mr Fitzpatrick and Mr and Mrs Creamer as they supported each other in the sadness of the reality that they now had to face: nonetheless a better one than what they had lived through for the past few years. They hugged me and thanked me profusely. Nice of them, but I was still left with a sense of how much I, or we collectively, had failed them in that time. I also got to show Mr and Mrs Breen the exact spot where their son's body had been abandoned. At their request we held a small Mass with just their immediate family and us present. It was performed by a gentle, lovely priest and was both moving and strangely healing.

Thank God for Con and his keen observation skills, as he identified at least one other adult present, whom I missed, in two of the videos. This person was never seen, but the camera was clearly held and moved around at times when all the others were visible. As a follow-up the technical team were asked to examine the hidden room and the equipment in it to identify unknown prints.

After the arrests of McKinnon, Whitely and McMurrough the real work began. Each separate prosecution file had to be carefully compiled. Not the part of the job I best enjoy, but hard experience has taught me how essential this is to a good outcome.

In truth, both Con and I would have much preferred to devote all our time to the two missing pieces of the overall case.

Who was the other person who held the camera at the murders?

We compiled a list of three possible individuals to follow up on when the information from technical branch became available. We knew it had to be one of them, but which?

Who was the other child victim? Number one in this series of murders! We had taken the best likeness from the video and were just waiting for the medical report before starting the unpleasant task of identification.

In the interim our energies were focused on completing our part of the admin work and handing it over to the prosecution service.

That night, however, I was going to Joan's for dinner. We had talked, a lot, but this would be the first chance to get together properly since the hospital scene with John Franklin, and I was excited and strangely nervous.

Just as I was leaving, an urgent call came in from McMurrough's solicitor, whose client had apparently been taunted and threatened by other inmates and felt unsafe. His solicitor was insisting that he be moved to more secure accommodation. Con and I talked about it and agreed to see him as a matter of urgency first thing in the morning. This urgency was, however, driven by the thought that if he felt so vulnerable we could use the opportunity to pry the answers we needed out of him. This would save us a lot of time-consuming leg work.

The following day suddenly seemed brighter if we could handle it in the right way. This is where Con and I usually work so well together.

I felt so comfortable with Joan, and Ronan was staying with his granny for the night. We settled to the meal talking mostly of incidentals. Dancing around our heightened awareness of each other in, I felt, harmony.

A pleasant antidote to work stress!

I just had to ask for an update on Brendan. I had heard much, but only in phone snippets.

Brendan had been discharged from hospital. John Franklin had at least provided good health cover for his family. Brendan was transferred to a small children's unit where hopefully he could start to come to terms with his trauma. A long road ahead, but if we all supported Ann and Maura we could get there. At least they reported that he seemed to be settled.

Joan also talked of Cormac and her chat with Kate in the hospital. He was doing well and due soon to be discharged home. He had started seeing a therapist and that was going to continue as long as deemed necessary. Kate was hopeful of a very positive outcome.

We smiled at each other knowing that while much was positive, there was going to be many a crisis to overcome.

'You know, Kevin,' Joan said finally, 'after everything we have gone through, just having those two outcomes sort of makes it all worthwhile.'

'That's funny,' I answered. 'There I was thinking that all of it was worthwhile because I met you.'

Joan looked at me, a serious, thoughtful expression on her face. Then she said 'I think, Kevin, that you are reading too much into the fact that Ronan is staying at his granny's. Still, why don't we leave the dishes for now and go explore the possibilities of our having a life together.'

As we stood up, she added, 'You can do the washing-up in the morning while I have a lie-on. Can't you?'

As we went hand in hand up the stairs, so reminiscent of our first time, it occurred to me that now wasn't the best time to mention that I had an urgent prison appointment in the morning!